Loving LAUREN

A SAPPHIC LOVE STORY ABOUT IDENTITY, HEALING, AND HOLDING ON

CARLY BRYANT

For more information, contact: **http://www.carlywrites.com**

Cover design by GetCovers.com
Editor: Leah Pugh

ISBN - eBook: 979-8-9997052-1-1
ISBN - Paperback: 979-8-9997052-2-8

First Edition: November 2025

Dedication

For every soul who's ever dimmed their light to fit,
for every heart that's ached to be seen,
You are not alone.
You are worthy.
You are whole.
You are already enough.
I see you.
I love you.
I promise, true love was never meant to hide.

Dear Reader,

I'm so honored and grateful that you picked up Loving Lauren, a slow, tender romance about two people learning how to be fully seen and loved. At its core, this book is about what it means to open yourself up to someone, even when it feels scary. Even when you're still figuring out who you are.

Sierra (she/her) is a pansexual female with a creative soul and a heart that loves big, even when she doesn't have all the words. Talented makeup artist Lauren (they/them) is a trans demigirl who has been hurt by people who were meant to care for them.

In this story, Lauren is referred to as she/her until they make their pronouns known. Their story is one of cautious steps, awkward moments, big feelings, and the love that grows through care, not pressure.

This book includes a queer friend group, messy emotions, and a lot of soft, quiet bravery. It also includes moments of pain, because that's real too. Above all, this is a story about healing and hope.

Content Warnings: I want you to feel informed before diving in, so here's what you can expect:

Transphobia (external, not within the relationship)

Family rejection

Pansexual identity invalidation

Light references to past trauma (not graphic)

Whether you're here for the romance, the representation, or the soft feels, I hope this story makes you feel something real and reminds you that you're worthy of a love that sees you exactly as you are.

With love and gratitude,

Carly

Contents

Chapter 1

Three years of playing it safe had left Sierra Turner excellent at capturing everyone else's life through a camera lens and terrible at living her own. Having perfected the art of staying invisible, Sierra felt comfortable behind the viewfinder, polite smiles, and the familiar lie that work was enough.

But some moments refuse to stay safely framed.

She'd been walking through the park for twenty minutes that afternoon, camera in hand, chasing the light. The late spring air was making her slow down, making her notice things... the way the sun broke through in scattered bits, how the grass grew greener in places, the sweetness of lilacs mixed with cut grass.

A couple picnicked under the blossoms. Kids circled an old oak nearby. She lifted her camera, framing shots without really seeing them. Photography had always been her anchor. Through the lens, life arranged itself. Mess turned into meaning. Lately, her art felt like the only part of her life that stayed steady. It was the one thing she could count on to make sense.

A breeze moved through the branches above, carrying a hint of jasmine. She watched the light shift through the branches, patterns that would never repeat. But just when she pressed the shutter, movement caught her lens.

Sierra swung toward the path and froze. A girl stood laughing in a swirl of sparrows, maybe five-five, with long black hair lifting in the wind. Something in Sierra's chest went still. The girl moved with the birds like she belonged to them, but when she thought no one was watching, her smile faltered, like joy was something she carried carefully.

Click. Sierra snapped another shot, then another, and again.

She could attribute it to the lighting, composition, or the symmetry of the motion, but none of that was true. Something about this girl tugged at her and left her a little breathless. She fit into the scene like a secret, as if light itself had chosen her.

The girl tossed her head back and laughed again, sunlight catching the tips. Sierra's finger froze on the shutter. Her stomach fluttered. Not a crush. Not yet, but more like recognition. A silent alarm went off inside her chest.

She imagined walking over, crossing the lawn with practiced steps, offering a compliment or a question. Maybe she'd ask about the birds. Maybe the girl would smile back. But by the time Sierra lowered her camera and stepped toward the path, the spot was empty. The sparrows had scattered. Only the rustle of branches remained.

· ♥ · ♥ · ♥ · ♥ · ♥ ·

Back at her apartment, Sierra eased the door open. It was quiet inside, the kind that sits heavy before the city goes dark. The air still held a trace of chamomile from the tea she'd left cooling that morning. Somewhere overhead, a single bulb hummed.

Then Salem shattered it all with a yowl that could wake the dead.

Sierra nearly dropped her keys. "Damn, Salem."

He strutted out from behind the couch, tail high, eyes wide. Another meow, this one somehow more indignant than the first. He circled her ankles then sat and stared up at her with an expression that could only be described as theatrical betrayal.

"You have food and water. You're not starving."

Salem blinked slowly. Unimpressed.

She crouched down and scratched behind his ears anyway, and he leaned into it with a purr that sounded like a small engine turning over. Drama king. But hers.

Her camera bag waited on the table, still zipped. She stepped over a pile of crumpled magazines, sidestepping a scatter of loose photo prints. Her fingers trailed along the back of the chair as she dropped into it. The SD card slid into place with a sharp click. Her screen lit up, casting a pale glow across her face. Image after image blinked into view... flowers, hedges, wide shots of the park.

And then: the girl with the birds.

Sierra leaned closer, zooming in until the photo took over her screen. The girl's head tipped back mid-laugh. Her hair had lifted in the moment, caught by the wind. A scatter of freckles crossed her cheeks, and her eyes—icy blue, touched with bits of gray and violet—seemed to hold light even frozen on the screen.

A stranger. Just a stranger. But something about her pressed into Sierra's chest like a thumbprint.

She leaned forward, palm to her forehead, tugging at the roots of her hair as if pressure might untangle the question in her mind.

What is it about this girl?

Sierra had spent three years avoiding this exact feeling—the pull toward something unknown, something that might actually matter. Maybe it was time to stop hiding. Maybe she was lonelier than she'd let herself believe.

The silence pressed down. Sierra pushed back from her desk. She needed to move.

Outside, the wind cut cool across her cheeks. Her sneakers found an easy beat on the sidewalk as she jogged through streets tilting toward night. Streetlights blinked awake here and there. She passed the coffee shop, neon light spilling into puddles, the damp smell of wet cement lifting as she went by.

She cut through the park toward that spot. Part of her still expected to see the girl leaning against a lamppost, maybe, or disappearing around the next corner, but the streets stayed empty. The girl, like the birds, had vanished.

· ♥ · ♥ · ♥ · ♥ · ♥ ·

Later, after peeling off damp clothes and washing the sweat from her skin, Sierra slid into bed. Her hair was still wet. Her thoughts were too. She stared at the ceiling, the soft hum of the city slipping in through the window.

Why can't I let this go?

No answer came. Only the echo of laughter and eyes she'd never seen before yet felt somehow familiar.

Chapter 2

Dawn was barely breaking when Sierra stepped outside with her camera bag and tea. The air smelled like rain coming. She took a slow breath, steadying herself before Jonas's SUV appeared at the curb, dark and still. He sat behind the wheel without looking over, fingers tapping an uneven rhythm against the steering wheel. His thermos balanced in the cupholder like an old ritual. He didn't look over when she opened the door and slid in beside him. He never did, because Jonas considered eye contact before sunrise to be cruel, almost a punishment.

Neither of them spoke, but they didn't need to. They worked like gears... tight, efficient, always turning. Early mornings, sharp light, and the shared language of aperture and instinct bound their dynamic.

The drive wound through a city still half-asleep, the sky bleeding pink and gold. Light slid across the windows like liquid honey, softening even the sharpest edges. Photographers called this fragile span their golden hour, a window where everything glowed. It only lasted for an hour or two, book-ending each day like a secret only photographers bothered to learn, and maybe that made it sacred. Sierra tipped her head toward it, letting the warmth sink in enough to take the edge off the tired feeling behind her eyes.

Jonas unpacked his gear with the economy that comes from doing it a hundred times. Camera bodies, lenses, light meters, reflectors. Sierra mirrored his movements, setting up lights and adjusting stands while he snapped test shots. They didn't speak, but their rhythm held.

Models arrived in shifts, their heels tapping over stone. The makeup artist came in behind them, arms full of powder brushes and bronzer palettes. She laughed at something one model said, but the sound faded fast.

Sierra clipped the reflector into place, then stepped back, squinting into the glare. Sequins on the dresses kicked the sunlight back at her, scattering it across the cobblestones. The models shifted into place... angles perfect, expressions locked in, the look you usually see sealed up behind glass.

Jonas gave directions in short, clipped phrases. He hated fuss. Sierra's focus drifted, and a growing unease lingered. Ever since yesterday's encounter in the park, she'd felt restless, distracted. The girl with the sparrows kept slipping into her thoughts at the worst moments. She couldn't name it, but it stayed there, tugging at the edge of her thoughts like a thread she hadn't pulled.

By the far wall, in the shade of a flowering trellis, an older woman relaxed. She wore her silver hair in a loose bun. A lilac cardigan buttoned to the top, a paperback balanced on her knees. Her attention wasn't on the models. Sierra's hands stilled.

That woman was more interesting than anything else in the courtyard. She didn't sculpt her expression or pose, but she radiated the type of presence that came from living... from being seen and choosing not to flinch.

Sierra grabbed her camera and clicked just once, but the sound startled the woman who looked over, met her eyes, and smiled. Not with curiosity, but with understanding.

Sierra lowered the camera. That was the moment she wanted to chase. Not runway-ready glamour. Not symmetrical beauty, but stories etched onto faces, fingerprints of time.

She wasn't sure this job with polished industry shoots, brand contracts, and name-dropping was her world anymore. She wasn't sure it had ever been, but it paid the bills.

The day had left Sierra restless. Even after the shoot wrapped and she'd helped Jonas pack the equipment, the feeling of searching for something more authentic lingered. She needed a distraction, something to shake off the dissatisfaction clinging to her.

That night, Sierra stayed outside her building a little longer, watching the sky lose its last streaks of light. The air clung to her skin, thick with humidity. She was rubbing the knot on her shoulder when her phone lit up. Three missed calls. With everything going on, she completely forgot about club night with her friends.

Before she could call back, she spotted them. Three figures under the busted streetlamp at the corner.

Raven leaned on the post as if it were hers to defend, arms crossed, black lace boots set wide. Raven's dark lipstick and sharp eyeliner were her signature. She had the look of someone who could win prom queen just to see if anyone would dare take it from her.

Calliope shifted her weight from one foot to the other, curves tucked into ripped jeans and a flannel jacket too big to be hers. Her green eyes caught the flicker from the bulb overhead. Spiky red hair stuck out as if she'd attacked it with a toaster and no second thoughts.

Jett was all charm and heat. He wore a grin that suggested he was always keeping a secret. His ebony skin glowed beneath the streetlight, his jawline clean and smug. He tossed her a wink.

"You're late," he called, grinning. "Fashionably late, I'll allow it, but next time you're buying the first round."

"Disappear on us again and I'm filing a missing persons report. Don't test me, Turner." Raven's eyes narrowed like she was only half-joking.

"It's club night, darling." Calliope looped her arm through Sierra's before she could blink. "The gods have decreed it. Your protest has been overruled."

"I didn't even say..."

"You don't get a vote," they chorused, Jett laughing, Raven smirking, and Calliope fluttering her free hand like she was casting a spell.

Neon Pulse throbbed with bass and heat. The sign out front buzzed in pink and blue, and inside smelled like perfume, vodka, and too many fresh stories already in the making.

They moved through the crowd in a blur—elbows, glitter, strangers pressed too close. The dance floor thudded like a second heartbeat.

At first, Sierra stayed cautious, body half-stiff with habit. The music didn't let up, and the lights kept blurring the edges of everything, yet she finally gave in. Calliope laughed and spun her. Jett reappeared just to throw a wink over his shoulder before dipping Raven in a move so exaggerated it almost worked. Raven shrieked with laughter.

Sierra lost herself in it all... the rhythm, the heat, the sense that maybe she wasn't drifting so far from herself after all.

Then she saw her. Across the dance floor, under a wash of purple light, was a girl with long black hair, her skin shining with sweat.

Sierra's heart leaped. *Could it be?* Her eyes caught the light right. Sierra's chest tightened with sudden hope. Her feet moved before her brain did, pushing through the crowd, pulse racing with possibility.

But the girl's face was a stranger's... not the girl from the park, not the one who laughed like she was part of the flock, surrounded by sparrows. The disappointment hit like cold water, leaving Sierra hollow in the middle of all that noise and heat.

"Sorry." She stepped back, heat climbing her cheeks.

Back at the table, no one asked her. They just made room.

"I thought I saw someone from the park. I took her photo while she was feeding the birds. She's been stuck in my head ever since." Sierra ran her fingers through her hair.

"Bird girl?" Calliope gasped like it was the juiciest gossip of the year. "Tell me everything. Was she tragic and beautiful? Mysterious and doomed?"

Raven squeezed her hand. "Ghost girl crush. That's so you."

"Babe, you're living in a rom-com and I'm absolutely here for it. Ghost girl has my vote." Jett gave a fist bump.

"I don't even know her name." Sierra admitted, her head in her hands.

Calliope nudged her. "Maybe the universe does."

They didn't mock her. They let her keep it to herself. Let her hold the ache without prying, and that, more than anything, made her want to cry a little in the best possible way.

She slipped into her apartment, shoes in hand, hair damp with sweat. Salem meowed from the couch as if she'd been gone for weeks. She scooped him up and whispered in his fur.

"I think I'm losing it, buddy."

He purred as if he didn't agree. She stayed under the shower until her skin flushed pink, then pulled on loose pajamas and climbed into bed with her hair still wet. Salem curled against her hip like a comma, and she whispered again to the ceiling.

"Maybe she wasn't real."

Even in saying it, she didn't believe herself. Some things don't feel imagined. They feel like prologues, and Sierra wasn't ready to let go of the beginning.

Chapter 3

Sierra stood in front of her bathroom mirror for the third time in twenty minutes, wiping off lipstick that was too much, then not enough. Her hands wouldn't stop doing that stupid trembling thing, and Salem sat on the toilet lid watching her like she'd lost her mind.

"Don't judge me. This is a big deal, okay?"

It was the first date in three years and the first date with a woman ever. The words kept looping in her head like a broken record. She always knew her attraction didn't have gender lines. She just never had the words to describe it. The last three years, she just ignored the thoughts, but she couldn't do that anymore. It was lonely. She needed to see if it was just attraction or if there could be more with someone other than her old high school boyfriend.

Three years. That's how long she'd been hiding behind her camera, telling herself work was enough. For her, photography was all the intimacy she needed. Capturing other people's moments, joys, and connections—keeping herself on the other side of the lens where she was safe and nothing could touch her. Where she couldn't get hurt again.

But then Monica happened.

Monica caught Sierra off guard at the bookstore last week. She was in the horror section, because where else would you be on a Tuesday afternoon? She was reaching for the new Stephen King when a voice behind her said, "Finally! Another woman who appreciates a proper nightmare before bed."

Monica was gorgeous in an effortless way that made Sierra self-conscious of her ratty band tee. She had thick auburn hair in a messy bun and wore glasses that made her look both studious and rebellious. They'd ended up talking for forty minutes about whether modern horror had lost its teeth compared to the classics. Then Monica just asked her out. Simple as that. Just like that.

Sierra's instinct was to say no, run, or make an excuse about being busy with shoots. But something stopped her. Maybe it was Monica's genuine smile. Or maybe she was just tired of being scared, but she heard the word "yes" coming out of her mouth. She couldn't take it back, and now, she was terrified all over again, getting ready.

Sierra finally settled on a soft black sweater that was casual yet nice enough to show she'd made an effort, jeans that actually fit, and the boots Thalia bought her she never wore because they seemed too fancy. She grabbed her camera bag out of habit, then set it down. Tonight was about being present, not hiding behind a lens.

She looked at herself one more time. This would work. Maybe.

Monica picked a trendy farm-to-table place downtown for the restaurant. The place had dim enough lighting to hide Sierra's nervous sweating but bright enough to see the menu. She was already there, waving from a corner booth, and Sierra's stomach did a weird flip thing that wasn't entirely unpleasant.

Monica said, "You came!" before standing up for an awkward should-we-hug moment before they both sat down.

"Of course I came." Sierra tucked her hair behind her ear, then untucked it. Then she tucked it again. She needed to chill.

Though part of her couldn't help wondering what it would feel like to sit across from someone else—dark hair, eyes that held storms and sunlight in equal measure. She shook the thought away. The park girl was a ghost. Monica was here, real, trying.

The conversation started stilted, both doing a polite dance around the appetizer menu. Then, Monica launched into a story about accidentally buying a foreign language horror novel online thinking it was in English and trying to read it with Google Translate. Sierra choked on her water, laughing. After that, it got easier.

They talked about everything. Monica worked at a veterinary clinic and had stories about cats that made Salem look angelic. Sierra told her about the community center and the one person who drew only eyeballs for three weeks. They discovered they both thought The Haunting of Hill House series was amazing, both agreed books are always better than their movie or TV adaptations, and they'd both cried at the same part of Hereditary.

Monica was smart and funny. When she listened, she tilted her head, making you feel like what you said was the most interesting thing in the world. When their entrees came, they kept talking through bites, gesturing with forks, looking ridiculous.

But, and there was definitely a but.

Sierra waited for the spark and pull she'd heard about that made your chest tight and scattered thoughts. That feeling she'd had standing in the park, watching a stranger laugh with sparrows, unable to look away. Monica was objectively beautiful and kind. They had tons in common. On paper, this should've been perfect. Yet sitting across from her felt like hanging out with Calliope. Comfortable, fun, and platonic.

The weird thing? She had a gut instinct that Monica felt it too. Somewhere between the main course and their splitting a piece of chocolate lava cake, the energy had shifted. Not bad, just different. Like they'd silently agreed they were forcing something that wasn't there.

Monica said, "So, this is the part where I'm supposed to suggest we go somewhere else to continue the evening, right?"

Sierra let out a nervous laugh. "Yeah, probably."

"But we're not doing that."

"No."

Monica grinned with the most genuine smile she'd given all night. "Thank God. I thought it was just me. You're amazing,

Sierra. Genuinely one of the coolest people I've met in forever. But..."

"But it's giving more book club vibes than date vibes."

Monica laughed so loud the couple at the next table looked over. "Exactly!"

They paid the check, split it evenly without any of that weird who-pays dance, and walked out into the chilly night air. The streetlights made everything look softer, more forgiving.

"For what it's worth, I'm really glad you said yes. Even if this wasn't... you know. You seemed so closed off at first, like you'd built this whole fortress around yourself."

Sierra blinked. "That obvious?"

"Little bit. But hey, you said yes. That's something."

Sierra said quietly, "Yeah. It is."

They hugged, a real one this time, not awkward at all. Just two people who'd figured out exactly where they stood with each other. Monica headed toward her car, turned back to wave, and that was that.

Walking home, Sierra felt something unexpected. Not disappointment, but... possibility. Like a door she'd deadbolted shut had finally cracked open, just an inch. She knew she was attracted to women, but now she could imagine herself in a relationship with one. That part was clear now. She spent half of dinner noticing the way Monica's collarbones in that sweater. But attraction wasn't everything. There had to be something else, something more.

Something like what she'd felt in the park that day. That pull, that certainty. Maybe she was being ridiculous, holding every potential connection up against one fleeting moment with a stranger she'd never see again. But now that she knew that feeling existed, she couldn't un-know it.

And she'd felt it with the girl from the park. If she could ever find her again.

She passed the park near her apartment, the one she usually rushed through without looking. Tonight she slowed down. The trees were budding, threatening spring's arrival. A couple sat on a bench, leaning into each other. An old man scattered seeds for the pigeons despite the sign saying not to. Normal life continued around her, a stark contrast to her lonely, self-imposed isolated world.

Three years was a long time to be scared. Maybe she was done with that. Maybe this thing with Monica, though not romantic, had reminded her what it felt like to try. To risk something. To sit across from someone and hope for magic, even if it didn't show up this time.

She'd know it when she found it. Whatever "it" was. Maybe it was the girl in the park. That is, if she could ever find her again. She felt weird standing in the lamplight, like something was coming. Like the universe was finally done with her hiding phase and had plans she couldn't see yet. Spring was coming. Change was coming. Hell, maybe love was coming. The thought scared her less than it would have this morning.

Salem waited by the door, doing his best impression of a cat abandoned for years instead of three hours.

"It was fine. Good, even. Just not... the thing."

She scooped him up. He purred against her chest, which she took as understanding.

Later, she looked in the mirror again while getting ready for bed. It was the same face as this morning, but something felt different. More open, maybe. Like she'd been looking at herself through a camera lens for so long, she'd forgotten what it was like to see clearly.

Her phone buzzed.

Monica: Thanks for tonight! Horror book club soon if you're up for it. I'll bring the wine if you bring your Stephen King opinions.

Sierra: It's a date. But like, not a date-date.

Monica replied with a laughing emoji.

Yeah. This was good. This was right.

She set her phone down and walked to her window, looking at the city lights. Tomorrow she had lunch with Thalia. Her stomach did another flip as she thought about telling her sister. *The time for change is now.*

Chapter 4

Sierra had rehearsed this conversation maybe thirty times. Maybe more. Didn't matter now. Sitting across from Thalia at Bean & Bloom, watching her sister methodically destroy a sugar packet like it was some kind of art installation, every practiced line had evaporated.

The café had the same vibes as on any regular afternoon. Like this was just coffee between sisters, not Sierra finally putting words to something she'd been carrying around for way too long.

Her sketchbook lay open on the table, pages full of half-finished charcoal portraits. One face in particular seemed to glare back at her - abandoned, annoyed. She couldn't look at it. Instead, she wrapped both hands around her latte even though her palms were slick with sweat.

Thalia looked up from the sugar packet massacre, silver hoops catching the light. "So first you've been acting all distracted and weird this week, and now you tell me you went on a date with a girl? I thought you were straight."

Sierra's stomach dropped straight to her shoes. She tucked hair behind her ear and let out a shaky breath. Her hair was a lighter blonde than the rest of her family, longer too, with a bit of wave that never sat the way she wanted. Their mom had given them the same blue eyes; Thalia's were vivid as sapphires, but Sierra's were gentler, like twilight. Same jawline, same chin.

"I get why you'd say that. I mean, there was Josh in high school, and this was my first date with a girl."

Thalia just waited, which was so Thalia.

Sierra kept going, trying to find words that would help her sister understand. "I've never been big on labels. I just connect with people. That's always been my thing."

"So, you're bisexual?"

Sierra met her eyes. "More like pansexual, I guess if I had to put a label on it. I fall for *who* someone is, not *what* they are."

Thalia reached across the table and grabbed her hand. Her grip was warm and sure. "I want you happy. That's literally all I care about. Whoever actually sees you, that's who matters. Mom and Dad will figure it out. They love you. Once you tell them, they'll come around."

"You really think so?"

Thalia paused, and Sierra caught the flicker of uncertainty in her eyes. "Okay, so Dad's going to need some time. You know how he gets with anything that doesn't fit his neat little boxes. And Mom..." Thalia sighed. "Mom's going to want to research it to death and probably ask a million awkward questions."

Sierra's chest tightened. "That's what I'm afraid of. They're not exactly... progressive. Remember when our cousin, Jake, brought his boyfriend to Christmas two years ago? The way they kept calling him Jake's 'friend' all night?"

"That was different. Jake sprung it on them without warning." Thalia squeezed her hand. "But yes, they're old school. Traditional. They still think happiness looks like a white dress and grandkids. But Sierra, they also drove hours to every single one of your art shows. They love you more than their comfort zone. It might not be immediate, but they'll come around. They have to. Did you tell Tobias?"

Sierra smiled for the first time since sitting down. "Tobias probably knew before I did. He's just too nice to say anything."

"Emotionally mature little shit. So unfair." Thalia let out a sigh.

"Right? Honestly rude."

Sierra sipped her latte, finally letting the sweetness and warmth do their thing. The coffee shop buzzed around them, all cinnamon smells and coffee machine hisses, and something tight in her chest loosened.

"I'm glad you told me." Thalia stirred her tea in slow circles. "After this week of thesis chapters nobody will read and grading essays, talking about something real feels like I can finally breathe."

Sierra grinned. "Grad school living up to all your dreams?"

·❤·❤·❤·❤·❤·

"Oh yeah. I've been surviving on coffee and pure spite for so long, I'm pretty sure that's what's in my veins now."

They both cracked up. They'd both been missing this.

The laughter faded, and Sierra's smile softened into something more serious. She picked at the cardboard sleeve on her cup. "So... about that date."

"The date wasn't life-changing or anything. No instant love connection. She was nice, but it made me realize how much I've been hiding behind work lately." Sierra glanced at her sketchbook, all those half-finished faces. "But there's something else. There's this girl I saw in the park earlier this week. I photographed her with these sparrows, and I can't stop thinking about her."

Thalia's eyebrows shot up. "Wait, so there's Monica from the date AND mystery park girl?"

"Monica was sweet, but when I was with her, I kept thinking about the other one. The one I don't even know." Sierra ran her finger around the rim of her mug. "I've been taking pictures of everything except what actually matters, and then I saw her and everything just... clicked."

Sierra set down her mug, something vulnerable crossing her face. "The light was hitting her just right, and she was laughing, and Thalia, I couldn't stop taking pictures. She was feeding these sparrows, and they were flying all around her like she belonged to them, and for a second it felt like I was watching something magical happen."

26

"Did you talk to her?"

"No." Sierra's laugh came out hollow. "By the time I worked up the courage to walk over, she was gone. Just vanished, like she'd never been there at all."

Thalia leaned forward, studying her sister's face. "So mystery park girl is why you finally felt ready to figure yourself out?"

"Maybe? I don't know." Sierra traced invisible patterns on the tabletop. "It was just this moment where everything clicked into place. Like I finally understood what I'd been missing all this time." She paused, looking almost embarrassed. "I even went back to the park looking for her. Multiple times. Like some kind of creep."

"You're not a creep. You're someone who felt something real."

"She's probably long gone. I'll never see her again." Sierra shook her head, but her eyes were bright with the memory. "But that feeling? That instant recognition, that pull? That's what I want to find with someone."

Thalia's smile was knowing and gentle. "You will. And who knows? Maybe the universe has a sense of humor about these things."

They sat there for a minute longer, not talking, just being sisters in the comfortable way they'd perfected over the years. The afternoon light shifted golden through the windows, and Sierra thought about dark hair catching sun, about finally saying the truth out loud, about how terrifying and necessary both things were.

"You know what's wild?" Sierra said quietly. "I spent so long trying to figure out who I was supposed to be that I forgot to just... be. And then I saw her for like two minutes, and suddenly I understood."

Thalia reached over and squeezed her hand one more time. "Then I'd say the universe is telling you something. Maybe mystery girl was exactly who you needed to see to finally see yourself."

"Maybe." Sierra's smile felt lighter than it had in months. "Or maybe I'm just losing it over a stranger with good lighting and excellent bird-feeding technique."

"Could be both."

They both laughed, and for the first time since this whole confusing, scary, beautiful thing started, Sierra felt like she might actually be okay. More than okay. She felt like herself.

Chapter 5

Sierra unlocked the studio and hit the buzzing fluorescents. The place smelled of pencil shavings and citrus cleaner. Here, the only thing that asked anything of her was the next blank sheet of paper. She let out a slow breath, the morning settling in around her. No need to define herself or explain who she was and wasn't. Here, she was just Sierra, a teacher, an artist. Someone who believed in crooked lines and second chances.

She moved through the room, dropping thick sketchpads and sticks of charcoal on each table. Outside the frosted windows, a breeze carried the low rumble of city buses starting their routes. Inside, calm stretched long and comfortable. These mornings felt like a reset—a pause before the day remembered how to get messy again.

The door creaked open, and Joe, her most loyal late-bloomer, stepped in with paint-splattered jeans and a hoodie that had long since given up on structure. He grunted a hello or something close to it, and made for his usual seat by the window, settling in like the spot had his name on it.

Before long, the others started trickling in. A college freshman wearing earbuds with an anxious expression settled near the front. Balancing his toddler, a stay-at-home dad unpacked charcoal pencils. A teen slipped into the back row without removing their headphones. Joe gave them a nod that might've been mistaken for a neck spasm but was, in fact, a hello.

Sierra stood at the front of the room and smiled. "Alright, everyone. Let's talk about shadow and light."

She dragged a soft line across a fresh sheet of paper; the charcoal skimmed. "I want you to think of shadow not as the absence of light, but as where the story lives. Light is easy. It's where your eyes go first. But shadow gives it depth. It's where everything interesting hides."

As she spoke, Sierra thought of sunlight catching in dark hair, the way it had turned those black strands almost silver at the tips. The girl from the park had existed in that perfect balance... bright laughter against the shadows of leaves, joy illuminated but somehow still mysterious.

They drew while Sierra walked between tables, leaning down to guide a trembling hand here, redirecting a line there. She complimented the effort, not just the results. In here, she wasn't looking for perfection. She was helping them find their rhythm, their voice, their boldness.

Halfway through class, a sound broke the silence. It was long. Joe's corner announced the truth, and everyone froze.

Sierra looked up as Joe's face turned crimson. He slid lower in his chair, like maybe he could disappear if he held still long enough. Nobody moved for a second.

Then the room broke. Laughter rolled through like a wave. The college student covered her face. The stay-at-home dad let out a snort, which startled his toddler. Even the teen cracked a grin.

Sierra cleared her throat, eyes twinkling. "Joe, I swear, if you turn this into a weekly series, I'm promoting you to hallway monitor." That set them off again.

Joe looked half-mortified, half-proud. "It's a good thing I'm already sitting down."

"Charcoal and comedy. You're hitting your stride." Sierra turned and walked back to her desk, grinning.

By the time class ended, the air felt looser somehow, like the group had stopped pretending life wasn't messy. They packed up supplies with lazy chatter and promises to practice at home.

Joe hung back, clutching his sketchpad as if it might shield him from the memory. "Hey. Sorry again for... you know... that noise."

Sierra waved him off. "You gave the class its most authentic moment of the day and that's art."

He laughed under his breath, a little embarrassed. "You're alright, Miss S."

"You too, Joe. One fart per class, though. I've got standards."

"Understood. I'll pace myself."

The door shut behind him. Sierra stood there for a moment, taking in the silence with a sense of comfort. She looked around the empty room, something steady settling in her chest.

This was where she belonged.

That evening, the smell of fried chicken hit her as soon as she walked into her parents' house.

The scent triggered a memory: oven-baked bread, holiday cinnamon, her mother's off-key humming as she basted a golden dish.

"Hey, sweetie!" Her mom stepped out of the kitchen, cheeks pink from the heat, hair pinned back in her usual no-nonsense twist. She hugged Sierra tight, then leaned back to study her face as if she were checking for signs of neglect.

Her dad leaned over from the recliner to kiss her temple. "There's my girl."

Thalia called from the dining room. "Dinner's ready, and if you let the rolls go cold again, I'm staging a coup."

Sierra strolled through the hallway, her camera bag tapping her hip.

The walls still held every oddball family photo her mom refused to replace, including a tragic one of Tobias with a bowl cut and both middle fingers bandaged from a mysterious "science project."

Tobias sprawled across the couch like a dethroned prince, with a comic book on his chest, wearing mismatched socks.

"You're late. The mashed potatoes were about to send out a search party."

Sierra nudged his foot off the armrest. "You ever gonna sit on furniture like a regular person?"

"Define regular." He flipped a page.

The table groaned under the weight of the dinner. Mashed potatoes drowning in gravy, green beans cooked with bacon, biscuits steaming in a basket lined with a faded kitchen towel.

Thalia offered the butter as currency and glared at Sierra until she accepted a roll.

Midway through passing the corn, Tobias grinned. "So, how's your charcoal cult? Still making people cry over shading?"

"It's an art class, Tobias."

"Sure it is."

Sierra smirked. "How's your doomsday armor made of duct tape?"

"In progress. Testing phase begins this weekend. There will be impact trials and quite possibly a fire element."

Their dad shook his head with a smile and said nothing.

"Great. I'll schedule 'fire hazard' between laundry and dishes." Mom glared at him straight-faced.

"Didn't we just call him mature?" Thalia looked at Sierra.

Tobias mumbled with a mouth full of chicken. "I am mature."

Later, while everyone reached for seconds, Thalia leaned in. "Have you talked to them yet? About, you know..."

Sierra pushed her potatoes around. "There's nothing to talk about. I'm not even seeing anyone."

"You don't have to be dating someone for it to matter."

"I know. But right now, it feels easier to wait."

Their mom glanced up, as if she'd caught a shadow of something unspoken, but didn't press. The conversation drifted to safer waters.

Thalia was quick to rescue. "Sierra was telling me earlier, one of her students let out a fart so loud it echoed off the walls. She said the entire class almost died."

Tobias perked up. "Legend."

"We survived. Barely."

They laughed, refilled drinks, fought over the last biscuit. As the conversation lulled, Mom turned to Sierra with that look—the one that meant she'd been storing up something to say.

"Speaking of your classes, honey, you know Mrs. Henderson from next door? Her son David just got promoted at the accounting firm. He's single, very responsible, and she says he's been asking about you."

Sierra nearly choked on her sweet tea. "Mom..."

Dad looked up from his plate. "David's a good kid. Steady job, bought his own house last year. The kind of man who'd treat you right."

"I'm not looking to date anyone right now," Sierra said carefully, her chest tightening.

"But sweetheart, you're twenty-six. You can't hide behind that camera forever." Mom reached over and patted her hand. "I just want to see you settled. Happy."

Thalia jumped in quickly. "Sierra's doing just fine on her own, Mom."

"Of course she is. I just think David would be perfect for her. He's very traditional. Family-oriented."

Sierra forced a smile and pushed her green beans around her plate. The word 'traditional' echoed in her head like a warning bell.

"Maybe we could all meet him sometime," Tobias suggested with false innocence. "You know, make sure he's worthy of our Sierra."

"Don't encourage them," Sierra muttered, but she was grateful for his attempt to lighten the mood.

They stayed long after the plates were empty, the conversation eventually drifting back to safer territory. The night etched itself into memory unbidden. Even without saying it out loud, the love was there. It was messy, imperfect, but dependable. The kind that holds, even when you're still figuring yourself out.

The following week blurred at the edges. Studio lights flicked on too early, and sketches piled up too fast. Sierra moved from one obligation to the next, her days dissolving into one long smear of charcoal, critiques, and tired eyes. Friday arrived like an afterthought, wrapped in soft exhaustion.

By four-thirty, she packed her camera and stepped into the thin, hushed light that comes before evening takes over. The park was muscle memory by now. She could walk it with her eyes closed. Same steps, same turns, same brief stops without thinking.

She stayed until the sun stretched long and low across the lawn, waiting for something she didn't have the words to name. Any movement in the distance made her breath catch for a heartbeat too long. A flash of dark hair. A glimmer of sunlight on pale skin, but it never resolved into the face she had tucked away in memory.

There was no one feeding the birds. No girl with dark hair laughing like joy belonged to her. Just sunlight losing its grip and the silent ache of another almost.

Her apartment door creaked open, and the hinges sighed as if they shared her mood. Salem emerged from the bedroom with his usual air of dramatic timing, tail high and flicking.

Sierra crouched to meet him. "I'm finished looking for her." Her voice was low. Tired.

Salem meowed, short and skeptical.

"Okay, probably." She added, letting the smallest smile sneak out.

She curled onto the couch with her tea, Salem launching himself into the crook of her legs, purring like an engine too stubborn to quit. Outside, the sky dimmed until it glowed with the fuzzed edges of traffic lights and faint stars.

She could still see her frozen in the sunlight, hair in motion, and eyes like the inside of a storm and the first breath of spring, all tangled together.

"I don't know what's wrong with me. She was some girl in a park."

But she knew that wasn't true.

Sleep came eventually, but the ache and the image of her eyes stayed.

Chapter 6

The next morning, Sierra walked into the café. Over the door, the bell gave a quick ring. Thalia was in their corner spot with her latte, waiting.

Sierra dropped into the chair across from her. "Is it weird this place feels more like home than my apartment some days?"

Thalia arched a brow. "Your apartment doesn't come with croissants or me."

They traded updates in lazy circles... Tobias's latest attempt at homemade resin coasters that ended in a minor chemical spill, Thalia's competitive trivia night group, Sierra's community center students learning to express themselves through abstract paint splatters. For a moment, she forgot the ache that had followed her all week. The stilled longing she couldn't name. Then the bell above the door chimed again.

Sierra turned, her body going still before her brain caught up.

There she was.

The girl from the park. Long black hair that curled under her ears, a soft chambray shirt rolled at the sleeves, and eyes that stopped time. Blue, yes, but threaded with something more. Violet or starlight. It didn't matter. They were unmistakable.

Sierra's voice caught in her throat. "That's her." Sierra whispered, like naming her might make her vanish.

Thalia nudged her under the table. "Go."

"I can't walk up to her."

"She has haunted you all week."

"I wouldn't even know what to say."

"You never do. That's part of your charm."

The girl moved to the counter, ordering with an ease Sierra envied. No fluster. No fumbling. Just calm. Sierra had already wiped her hands on her jeans twice and was about five seconds from bolting.

"Go." Thalia was quieter this time. Her fingers brushed Sierra's arm. "You'll regret it if you don't."

Sierra stood before she could overthink. Her feet moved first, but her heart scrambled to catch up. She crossed the room.

"Hi. Sorry if this is weird. I'm Sierra. I... um... I was taking photos in the park last week, and I think you're in a few. They came out beautifully, and I'd love to show you, or send you copies."

The girl turned. Her smile held a simple warmth, the kind that made it hard to keep your guard up. When she spoke, her voice seemed to close the space between them.

The girl's smile widened. "I'd love to see them."

They walked close, their arms bumping for a second. Hardly anything, but it ignited something in her, as though a part of her had been waiting for it without knowing.

Back at the table, Sierra slid the memory card into her laptop. Her hands felt clumsy. Images emerged—branches bowed under spring blooms, pigeons suspended mid-wing-beat, a smile forming then vanished.

And then her.

Feeding sparrows. Laughing at nothing. Caught in the sun like a secret.

The girl leaned in, her breath soft against Sierra's cheek. "That was a good day. I'd almost forgotten how it felt." She turned, her expression full of wonder. "You're incredibly talented."

Sierra's heart stuttered. "Thank you."

They both sat, knees nearly touching. "This is my sister, Thalia. She's already judging me."

"Only a little." Thalia smiled a little too big. "Hi, I'm the cooler sibling."

The girl laughed warmly. "I'm Lauren."

"Nice to meet you, Lauren." Thalia stood. "I have to run, but Sierra's got excellent taste in photography, and other things." She gave Sierra's arm a quick squeeze. "Text me later."

When Thalia headed out, Sierra's eyes went back to Lauren. She was tracing the rim of her cup with a slow, absent motion.

The details stood out... the chipped black polish on her nails, the slight pull in her hands, how her eyes stuck on the photos a little too long before glancing away. Something in her expression suggested she wasn't fond of being the center of attention. Every time Lauren smiled, something in Sierra shifted.

"My camera loves you. If you ever want portraits or headshots, I would love to help you out."

Lauren looked up, her face brighter. "I'd love that."

Sierra pulled out her phone. "Want me to text you the ones I've already got? I can add your contact info."

Lauren held out her hand. "Let me do it."

Their fingers brushed as she took the phone. Sierra's pulse quickened. Lauren typed something in, then passed it back with a half-smile.

Sierra glanced at the screen and grinned. *"Lauren (aka Your Muse)."*

Lauren shrugged, playful. "I'm teasing."

Sierra laughed, her thumb brushing the edge of the screen. "Definitely memorable."

Lauren checked her watch. "I hate to dash, but I'm already running late."

The way she said it was quick, almost rehearsed, and it made Sierra pause. Her eyes held a guarded look, a flicker that hinted at something deeper, but she didn't press.

Lauren stood. "We'll talk soon?"

"Definitely."

She offered one last smile before turning toward the door. As she walked away, Sierra stayed frozen in place, hand still resting on her phone as if it might disappear. When the bell chimed again, it felt final.

Sierra pressed her hand to her chest. Her heart thrummed, but fear played no part. It was something else altogether. Hope.

Chapter 7

That afternoon, Sierra hovered over her phone, thumbs tapping in a rhythm only she could hear. Twenty-four hours. Was it too soon? She paced while Salem judged her from his perch atop the couch. She typed, paused, deleted, and typed again:

> **Sierra:** Hey Lauren, these turned out incredible. You're so photogenic you made it easy.

She stared at it and then hit send. Her phone buzzed almost instantly.

> **Lauren:** I loved them! Could you shoot for my makeup page? Client shoot Friday at 2 PM in my home studio. Want to join?

Sierra grinned at the screen like a complete dork and typed back a breathless *yes*.

·♥ · ♥ · ♥ · ♥ · ♥·

Lauren's makeup studio took up one corner—white muslin over windows, ring light against the wall, palettes cluttered across the table. The entire space glowed with the perfect soft light photographers dream about. The air carried a mix of vanilla and the sharp bite of alcohol cleanser, a scent Sierra already linked to her without thinking.

Barefoot and wearing an oversized smock freckled with color, Lauren leaned over a model whose smooth brown skin set off luminous green eyes. Her movements were steady, like those of a painter, each brushstroke coaxing shimmer into shape along the curve of a lash line.

Sierra lowered into a crouch behind her camera, finger resting above the shutter.

Click. Click. Click.

It wasn't just the model who was captivating, but Lauren too. There was something magnetic in the way she worked. The precision, the softness, the trust between her and the client. Watching her felt like watching art in motion, as if Lauren had reached inside the model and pulled confidence forward to sit on her skin.

Between shots, Lauren snapped behind-the-scenes photos on her phone, stealing moments of the process. Once, Sierra caught her pointing the lens toward her instead. Their eyes met, and Lauren smiled before turning away with a small laugh under her breath.

"These are going to be amazing." Lauren touched Sierra's hand. Her voice was light, but her eyes held something warmer. "I mean it. You're making me look real good right now."

Sierra's heart skittered. "I could say the same."

The shoot kept its energy light and playful. The model shifted from fierce to goofy without warning, tossing a wink toward Sierra or striking a mock runway pose with a hair flip. Lauren laughed more freely now, her voice rising above the shutter clicks. When Sierra caught a frame where Lauren was adjusting a collar with her tongue poking out in concentration, she couldn't help but smile behind the camera.

After it wrapped, Sierra grabbed her laptop and slid the SD card in with careful fingers. Images bloomed onto the screen, one after another. The model's cheekbones gleamed, glitter catching like frost. There was Lauren too, mid-motion, hand on a brush, or reaching to tuck a strand of hair. Sierra stole a glance at Lauren, chin nearly brushing her shoulder.

Lauren's expression softened with each photo. "These are... damn. You're seriously talented."

Sierra felt the compliment curl through her like a warm hug. "You're the one doing all the magic."

"I push powders around, but you're the one catching lightning." She hesitated, then tugged out her phone. "Look, I got some of you too."

Lauren flipped through a few quick snapshots of Sierra behind her camera, head tilted in focus. One where she was laughing with the model and another mid-squint as she adjusted her lens. The angles weren't perfect, but the feeling was there.

Lauren questioned with self-doubt. "These are cute, right? Not professional or anything, but good vibes."

Sierra smiled. "They're more than cute, and they're honest."

Lauren glanced up. "Do you mind if I post a couple of these?"

"Only if you promise to tag me."

Lauren's eyes sparkled. "Well obviously I will."

A few taps later, Sierra's phone buzzed.

Lauren: *My girl @SierraFrames absolutely crushed this shoot today. Camera magic. I can't wait to do it again.*

Sierra stared at the words on her screen, warmth blooming across her chest. *My girl.* Her cheeks ached from smiling.

As they packed up the equipment, their hands brushed over a compact. The touch was brief, a little clumsy, but neither of them pulled away too fast. They shared a look, a flicker of unspoken emotion that both of them felt.

"You have an eye for this." Lauren's voice had dropped to something gentler. "It's not just technical. You see people."

Sierra blinked. "That means a lot, especially coming from someone who makes people feel beautiful for a living."

Lauren looked like she had something else to add, but she just nodded. "We make a good team."

·♥·♥·♥·♥·♥·

Back at home, Sierra sank into her couch, still riding the high. Afternoon sun spilled across the floor. Salem sprawled on the cushion with his usual disdain. Sierra set her tea on the coffee table, reached for her phone and dialed Thalia without thinking.

"Thalia, I'm on cloud nine, and I can't feel my feet."

"That sounds dramatic, even for you, so what happened?"

Sierra flopped backward, staring at the ceiling as if it held answers. "Lauren asked me to shoot a makeup session and it was amazing. Like, actually amazing, but it wasn't just the shoot. I mean, that was great, but... being around her."

"She's kind of magnetic, isn't she?"

"Magnetic isn't even the right word. It's like she walks into the room and the light listens."

Thalia let out a small sigh. "Okay, poet. So, are you going to ask her out or are you going to talk about her like a Victorian diary for another month?"

Sierra buried her face in a throw pillow. "I don't want to ruin anything, but we're working together again next month. It's a collab series, so I'll see her a lot."

"Then ease into it and maybe suggest coffee or tea. There's less pressure that way."

Sierra sat up, heart fluttering again. "It's casual, smart, and friendly but could be flirty."

"Exactly, Sierra, so don't overthink it."

Which of course meant she was now going to do nothing but overthink it. Still, Sierra opened her messages and started typing.

> **Sierra:** Hey Lauren. I'm still buzzing from Friday and was wondering if you'd want to grab coffee Wednesday morning? I promise great espresso, and I'd love to pick your brain about makeup secrets.

She stared at the message for way too long and then finally hit send. Seconds later.

> **Lauren:** Hey Sierra! I'm still not over how amazing those shots turned out. Coffee on Wednesday sounds perfect. How about 9 AM at Bean and Bloom? I'd love to trade makeup tips for photography secrets. Can't wait!

Sierra read it twice, then read it again, and her whole body tingled.

She picked up Salem, stood up in the middle of the living room and spun once, bare feet sliding on the hardwood. Salem blinked at her as if she'd lost her mind.

"I'm in trouble, Salem, but it's the best kind."

He blinked, flicked his tail, and pawed at her chin as if he disapproved of this nonsense.

She laughed, setting him down with a kiss on the top of his head. Still smiling, she pulled her hair back into a bun, tucked her phone into her pocket, and took a deep breath.

Coffee on Wednesday, a new shoot on the horizon, and maybe... something more.

Chapter 8

Monday afternoon sunlight filtered through Sierra's gauzy curtains, casting soft stripes across the hardwood. Her coffee table had become a gallery of glossy prints, each one a tiny celebration of the shoot with Lauren.

There she was. Winged liner sharp enough to earn its own security clearance. Lashes shimmering beneath diffused light, glitter suspended like stars mid-blink. Sierra arranged three of her favorites into a crisp white folder and studied them like a curator prepping for an exhibit.

"Love the glow on her cheek. That catchlight in her eye is perfection." She paused, lips quirking. "And this pigment? Full-blown mood."

She snapped a photo of the mini-portfolio with her phone and smiled. Even if conversation stalled on Wednesday, she'd have these as her safety net. A visual reminder that this wasn't just a crush; it was a collaboration. She cared about Lauren's work as much as she cared about her own. Probably more. Okay, maybe it was a tie.

Sierra flopped onto the couch, one arm draped dramatically across her face. When exactly had she become the person who got butterflies over eyeliner?

That evening, she stood in front of her bathroom mirror, phone in selfie mode, like she was auditioning for the role of *mildly deranged romantic* on some off-brand reality show.

She tried out lines in a stage whisper.

"So, how long have you been... brushing other people's eyelids for money?" She winced. Too weird.

"What's the difference between warm and cool tones again? Because apparently I've been doing everything wrong for a decade." Nope, sounded like a pop quiz.

She leaned in, blinked at herself. "Do you have a favorite brush for blending existential dread?" That one hit too close.

Finally, she dropped the performance, stared at her reflection as if it were Lauren. "I think you're incredibly talented, and your looks are next-level inspiring. Like NASA should study your cut creases."

She cringed. "Um. You're amazing?"

A beat of silence—and then a full-on laugh exploded out of her, the kind that made her double over the sink, gasping.

From the hallway, Salem peeked around the corner, tail flicking once like an editor rejecting her entire emotional monologue. He stared with regal disdain, then turned away as if to say, *Honestly. Get it together.*

·♥ · ♥ · ♥ · ♥ · ♥·

Tuesday morning arrived with coffee and a false sense of confidence.

Sierra sat cross-legged at her desk, scrolling through Lauren's Instagram. A reel caught her attention: Lauren applying a holographic highlighter that shifted colors with a tilt of her wrist, like bottled moonlight. The caption read: *You glow differently when it's personal.*

Sierra tapped a comment... *That glow is unreal. Actual witchcraft.*

She added a single red heart and stared at it, debating. Enough to be flirtatious? Too much? Not enough? She hit send and shut off her phone before her thoughts could start circling the drain.

By mid-afternoon, she'd wandered toward Bean and Bloom without really deciding to. The lunch hour had cleared out, and it was too early for the dinner crowd. The bell over the door gave a quick jingle, and the smell hit her right away—espresso, cinnamon, and warm air that seemed to reach for her like an embrace.

The table near the window, her favorite, was free. Tucked far enough from the main flow to feel private but still catching that late golden light. The espresso machine gave its slow, steady hiss. Behind the counter, shoes squeaked faintly on tile.

Outside, the city moved in rhythm: a bus sighed at the curb, leaves skittered across the sidewalk, a couple strolled past, coffees in hand.

She slid into the booth and let herself picture tomorrow. Lauren sat across from her, that soft half-smile curling her stomach into knots. Sierra smoothed her sleeve, pulled out the folder of prints, trying not to imagine knocking over her latte from sheer nerves. She closed her eyes and tried to picture it all going well. That helped. Not much, but a little.

She took a few discreet pictures of the space with her phone, catching the glow on the wood, the curve of the window frame, the streak of sunlight across the table. Just in case she needed proof later that she'd been brave enough to sit here and imagine.

That night, the familiar chaos of movie night filled her apartment. Raven arrived first, wearing crushed velvet leggings and a hoodie that read *Hex the Patriarchy* in jagged silver font. Calliope came next, arms loaded with fancy popcorn and zero chill. Jett showed up fashionably late, eyeliner glittering like he'd kissed a disco ball and dared it to kiss back. His hair was slightly mussed, shirt buttoned one hole off, and he had that satisfied glow of someone who'd had a very good afternoon.

Jett flung himself onto the couch dramatically. "Alright, babes, tonight is sapphic central. Find me the cheesiest rom-com on here, extra gooey. I want subtitles just for the longing stares."

Calliope held up a wine bottle like a trophy. "With live commentary, darling. I will narrate every smoldering glance like it's Shakespeare in Verona."

By the time the heroine locked eyes with her rival-turned-lover, Sierra was clutching a throw pillow and pretending not to feel anything at all.

Calliope lobbed a popcorn kernel at her. "Observe, Miss Soft Eyes. Lesson one: the stare. Lesson two: the strut. Lesson three: thirst so subtle it belongs in a museum."

Sierra's cheeks flushed. "Someone's projecting."

Raven didn't miss a beat. "Calliope, please. Your idea of flirting is a bottle of tequila and a tragic backstory. Not a love language."

"Bold of you to assume I'm not doing that on purpose." Calliope smirked, stealing the popcorn back.

Jett leaned over and offered Sierra a fist bump. "Look at you, Camera Girl, not even fake-chill anymore. That's growth, babe. I'm proud."

Jett's phone buzzed. He glanced at it, smirked, and typed back quickly. "Sorry, scheduling tomorrow's entertainment." He waggled his eyebrows. "Some of us don't pine for weeks over coffee dates."

Sierra took the bump and laughed. Her defenses had collapsed somewhere between the slow-burn plotline and the third bowl of popcorn. Being this exposed felt good. Good to be seen and teased and still safe.

She slumped back into the cushions. "Okay, fine. I might have a tiny crush."

Raven snorted. "Tiny? Try epic saga, sweetheart. You skipped crush and went straight to trilogy."

"You know." Jett stretched like a cat across the back of the couch. "If Makeup Goddess hurts you, say the word and her bumper gets a love note. Courtesy of my keys."

Raven raised a hand. "And I'll hex her—with consent, mostly."

Calliope lifted her wineglass. "And I'll drink wine. Supportively."

Sierra shook her head, heart full. "Good to know I've got options."

"You've got a damn army." Calliope passed her the popcorn. "Go win your girl."

By Wednesday morning, her nerves had reached peak levels. The vibrating panic where even her playlist felt too loud.

She laid her outfit out on the bed as if it were part of a ritual. A cute top that hugged her curves in all the right places. Check. Jeans that made her feel confident but not like she was trying too hard? Also check. Boots that added a whisper of height without threatening to send her flying over a sidewalk crack? Absolutely yes.

She added a delicate gold necklace with a tiny camera charm and paused, fingers grazing the pendant. It felt small but steady. Like her. Like the version of herself she wanted to bring into this.

Then came the finishing touch: her favorite rose-tinted lip balm. Just a hint of sheen, a nod to Lauren's world of shimmer and polish.

Her camera bag sat by the door, already packed with charged batteries, both her 50mm and 85mm lenses, a spare SD card, and the little notebook she'd filled with worst-case-scenario conversation prompts.

She flipped it open.

- Compliment her artistry

- Ask about her favorite product

- Don't accidentally trauma-dump

- Smile like a normal person, not a horror movie doll

- For the love of God, breathe

Sierra exhaled hard, then pressed play on her "calm confidence" playlist—acoustic songs that reminded her of warm light through windows and soft certainty. She rolled her shoulders back.

It was just coffee. It was casual. A low-stakes, very chill hangout with the girl whose smile short-circuited her entire brain. And maybe, if the universe felt like being generous for once, it would blur into something more.

Chapter 9

Sierra arrived at Bean and Bloom twenty minutes early. Not fashionably early. Not *I was in the area* early. Full-blown, I-planned-this-with-the-precision-of-a-NASA-launch early.

She ordered a lavender chai latte because it sounded artistic and vaguely romantic. With one sip, she regretted everything. It tasted of flowers and anxiety.

Cradling the warm cup as if it might suddenly reveal wisdom, she sat at her favorite table near the window, then closer to the counter, then back to the window again. She pulled out her phone. Put it away. Opened her portfolio folder. Closed it. Checked her hair in the napkin dispenser's reflection. Dropped two sugar packets trying to look casual.

"Okay, Sierra. You are calm, composed, and drinking this purple regret tea like a woman who absolutely has her life together."

The door chimed. Sierra looked up and forgot how to breathe. Lauren stepped inside, and suddenly the whole café felt warmer. Cropped denim jacket. Soft gray tee. Black jeans that made Sierra want to write a poem. Her long black hair looked messy enough to look effortless. There was shimmer on her cheekbones and a calm in her smile that made Sierra's stomach forget how to be still.

The tote bag slung over Lauren's shoulder revealed the tell-tale end of a brush handle poking out, like a flag announcing she'd come in peace with pigment.

Lauren spotted her, and her smile widened, easy and warm. "I knew you'd be early."

Sierra stood up, nerves scrambling. "I like to survey the caffeine landscape. Very tactical."

Lauren laughed. "How's the survey going?"

"I panicked and ordered lavender chai. It tastes as if regret wore perfume."

"Bold move." Lauren said, setting her bag down and pulling out the chair across from her. "I'll go with an oat milk latte, but I respect the chaos."

Sierra smiled, the tightness in her chest easing. "Chaos is part of my brand. Right up there with bad impulse decisions and deeply awkward silences. I'm basically a lifestyle influencer."

Lauren chuckled and tucked a strand of hair behind her ear, revealing another flicker of highlighter. The light hit right. Sierra had to blink.

"Let me grab my drink. Don't vanish." Lauren rose with the same unhurried grace.

Sierra nodded, trying not to vibrate out of her seat. She thought about texting Thalia something dramatic like *Abort mission, she's prettier in natural light,* but preserved her dignity.

Lauren returned a few minutes later, latte in hand, and settled across from her again.

"This is for you." Sierra pushed the small white folder across the table. "A few shots from the shoot. I thought maybe we could go over them?"

Lauren opened it. Her expression shifted as she flipped through the glossy images. Her gaze softened, mouth parting slightly. "These are stunning. You made the shimmer look like stardust, and I look calm here. That never happens. You have a genuine gift."

Heat rose in Sierra's cheeks. "I try to capture what's already there. Most people don't realize how much they're saying without words. But you..." She paused, then pressed forward, "You say a lot. In the best way."

Lauren looked up, lips curled into something amused and knowing. "Do you rehearse compliments before coffee dates?"

"I tried. My cat judged me. Harshly."

Lauren grinned and leaned in, eyes catching on the charm at Sierra's collarbone. "That's a cute necklace."

Sierra opened her mouth to respond, but Lauren reached out first. Her fingertips brushed the tiny gold pendant, a camera charm, barely grazing her skin.

"A camera. I love it." Lauren's eyes still on it.

Sierra forgot how to inhale. The brush of contact was featherlight, but her entire chest hummed as if she'd touched a live wire.

Lauren's gaze finally lifted. She didn't apologize. Just smiled. Soft and unbothered. A little dangerous.

Sierra cleared her throat. "It was a gift from me to me after my first paid shoot. Not expensive, but it's meaningful."

Lauren nodded. "It suits you. Quietly powerful and intentional."

They sat in silence for a moment, sipping their drinks as the café buzzed around them. The espresso machine hissed. A barista laughed behind the counter. Morning light filtered through the windows, scattering leafy shadows across the floor.

Sierra glanced up. "What's your favorite part of your job that no one ever asks about?"

Lauren blinked, clearly surprised. Her shoulders relaxed as she leaned back, eyes thoughtful. "No one ever asks that. I think it's when someone looks in the mirror and says, 'I didn't know I could look like that.' Not because of the makeup, but because of the shift. Like you held up a version of them they'd never seen before."

Sierra felt it. That silent click of something falling into place. Not an attraction. Not even understanding. Recognition.

"That's what I love about photography. Those moments. The pause. That blink when someone sees themselves differently."

They sat in it for a while, whatever this was. Whatever it was becoming.

Lauren traced the rim of her cup with her finger. "Can I ask you something? How did your family react when you decided to become a photographer? Like, as a career?"

Sierra's smile faltered slightly. "They're... practical people. My parents wanted something more stable. Dad still asks about my 'backup plan' sometimes. Mom still introduces me as 'our daughter who takes pictures' like it's a hobby that got out of hand."

"That sounds lonely."

"Sometimes, but my siblings get it. Especially my brother Tobias. He's the one who actually convinced me to take my first paid gig. Said I'd regret not trying more than I'd regret failing." Sierra's expression softened. "What about your family?"

Lauren's fingers stilled on her cup. Something flickered across her face, too quick to read. "It's complicated. But I love that your brother saw your potential before you did. That's rare."

The way Lauren deflected made Sierra want to ask more, but she sensed a boundary. Instead, she asked, "What made you choose makeup artistry? Was it always the plan?"

"God, no." Lauren laughed, but it held a note Sierra couldn't identify. "I was supposed to be a lot of things. But makeup... it was the first time I felt like I could help people see themselves the way I saw them. Like I could give them permission to be beautiful. I was obsessed with watching makeup artists online. Nikkie de Jager was huge for me. Seeing someone who was so confident and talented and herself. She made me believe I could do this, too."

"Permission?"

"Some people need it. The world tells us we're too much or not enough, and makeup becomes this armor. Or this revelation. Both, maybe." Lauren's eyes met Sierra's. "Photography does that, too, doesn't it? Shows people versions of themselves they didn't know existed?"

Sierra felt that recognition again, deeper this time. "All the time. My art students especially... they'll create something and look at it like they can't believe it came from them."

"Exactly." Lauren leaned forward. "It's not about the makeup or the camera. It's about the moment someone realizes they've been holding back."

Lauren tilted her head. "You're easy to talk to. Like suspiciously easy. Are you a therapist in disguise?"

"Only if we bill by awkward monologue. I've got enough material for a ten-part series."

Lauren laughed again and glanced at her watch. "I hate this part. I have a client in forty."

"Real life ruins everything." Sierra managed a small smile.

Lauren grabbed her bag, then paused. "I liked this. We should do it again. Not only for work."

Sierra's heart threatened to break through her ribs. "Yeah. I'd love that."

Lauren reached out and gently touched her wrist. Her fingers lingered.

"See you soon, Camera Girl."

Then she turned, walking toward the exit with all the devastating calm of someone who knew exactly what she was doing. The bell over the door chimed. Sunlight poured in, and she was gone.

Sierra sat there, clutching her chai of poor decisions, her brain looping the same phrase over and over.

She called me camera girl.

From across the café, the barista gave her a look that said, *girl, yay.* With a hesitant smile, Sierra offered an awkward thumbs-up to signal she was okay, and somehow, beneath it all, she was.

Chapter 10

Friday night. Sierra bit her lip and stared at her phone, thumb hovering over Lauren's contact. Salem watched from the windowsill like a judgmental roommate who'd seen this whole thing unfold in slow motion.

"Okay. Worst case, she says no."

She tapped *call* before she could overthink it to death.

Lauren picked up on the first ring. "Hey, Sierra."

That voice. Like soft velvet and static electricity. It lit up something in Sierra's chest.

"Hey! I, um, was wondering if you wanted to come out tonight. Just a casual club night with my friends. No pressure."

"Only if there's dancing involved." Lauren's reply was smooth as always.

Sierra grinned. "Oh, there will be. See you at nine?"

"I'll be there. Text me the details."

As soon as she hung up, Sierra face-planted into a throw pillow with a muffled groan. "What am I doing?"

From the windowsill, Salem blinked once, slowly and deliberately, like he'd been asking himself the same question for weeks.

The line outside *Neon Pulse* buzzed with weekend energy. Strobe lights leaked from fogged windows, painting the sidewalk in bursts of saturated pink and electric blue. Sierra arrived first, tucked into her signature black leather jacket, a cropped tee underneath and ripped jeans that clung just right. Mascara. Lip gloss. Bold on the outside, nerves sprinting laps on the inside.

Calliope had once described *Neon Pulse* as "half club, half fever dream, all chaos." She wasn't wrong. The bass throbbed up from the concrete, a heartbeat for the entire building.

Lauren showed up in boots and a black top threaded with glitter that caught the lights, like she was born to sparkle. Her eyeliner was sharp enough to file a restraining order, and she styled her hair to perfection, sweeping it slightly to the side. Sierra's heart thudded.

"You clean up alright." Lauren grinned as she stepped closer. Somewhere between harmless and devastating.

Sierra blinked. "You're glowing."

But there was something — a flicker in Lauren's eyes. Like a shadow passed behind the shine. Bracing. Guarded. It disappeared so fast, Sierra wasn't sure she hadn't imagined it. Still, it lingered in the back of her mind as they headed inside.

The bouncer gave Sierra a nod and waved them all inside. Regulars got perks.

The bass rattled their ribs the second they crossed the threshold. Calliope tossed a drink to Sierra and dragged her onto the dance floor. Raven wore velvet pants and a sheer top layered over a mesh bra. Jett sparkled from head to toe, thanks to an aggressive amount of glitter gel and an abundance of confidence.

They pulled Lauren into the fold as if she'd always been there.

Jett gave a theatrical bow. "So, you're Lauren. We've heard things."

"Good things, I hope?" Lauren arched a brow.

Raven clinked her drink against Lauren's. "We'll decide by midnight."

Calliope was already smirking. "She passes the vibe check. Let's see if she can dance."

Lauren's grin was all teeth. "Careful what you wish for."

The chaos began immediately. Jett spun as if he were headlining his own music video. Calliope fake-serenaded the bartender with an empty glass as a mic. Raven invented a dance move that may or may not have summoned spirits. Sierra, never one to blend in, made the rounds with her signature twerk, initiating everyone in her orbit like some holy rite of queerness.

"Oh no!" Calliope shouted over the beat. "She initiated you, Lauren! The booty has blessed you!"

Lauren doubled over laughing, one hand on Sierra's arm for balance. "I'm honored. Truly." She snapped a photo of the moment — Sierra mid-twerk, chaos swirling behind her, then another of the group tangled in glitter and sweat.

She pulled Sierra close for a selfie, draping her arm casually across her shoulders. "Smile."

Then, without warning, Lauren kissed her cheek as the camera clicked.

The second after, her thumb hovered over the screen. Too much? Was she overstepping?

But then she smiled, hit *post*. "I'm uploading and tagging everyone. If I'm crashing your friend group, I'm going all in."

"Congratulations." Raven stole a sip of Lauren's drink like it was her right. "You're officially one of us now."

"I get my coven patch later?" Lauren deadpanned.

"Exactly. First you survive the night. Then Calliope's unsolicited relationship advice. Then brunch." Jett winked at Calliope.

Calliope threw a lime wedge at him.

They collapsed into a booth in a tangle of limbs and glowing skin. Someone ordered a round of shots. They toasted to "glorious chaos" and downed them with no coordination, no regrets.

As the next high-energy track faded, the DJ slid into a dreamy, slow tempo. The lights dimmed, and the tempo dropped like a sigh.

The group peeled away, flopping into the booth to recover.

Sierra stayed. She turned to Lauren, who was still beside her, sipping what remained of her cocktail.

"We should probably sit this one out."

Lauren didn't move. "Why? You afraid to slow dance with me?"

Sierra hesitated. "Maybe."

Lauren stepped closer, hand extended. "Good thing I'm not."

Sierra didn't even try to play it cool. She slipped her fingers into Lauren's and followed her onto the middle of the floor.

They settled into each other's arms, finding a rhythm without even trying. Lauren rested her head on Sierra's shoulder. After a long moment, Sierra pressed her cheek against Lauren's hair, breathing her in. They fit.

Sierra held her as if she were both precious and fleeting.

Around them, their friends couldn't help themselves.

"Y'all are *disgustingly* cute!" Jett called.

Calliope whistled. "You'd better spin her, Sierra!"

"Shut up!" Sierra called back, but she never loosened her hold.

Lauren laughed against her neck. The sound was soft and private, like a secret just for her.

Across the booth, Raven lifted her glass. "Carry on. I live for a good rom-com moment."

As the song wound down, Lauren pulled back slightly and tucked a strand of hair behind Sierra's ear. Her eyes lingered, quiet and unreadable.

"Let's grab another drink."

Under the slow pulse of neon light at the bar, Sierra brushed Lauren's arm by accident and felt it everywhere.

Lauren passed her a drink, fingers lingering longer than they needed to. Still no kiss. Not yet. But every glance, every brush of skin, said they both felt it.

Lauren didn't just blend into the friend group. She filled the gaps Sierra hadn't realized were still empty. The quiet ones. The ones between comfort and curiosity. It wasn't just physical; Sierra wanted to memorize every version of her, and she would. If Lauren let her, Sierra would learn her shadows, her stutters, her favorite brand of chaos.

They spilled out of the club after two, still laughing, still glowing. A flickering streetlamp buzzed above them as if it were in on the joke. The night air felt like a reset. Crisp and full of leftover adrenaline. Sierra's boots clicked against the sidewalk.

"I had fun tonight." Lauren bumped her shoulder gently.

"Me, too." Sierra tucked her hair behind her ear. Tried not to smile too big and failed.

There was a beat. Just enough time for a kiss, if either of them dared, but headlights cut across the sidewalk as their ride pulled up.

Lauren opened the car door with a small, teasing bow. "After you, Camera Girl."

Sierra climbed in, heart skipping like it was scoring a teen drama.

They dropped Lauren off first. Before stepping out, she gave Sierra's hand a gentle squeeze, quiet but deliberate. Then she disappeared through the lobby doors, and Sierra stared after her, lips parted, heart very much not okay.

Back home, she collapsed onto her bed still fully dressed. Salem jumped up beside her with a grunt and made himself comfortable.

Her phone lit up with notifications. Her cheek was still warm where Lauren had kissed it. She looked at Salem, eyes wide and dazed.

"What even is my life right now?"

The cat blinked once, unimpressed.

Sierra grinned and stared at the ceiling, the echo of Lauren's laugh still buzzing in her ears.

Chapter 11

The morning after the club, Sierra's phone lit up with chaos. It was a buzzing that came only from one place.

◻ **The Chaos Coven** ◻

> **Raven**: So. Spill it. Don't make me drag it out of you.

> **Calliope**: Confess, darling. My wine is poured and waiting for gossip.

> **Jett:** Sooo... was it lip action or just long stares and tragic poetry?

> **Sierra:** Rude. We danced, we talked, and maybe I fell a little harder.

Jett: Sooo... was it lip action or just long stares and tragic poetry?

Sierra: Rude. We danced, we talked, and maybe I fell a little harder.

Jett: That's it? No steamy details? You're killing me here.

Sierra: Unlike some people, I don't broadcast my love life to the group chat every weekend.

Raven: Drag him harder. Man lives for attention.

Calliope: Sierra, queen, you voiced the collective truth.

Jett: Hey, I'm an open book. And that book has excellent reviews. Okay, but seriously, she's officially one of us, right?

Calliope: Without question. Time for a rebirth. Rise, new chat, rise!

Jett: RIP Chaos Coven. May she rest in memes and midnight thirst traps.

Raven: Long live... wait, what do we call it?

Calliope: The name must be iconic. Etched in legend. Sparkle included.

Sierra: What about *The Inner Circle*?

Jett: Say less.

Sierra: Making it now. Hold, please.

A moment later, she invited Lauren into the group chat.

◻ **The Inner Circle** ◻

Jett: New chat. Who dis? Upgrade unlocked.

Calliope: Welcome to The Inner Circle, Lauren. No takesies backsies.

Lauren: I am honored. I've heard stories.

Raven: Lies. Except the cartwheel in boots. That disaster is canon.

Sierra: It was a spontaneous moment.

Lauren: Honestly? I respect the chaos.

Jett: We have one sacred tradition.

Raven: Weekly movie night. Sierra's place. Attendance mandatory. No excuses, no mercy.

Calliope: Horror week, darlings. Bring snacks or risk becoming them.

Lauren: I'm so in.

Sierra: You better be. I'm already prepping the vibe.

Lauren: I'll bring gummy bears and the spirit of a final girl.

Jett: She gets it.

Raven: She really does.

After the flurry died down, Sierra tapped Thalia's contact and curled into the corner of her couch, knees to chest. The second her sister answered, Thalia didn't waste a beat.

"I saw the photos. You two looked like a music video set to slow-motion heartbeats."

Sierra groaned and hid her face in her sleeve. "She kissed my cheek for a selfie, and I short-circuited. Like, full system crash."

"She fits in. You can tell from the pictures alone. It's easy."

"Yeah. It's scary how easy." Sierra chewed her lip. "Like we've known each other longer than we have."

"You sound smitten."

"I'm trying not to be. Not too fast."

Thalia's voice softened. "You don't have to rush or resist it. Just enjoy it for what it is. Let it unfold."

Sierra smiled. "I'm trying. Maybe failing but trying."

That evening, her apartment smelled of cinnamon candles and nacho cheese. Not a good combination. She fluffed throw pillows, straightened the blanket draped over the couch, then fluffed the same pillows again. Salem weaved between her legs, meowing like he was running quality control.

"You're judging me, aren't you?" She scooped him into her arms. He blinked slowly. Confirmed.

She put him down and went into the kitchen, where gummy worms were in a skull-shaped bowl, popcorn bags were ready for the microwave, and soda was chilling in the fridge. She took a deep breath. Warm lighting illuminated the room. She set the horror-themed coasters, and now all she had to do was breathe.

Tonight was going to be fun. Maybe even magical.

Calliope showed up first, wearing a cape and holding three DVDs like ancient spell books. "I bring cursed offerings. A possessed doll, found footage chaos, and this one's called *It Watches*. No description. Vibes only."

Jett came next with skull-shaped cookies, soda, and dramatic flair. "Because I love you all, and I understand aesthetics."

Raven marched in and immediately took over the smart bulbs and set them to a bloody red glow. "It's giving haunted house vibes now. We love to see it."

Then came Lauren.

She wore a black hoodie and low-rise jeans, her makeup soft but sharp—lavender shimmer on her lids, a line of kohl so precise it could cut glass. She carried bags of gummy bears, which she presented like an offering to a gothic deity. "Did I miss the blood ritual?"

"You're just in time." Sierra bumped her shoulder gently. "The altar's in the kitchen."

Lauren's grin hit somewhere between charming and devastating. Sierra might have blacked out a little.

They settled in and sprawled on beanbags, tucked under blankets, snacks within reach. They picked *It Watches*, mostly because no one could remember seeing it and the title sounded like a dare.

Twenty minutes in, a violin paired with a jump scare made Sierra jolt so hard her popcorn went airborne. She reached for the bowl and found Lauren's hand instead.

Lauren laughed softly. "You okay?"

Sierra nodded, but her pulse had already betrayed her. Lauren didn't let go. Instead, she laced their fingers together and kept them there—steady, warm, quiet. Sierra's whole body hummed like a struck tuning fork.

For the next hour, she barely registered the film. All she could think about was the press of Lauren's hand against hers. The way her thumb occasionally brushed Sierra's knuckles like it meant something. Like maybe it meant everything.

When the credits rolled, Jett sat up and pointed at the screen. "Okay, what was that ending? Who was watching? I have questions."

Calliope groaned and grabbed her coat. "They won't answer any of them. That's the charm."

Raven shook her head. "It was vibes over plot. I respect it."

Lauren stood and pulled out her phone. "Group photo before you vanish. It's law now."

They posed on the couch, half-asleep, full of sugar, with arms draped over each other like family. Lauren leaned into Sierra at the last second and snapped the pic.

"That one's going in my story. Caption: *Survived my first Inner Circle initiation.*" Lauren beamed.

Calliope pointed as she walked to the door. "You're in. Don't forget. No take-backs."

"Officially cursed." Jett added while yawning. "Welcome."

They left in a flurry of hugs and waves. Sierra saw them out with a warmth in her chest she didn't know how to name.

After the door clicked shut, silence settled in. Lauren lingered in the entryway, keys in hand. The shadows from the red lights danced on her face.

"Thanks for inviting me." Lauren's voice was soft.

Sierra wanted to say more. *Stay. Don't go. Let this be something real.* But the words caught in her throat.

"I'm glad you came."

Their eyes met. The moment stretched, silent and electric.

Then Lauren stepped back with a smile. "Goodnight, Sierra."

"Night."

Sierra watched from the window as Lauren disappeared down the sidewalk, arms wrapped around herself, the bag of leftover gummy worms swinging at her side.

She didn't know what came next, but she hoped, more than anything, that this was the beginning.

Chapter 12

Three days after movie night, Lauren sat cross-legged on their bed, phone balanced on their knees. They'd been thinking about Sierra constantly. Her laugh during the horror movie, the way she'd held their hand without hesitation, how effortlessly she'd fit into the group. But underneath all that warmth was the weight of what Sierra didn't know yet.

Lauren stared at the message draft for ten straight minutes.

> **Lauren:** Dinner at my place? Just us. There's something I want to tell you.

They deleted it. Rewrote it. Rephrased it. Then finally sent it with trembling fingers, heart thudding against the ribs like it knew what was at stake. This part was always the hardest.

They'd been here before... the late-night invite, the careful setup, the practiced calm that never quite reached their pulse.

It always started hopefully, but it rarely ended well. Some people got quiet; others made excuses. While some simply disappeared.

Lauren had learned not to expect anything. Not rejection, not understanding, and certainly not kindness. Just... silence, mostly, but sometimes violence. Too frequently, it was a slow drift into absence. They weren't worried about violence from Sierra at all, but the thought of losing someone already so precious to them seemed unbearable. But Sierra didn't leave Lauren on read. The reply came a minute later.

> **Sierra:** Yes. Just say when. And I'll bring wine.

Lauren let out a shaky breath and read the message again, and again. It didn't erase the fear, but it softened something. Just enough.

They placed the phone down gently, as if any sudden movement might jinx it. Tomorrow, Sierra would come over, and Lauren would finally say the words out loud. They didn't know what would happen next, but for the first time in what felt like forever, they wanted to find out.

Lauren's apartment smelled like lemon, rosemary, and the faint edge of nervous energy she couldn't shake. They had already checked the oven timer three separate times and rearranged the couch pillows twice, trying to convince themself it was all no big deal. Just dinner. Just Sierra. No pressure.

But their hands trembled anyway as they lit the candle on the table, the flicker catching the gold rim of the wineglasses. A playlist played low in the background, soft acoustic and lo-fi jazz woven together. Everything looked warm and inviting, but inside, they were bracing.

Lauren had hosted friends before. They'd dated casually, but tonight felt different. It felt like the air had shifted, like something important was waiting past the clink of silverware and flutter of nerves.

When Sierra knocked, Lauren exhaled and smoothed their palms down the sides of their jeans. She opened the door with a smile already halfway there.

"You're early." Lauren tilted their head in gentle tease.

Sierra grinned, holding up a bottle of wine like a prize. "I missed seeing your face."

Lauren's breath caught for a second, but they stepped aside and let her in. "Well, in that case."

Dinner was warm. Easy. Laced with the laughter that cracked open places Lauren hadn't realized they'd been holding closed. Sierra told stories with her whole body, eyes bright, and hands animated. She complimented Lauren's cooking like she meant it, and Lauren, normally shy about praise, soaked it in without shrinking.

But underneath the banter and the sips of wine, there was a slow pressure building. Not tension in a bad way, but more like potential energy. Like a held breath. Like if either of them reached a little further, the entire night would shift into something else, and Lauren wanted that, but not before she said what needed saying.

They cleared the dishes together, the rhythm between them so natural it felt rehearsed. When they settled on the couch with fresh glasses of wine, Lauren tucked their legs beneath them and turned toward Sierra, one hand still holding hers.

Lauren's throat tightened. "I need to tell you something."

Sierra's expression softened in an instant. She angled toward her. Her fingers gave Lauren's an encouraging squeeze.

Lauren looked at the candle flickering between them, then back at Sierra. "I'm transgender... a demigirl. Also, I prefer they/them pronouns. I didn't bring it up before because I wait to see how people treat me first, but I want you to know before this went any further."

They paused. Let the words land. Let them live in the room.

"I've known since I was little that I didn't fit what everyone expected of me. When I was three, I cried about wearing blue and not wanting to cut my hair. I didn't want to play with the boys. I didn't entirely fit in with the girls either, though I felt more like myself there, but mainly I felt like I didn't belong anywhere all the time. That's why I chose they/them for my pronouns."

Sierra was silent while she listened, truly listened, and it made Lauren's chest ache.

"To my parents, I was just wrong. I didn't understand why. As I got older, I started letting more of my true self come through. Small things, then bigger ones. When I was in high school, I found a group of friends who didn't just accept me; they celebrated me. They helped me find the courage to be myself. That support kept me going when everything else fell apart."

They glanced down, voice quiet. "My parents didn't take the changes well. By sixteen, they'd kicked me out. I stayed with friends, worked part time, and finished school. I scraped by, but I made it. My parents and I haven't spoken since."

They felt her hands shake and tried to still them.

"I don't talk about this much. I've been careful. People have been cruel. Sometimes they smile while they do it, and it makes you question everything. Makes you wonder if you're ever going to find someone who sees you fully and still stays."

Their voice nearly cracked on the last word.

Sierra reached out and gently tucked a piece of Lauren's hair behind their ear. Her fingertips lingered against their skin before she leaned in, forehead resting lightly against Lauren's.

"I'm so sorry you had to go through that. You didn't deserve it. None of it."

Lauren blinked, a tear slipping free before they could catch it. Sierra wiped it away with her thumb.

"I meant what I said. You didn't owe me that part of yourself, but I'm glad you shared it, and if I mess up your pronouns..."

"I'll throw a pancake at you," Lauren said with a grin.

"Blueberry, I hope."

"Obviously."

Lauren let out a shaky breath, the weight of their unease lifting inch by inch.

"Eventually, I'll tell you everything, but I need to take things slow. I hope that's okay."

Sierra pulled them into a hug that wasn't careful. It was solid and full, the kind you only give to someone you're not planning to let go of soon. They stayed that way for a long time, hearts pressed together, music humming quietly in the background like a heartbeat outside their own.

Sierra didn't move right away. She stayed curled beside Lauren, their fingers still laced together.

"I meant what I said. You didn't owe me that part of yourself, but I'm glad you shared it."

Lauren exhaled softly, the breath that only came after holding something in for too long. "It's always been... complicated. Telling people. There's this moment right after where I'm not sure if they're going to stay or shut down or worse. Like I have to prepare for anything."

"I'm not going anywhere. Not unless you ask me to." Sierra kissed their hand.

Lauren looked at her. This was the safest moment they'd had in a long time, maybe ever.

They stayed there like that for a few moments more, wrapped in low light and warmth. For once, Lauren didn't feel braced or guarded or halfway undone. Just whole.

Eventually, Sierra stirred and reached for her coat with reluctant hands. "I should head out. If I'm gone much longer, Salem will stage a mutiny." Sierra's voice was hushed, like anything louder might break the spell.

Lauren nodded, rising with her. They walked to the door side by side, fingers grazing again in a way that felt both familiar and electric.

Sierra paused in the doorway. "Thank you for trusting me."

Lauren looked at her steady eyes, the softness of her mouth, the space she left for every part of them. They reached up and cupped Sierra's face gently in both hands.

No hesitation or second-guessing. They kissed her. Soft, sure, and rooted. Not a question, not a maybe, but an answer.

When they pulled back, they smiled. "Good night, Sierra."

Sierra's voice was steady, but her eyes were shining. "Good night."

She turned and walked down the hallway, fingers brushing her lips as she went.

Lauren closed the door gently behind them and leaned against it, breath caught, eyes wide, heart full.

They wondered if they'd finally found someone who saw the whole of them... and stayed.

Chapter 13

The days that followed Lauren's revelation unfolded like soft pages in a favorite book: unhurried, familiar, and full of warmth. No dramatic shifts, no grand declarations. Just the steady rhythm of two people learning the shape of each other's lives and finding, somehow, that they fit.

Mornings began with sacred caffeine rituals. Lauren always arrived with Sierra's favorite lavender oat milk latte in hand, smirking like it was no big deal. "It's easier than watching you try to froth milk like a medieval alchemist," she teased. Sierra would glare playfully, steal her hoodie, and mutter something about betrayal. Lauren would let her.

Afternoons were slow strolls downtown, the kind that made the hours feel like honey. They wandered in and out of thrift shops and indie bookstores, fingers brushing until they laced together without a word. They bickered about the merits of Salem owning a cat-sized beanbag chair versus a faux-leather throne. Lauren insisted Salem was clearly a chaise lounge kind of man, while Sierra countered he deserved options. The stakes were low. The joy was genuine.

In the evenings, Sierra curled up with her sketchbook while Lauren painted their nails with a bold confidence. They scrolled through photo edits, shared silly voice notes, and read each other's texts in bad accents that devolved into giggles and sidelong glances that said more than either of them could.

They didn't label it. Didn't ask what this was or where it was going. But there was something in the way Sierra leaned into Lauren during a horror movie, or how Lauren always grabbed Sierra's hand, like they both knew. It was as if someone had already written it. Not in ink, but in breath, in glances, and in what was blooming between them.

Movie night came around again. Same crew, same brand of beautiful chaos. Calliope brought enough takeout to feed a small country. Jett arrived wearing silver alien antennae with a matching glitter lip. Raven took one look at the movie selection and threatened to unplug the TV if it turned out to be "another plotless gore-fest with zero budget and three brain cells between the cast."

They landed on a campy alien horror flick that leaned so hard into absurdity it practically came with its own laugh track. Within the first five minutes, someone tripped while running from absolutely nothing, the alien hissed in auto-tune, and Sierra felt the couch shake from collective groans.

Sierra claimed her usual corner of the sectional, and Lauren slid in beside her like it was the most natural thing in the world. Their legs aligned, knee to ankle, and neither of them budged. The contact was quiet, grounding, warm.

At the first jump scare, Lauren leaned into Sierra. "If she trips again, I'm siding with the alien. Let natural selection do its thing."

Sierra snorted so hard everyone cackled. Calliope clapped. "Honestly, worth it for that reaction alone."

By the time the credits rolled, Sierra's head had drifted to rest on Lauren's shoulder, and Salem had appointed himself their shared lap king. The glow from the TV cast soft shadows across the room, and for a moment, everything felt suspended in time.

Jett broke the silence. "So... I have a date this weekend. Hot white guy. Works in tech. Has a sleeve tattoo and knows how to make banh mi."

Calliope gasped. "A man who's hot and can cook Vietnamese fusion? Marry him immediately."

Raven nodded solemnly. "If he can make pho from scratch, he's a warlock."

Jett smirked. "We'll see. If he wears socks with sandals, it's over."

Sierra smiled, warm from the inside out. She didn't say it aloud, but her chest ached in the softest way, because Jett was glowing a little, and it reminded her how rare it was for any of them to feel seen outside of their circle, let alone hopeful.

Calliope motioned lazily between Sierra and Lauren. "Anyway, y'all looked like you stepped out of a romance movie tonight. Soft lighting, tender glances, feline mediator. It was a whole vibe."

"Babe, you two are giving serious Netflix vibes. Award-winning, queer, critically acclaimed. I'm obsessed." Jett nodded.

"Already renewed. Obviously." Raven agreed.

Sierra tried to play it cool, but the tug at her mouth betrayed her. She met Lauren's eyes, and in that glance, something passed between them. Not flashy or loud, but steady and certain.

When the group finally drifted out into the night, the apartment felt too quiet, too still. Lauren lingered, helping Sierra gather empty cups and re-stack pizza boxes. They moved in sync, like muscle memory.

Sierra handed over a hoodie for the walk home. Their fingers brushed, and for one moment, neither of them let go.

The call came the next morning. Jonas. Her mentor, her boss, her favorite human hurricane.

"I've got a last-minute assignment upstate." Jonas' voice crackled with urgency. "Four days. Travel, hotel, all expenses covered. Fast-paced, high-profile. You in?"

Sierra blinked, still in bed, hair wild, heart suddenly wide awake. "Wait. Seriously?"

"Do I ever joke about paid gigs and fancy room service?"

"Sometimes, but I'm still in."

She hung up, adrenaline buzzing through her. It was the opportunity she'd been chasing — real-world experience, an open door, a challenge wrapped in chaos. She should've been jumping up and down.

But her gaze drifted to the photo on her wall. The one Lauren had taken. Sierra mid-laugh, sunlight gilding her hair, the joy in her face so unfiltered it almost startled her. She hadn't realized until now how much that moment meant. How much they meant.

She grabbed her phone.

> **Sierra:** I have exciting news, and I hate it.

> **Lauren:** That's the most on-brand thing you've ever said. Tell me everything.

By nightfall, Lauren was curled up beside her, tucked into the blanket nest they'd unconsciously made together. Take-out containers littered her table like confetti, and Salem had given up and was sleeping on the floor in protest.

Sierra nudged Lauren with her foot. "Four days, and I leave on Friday."

Lauren stilled, then nodded. "That's amazing... terrible, but amazing."

"I'll try to check in, but Jonas runs on pure chaos and gas station espresso. So, I might vanish into the void a little."

Lauren's voice was quiet. "Just come back in one piece, okay?"

They hugged long and tight. The hug where your hands forget how to let go. Neither of them said the thing out loud. This already felt like goodbye.

The trip was beautiful, brutal, nonstop. Sixteen-hour shoots, fleeting bursts of amber light, and hotel suites so plush they almost made up for the exhaustion. Almost. Sierra fell into bed each night with sand still in her shoes and edits still buzzing behind her eyes.

She meant to call. She meant to text, but every time she found a moment, something came up.

When her flight finally touched down, she didn't even unpack. She dropped her suitcase by the door, thumbed open her phone, and hit Lauren's name.

No answer.

She stared at the screen. No missed calls. No new texts. Nothing.

Her chest tightened, ribs cinching as if they were bracing for bad weather.

Bean & Bloom was next. Their usual table sat empty, as did the one by the window. The barista shook her head when Sierra asked if Lauren had been around.

That night, Sierra went to their apartment.

When the door finally opened, Lauren looked dimmer. Washed out. Like someone had turned the brightness down.

Their eyes met.

Sierra didn't hesitate. She stepped forward and pulled them into a hug. "I missed you," she whispered.

Lauren nodded into her shoulder, their voice barely audible. "I missed you, too."

They talked little that night. Words felt too small for the ache of missing someone who had slowly become essential.

Instead, they curled up on Sierra's couch under a shared blanket, the glow of the TV casting soft shadows across the room. Outside, the world kept spinning, but inside, everything stilled.

Lauren's head rested on Sierra's shoulder, warm and familiar. Sierra turned slightly, brushing her lips against their temple.

"You okay?" her voice was barely above a whisper.

Lauren hesitated, breath hitching a little. "Didn't think I'd miss you this much. That's all."

Sierra shifted to see them better. "I'm so sorry that I didn't call or text. It was a brutal time. I missed you, too. I didn't see you coming, but now I can't imagine doing any of this without you."

Lauren let out a quiet laugh, rolling their eyes, but it was gentler than usual. "You're lucky I have a soft spot for cheesy."

"I am lucky. Lucky to have found you, and I might be cheesy, but I mean every word."

They leaned into each other, then, foreheads resting together, breath shared like a secret neither of them wanted to end. The closeness that didn't ask for more. It just was.

The movie ended unnoticed. The screen dimmed, and the room hushed. Lauren's hand found Sierra's under the blanket, their fingers threading instinctively. Sierra squeezed once, like a promise.

Home, she thought. *This is what it feels like.*

Chapter 14

The days after her trip felt different. Their rhythm was off, trying to find its beat again.

Lauren didn't show up with coffee the next morning. Sierra brought them instead. They wandered downtown, but it wasn't spontaneous like before. Sierra had to nudge Lauren to join her. At the second shop, Lauren finally reached out and took Sierra's hand, their fingers lacing like they remembered how.

The ease hadn't vanished; it had shifted to something softer and more cautious.

Sierra noticed the pause before Lauren laughed, the hesitation before their jokes landed. So, she filled the space with warmth. Sent more voice notes. Invited them to sketch with her on the porch. Asked about new makeup ideas, even if she didn't understand half the terms.

One night, Lauren brought over their laptop and played an old black-and-white movie Sierra had never seen. They curled on the couch, a bowl of peanut butter pretzels between them, Salem snoring on Lauren's lap.

"You always bring snacks I end up addicted to." Sierra reached for another.

Lauren grinned faintly. "I enjoy knowing you'll think of me when you eat them."

Later, Sierra pulled her sketchbook onto her lap and quietly started sketching. Not with intention, just movement. Lines. Curves. Familiar shapes.

Lauren noticed. "Is that me?"

Sierra didn't look up. "It's not finished."

"Doesn't have to be. I still see myself."

That was the first night they laughed without hesitation again. Something uncurled. It wasn't perfect, but it was real and growing.

Movie night rolled around again. Sierra called Lauren that afternoon.

"You're coming to movie night, right?" Sierra held her breath.

"Of course. I can't risk being kicked out of the coven. Plus, I miss you."

Sierra's heart swelled. "I know it's rough going back home so late. You're welcome to stay. You can even have my bed, and I'll sleep on the couch."

"I'll think about it." Lauren's mind was racing.

"See you soon."

· ♥ · ♥ · ♥ · ♥ · ♥ ·

The night was full of chaos and comfort. Calliope arrived with a tray of cupcakes. Raven made drinks labeled "emotional support beverages," and Jett, still glowing, walked in humming and clutching a matcha latte like it was sacred.

This time, the movie was a coming-of-age indie with too much voiceover and not enough plot. No aliens. Just angsty bike rides, metaphors, and lingering shots of raindrops on windshields.

Sierra claimed the corner of the couch again, and Lauren settled in beside her without hesitation. Their legs found each other, as always. Easy. Familiar.

Calliope tossed a pillow at Sierra halfway through the film. "Okay, but the real question is, how was the trip? You vanished."

Sierra looked sheepish. "It was amazing. Exhausting. Beautiful. Jonas is still a menace, but I learned so much. I missed you guys."

"And we missed you." Jett bit into a cupcake. "But I also got distracted by a certain someone named Ellis."

Raven perked up. "Hot Ellis?"

Jett grinned. "White-boy name. Latin-boy moves. Absolute menace on the dance floor."

"Ohhh, so that's why you were MIA in the group chat." Lauren poked him.

"I was hydrating." Jett wiggled his eyebrows.

Sierra laughed and leaned her head against Lauren's shoulder, the weight of the past few weeks settling into something soft.

When the credits finally rolled, Raven stood and stretched. "So was that a film or an extended perfume commercial?"

Calliope nodded. "Very vibes over plot. But honestly? Sierra and Lauren were the real feature."

Jett raised his matcha. "Gorgeous, you two are giving me all the rom-com feels again."

Sierra groaned. "You guys are impossible."

Lauren smiled and bumped her shoulder lightly. "They're not wrong."

The room buzzed with laughter and warmth, the kind that only comes from people who know each other's stories and keep showing up to hear more.

Sierra carried the empty chip bowl into the kitchen, weaving around scattered blankets and half-empty soda cans. Raven trailed after her, with a hesitant look on her face. Sierra pulled open the cabinet for more snacks, and that's when Raven spoke up, voice low.

"Hey Sierra, can I ask you something kind of personal?"

Sierra glanced over her shoulder and smiled. "Always."

Raven shifted her weight, fingers fiddling with the hem of her sleeve. "How did you know? That you were pansexual, I mean. I keep thinking I'm bisexual or pansexual, but mostly I just feel... confused."

Sierra set the new bag of pretzels on the counter and stepped closer, wrapping Raven in a quick, reassuring hug. "I don't think there's a neat answer. For me, it wasn't some lightning bolt moment. It was looking back and realizing my crushes never cared about gender. It was about how someone made me feel. Hearts, not parts."

Raven let out a shaky laugh, like she'd been holding her breath. "That actually makes sense. I still feel lost at times."

"You don't need all the answers today," Sierra said gently. "Questioning is valid on its own. You don't have to rush into a label unless it feels right for you."

Raven's shoulders relaxed, the tight line of her mouth easing into something softer. "Thanks. You make it sound a lot less complicated."

"That's because it is less complicated." Sierra nudged her playfully with her elbow before grabbing the pretzels again. "You get to decide what feels true for you, nobody else."

Raven smiled, this time brighter, and helped Sierra carry the snacks back into the living room.

After the others departed, Lauren and Sierra were still cuddled on the couch; neither of them moved.

"Have you thought any more about staying? You can have my room." Sierra's voice was barely above a whisper, heat creeping up her neck as she avoided Lauren's gaze.

Lauren's smile was shy but sure. "I would love to stay. Together. Nothing has to happen, but I'd love to cuddle."

They brushed their teeth side by side like they'd done it a hundred times, their shoulders bumping gently in the mirror. But tonight felt electric. Every accidental touch sent sparks through Sierra's skin. Salem circled their ankles like a sleepy chaperone, purring softly in the warm bathroom air.

Back in the bedroom, Sierra reached for the hem of her sweatshirt. She pulled it over her head slowly, the fabric catching for a second and revealing the soft skin of her stomach, the curve of her ribs. Lauren stepped into the room and stopped mid-step, their breath catching audibly.

"Oh sorry." Lauren turned away quickly, then paused, their voice dropping to something barely audible. "Actually, Sierra?"

Sierra lowered the sweatshirt and turned, pulse racing but calm. "Yeah?"

Lauren's voice was quiet, their eyes searching hers with an intensity that made her breath hitch. "Can I show you something? Can I show you me?"

Sierra's heart stuttered. The weight of what Lauren was asking settled into her bones. It wasn't just physical vulnerability, but complete trust. Her mouth went dry, but she nodded, understanding that this moment would change everything between them.

Lauren stepped closer, close enough that Sierra could feel the warmth radiating from their skin. They lifted their shirt first, slow and deliberate, revealing their chest inch by inch.

Sierra's breath caught in her throat, not from desire, but from the sheer magnitude of trust being placed in her hands. This wasn't just about physical vulnerability. This was Lauren saying *I trust you with all of me, even the parts I'm still learning to love myself.* Her chest tightened with something fierce and protective as her eyes traced the line of their collarbone, the smooth expanse of skin, the way their breathing made their ribs rise and fall. Every curve, every part of Lauren that they'd hidden from the world was now visible to her, and Sierra felt honored in a way that made her want to cry.

Then, with a small, shaky breath, Lauren slipped their pajama pants down.

Sierra didn't flinch. She'd photographed hundreds of people, seen bodies as art and form and light, but this... this was sacred. She didn't hesitate but stepped closer, the space between them charged with vulnerability and trust, and placed her hand gently over Lauren's heart. She could feel it racing beneath her palm.

"You're beautiful, Lauren. All of you."

Lauren's lips parted, a soft gasp escaping. Their eyes shimmered with unshed tears. Sierra's acceptance made them feel more like themselves than ever.

"I would like breasts, but I can't afford surgery, and honestly, I'm not sure I want to have it. Surgery terrifies me. When I was little, my mom had a complication with her surgery. I don't know what exactly, but ever since then, the thought of going under the knife gives me panic attacks. I have concerns with hormones, too."

Sierra's heart cracked open. She could hear the longing in their voice, could see the conflict written across their features—want battling with terror. Her own hands trembled as she reached out, because how do you touch someone's pain gently enough not to bruise it further? *Surgery terrifies me,* Lauren had said, and Sierra felt that fear like a physical thing sitting between them. She wanted to wrap Lauren in her arms and promise that nothing bad would ever happen to them, but she knew that wasn't her promise to make.

Sierra's thumb brushed across their cheek, soft and reverent. "You deserve whatever makes you feel whole, not what the world expects. I'm with you wherever that leads."

The words came from the deepest part of her, the part that had fallen irrevocably in love with Lauren's laugh and their kindness and their courage. Sierra realized in that moment that she would stand beside Lauren through whatever journey they chose—surgery or no surgery, hormones or no hormones. She would love them through every evolution of becoming.

Lauren exhaled shakily, something tight in their chest unspooling. "That's why I told you, because I want you to see all of me."

Sierra leaned in, pressing a feather-light kiss to their forehead. Then another to their jaw, feeling their pulse jump beneath her lips. Then another on their mouth, slower, deeper, tasting the salt of tears and something sweeter. Her hands rested at their waist, fingers splayed against warm skin, grounding them both.

"Can I touch you?" Sierra whispered against their lips.

Lauren's answer was barely audible but certain. "Please."

They moved without urgency, slipping beneath the covers with deliberate care. The cotton sheets were cool against their heated skin. Sierra's fingers traced the line of Lauren's shoulder, down their arm, memorizing the texture of their skin. Lauren shivered at the touch, their breathing growing deeper.

"Is this okay?" Sierra's voice was soft, reverent.

"More than okay," Lauren breathed, their hand finding the curve of Sierra's waist.

They kissed again, long and carefully, full of everything they hadn't said yet. Sierra's hand moved slowly across Lauren's chest, over their heart that beat wild and fast, down to rest on their stomach. Lauren's soft gasp made Sierra's own pulse skip.

"Sierra," Lauren whispered, their voice catching. "I never knew it could feel this safe. Can we take this slow and just cuddle tonight?"

Sierra pressed closer, her forehead against Lauren's. "Of course we can."

They lay tangled together, with hands that explored each other. They gazed into each other's eyes. Gave gentle kisses. Tonight was about feeling the intimacy they craved. There would be plenty of time for sex.

They curled into each other, skin to skin, breath to breath. The room was hushed except for the soft hum of the city outside and their synchronized breathing. Sleep came slowly, like a tide returning to shore. Not just safe. Home.

Chapter 15

The invitation was hand-delivered.

Well, okay, slid under Lauren's door with way too much glitter glue and a dramatic "TOP SECRET" sticker, but still.

Inside was a folded piece of thick cardstock, hand-lettered in silver gel pen:

Private Viewing Tonight Only:
A Celebration of Softness
Featuring the work of Sierra Turner
Location: Your favorite gallery
(a.k.a. Sierra's living room)
Time: 8 PM sharp. Bring your curiosity
Wine will be served.

Lauren had never been good at surprises. Sierra? She excelled at them.

On the walk over, Lauren kept one hand pressed to the envelope, as if it might disappear. Their heart thudded with something heavier than nerves. It felt like being chosen. Seen. Like they were walking into a moment that would change something.

Just before eight, Lauren knocked on her door, still a little breathless from the anticipation. Sierra opened it, wearing a black fitted tee and jeans that hugged her hips just right. Two glittery clips held her hair back, and they caught the light when she moved. Salem wound around her ankles like a velvet rope, granting Lauren entry.

After the tenth outfit change, Lauren had decided on a miniskirt, t-shirt, and the spiked choker Sierra once called "dangerously kissable." When Sierra saw it, her smile faltered enough to give her away.

The transformation of the apartment was complete. String lights lined the ceiling. A playlist of warm jazz hummed from the speakers. She moved the furniture aside. Hanging from twine strung across the walls were candid, curated, intimate snapshots. They were all of Lauren.

Sierra stood beside her, bashful. "I wanted to show you how I see you. Not just through a lens. Through everything."

Lauren moved through the room. Here they were mid-laugh, eyes crinkled. There, brushing hair from their face during a shoot. One sleeping with Salem curled protectively on their chest. Another, looking straight into the camera, unguarded, soft, and entirely themselves.

Lauren swallowed. "It's beautiful. I don't even recognize myself."

Sierra's voice softened. "That's because you're not used to being seen."

Lauren turned to her, overwhelmed. "I think I'm falling in love with you."

Sierra didn't even hesitate. "Good, because I already know I am."

They poured wine, their glasses clinking softly. Sierra laughed when Lauren took a confident sip. "This is definitely a... red wine. Very red. With grape flavors."

"That's a Merlot, you beautiful disaster." Sierra grinned.

Lauren shrugged. "I understand art. Grapes, not so much." It was easy; the kind of easy that makes you realize how rare that feeling is. They sat on the couch, fingers laced, quiet pressing around them like cotton. The air between them changed, not heavier, not charged. Just real.

Lauren's thumb brushed Sierra's wrist. "Can I kiss you now?"

Sierra nodded, breath catching. "I was hoping you would."

It started slow, lips grazing like a question. Then deepened, slow and certain. Hands explored the curves of arms, ribs, waist. Soft laughter when they bumped noses. Lauren tugged at Sierra's shirt. "Can I take this off?"

"Only if I can take off yours."

Their clothes fell away in pieces, not hurried, revealed like secrets. They stood in nothing but underwear, eyes meeting between every motion. A pause. Then they climbed under the covers together.

There was no choreography. Just instinct. Sierra's hand traced the line of Lauren's back. Lauren's fingers combed through Sierra's hair. A kiss on her jaw. Another, lower. Their limbs tangled and re-tangled as they learned each other's warmth by heart.

Sierra kissed the slope of Lauren's shoulder. "You make me feel like home."

Lauren blinked; tears threatening. "You make me feel whole."

They held each other, skin to skin, hearts stuttering in sync. No rush. No expectation. Just presence. Reverence.

Eventually, Lauren whispered into Sierra's neck, "This scares me."

Sierra held Lauren tighter. "Me, too."

They stayed like that for a long time, tangled in cotton sheets and something sacred.

And when Lauren finally drifted, wrapped in Sierra's arms, Sierra kissed their temple and whispered, "Stay with me."

Lauren didn't open their eyes. They didn't have to. "Always."

Chapter 16

The weeks that followed melted together like honey on warm toast. Those perfect stretches of time that embed themselves in your bones, all golden light, and quiet contentment. Sierra and Lauren had crossed an invisible threshold. This wasn't just dating anymore; they were constructing something deliberate, something that felt like home.

Their days started with drowsy voice messages exchanged before either was fully conscious. Sierra would whisper updates about Salem's latest plant massacre, her voice thick with sleep, while Lauren's morning greetings came wrapped in that scratchy, just-rolled-out-of-bed rasp that made Sierra's chest tighten in the best possible way.

Work pulled them in different directions. Sierra stayed buried in photo edits and shoot preparations, Lauren was bouncing between content creation sessions, makeup appointments, and brand collaborations. But somehow, no matter how the day fractured their attention, they always gravitated back toward each other. Sometimes it meant stolen lunch hours on park benches, sharing greasy fries while trading Salem photos like precious currency. Other evenings found Sierra appearing at Lauren's door after marathon shoots, collapsing onto their couch while Lauren worked magic on her aching feet and they half-watched horror movies they could recite by heart.

Lauren had woven Sierra into their online world with increasing boldness, though always with the careful consideration of someone handling something precious: a shared latte, Sierra caught adjusting her camera in the soft amber wash of evening light, Salem mid-swipe at a feather toy — all of it documented with the reverence usually reserved for museum pieces. Lauren's captions carried their signature blend of tenderness and humor, and even though Sierra had enthusiastically consented to every post, seeing their private moments broadcast to thousands still sent butterflies rioting through her stomach.

Movie nights with the Inner Circle maintained their sacred weekly rhythm. Themes rotated democratically: chaotic musicals one week, nostalgic teen comedies the next. Sierra always ended up pressed against Lauren's side, their legs tangled comfortably, shoulders brushing with every laugh. The night Lauren accidentally launched popcorn across Sierra's lap and spent several unapologetic minutes brushing away imaginary kernels from her thighs; the tension had become so palpable that Calliope launched into a theatrical chant of "Just kiss already!" until Jett silenced her with a well-aimed throw pillow.

Then came that Friday evening that would later feel like a turning point. Lauren captured Sierra barefoot in the grass during an impromptu photo session in the park, as if she were made of pure starlight. Lauren knew right then that would shift everything.

The photo appeared on their story that night: the two of them pressed cheek-to-cheek, grins splitting their faces, late sunlight wrapped around them like a benediction. Sierra's hand rested over Lauren's heart, her fingers splayed across their chest. The caption was beautifully simple:

@laurenluminary *Found the one. No filter needed.*

They tagged Sierra, and the response was immediate — an avalanche of hearts, flame emojis, excited "finally!", and messages of support that made Sierra's phone buzz constantly for hours. She'd given her blessing for the post, had even helped Lauren choose which photo to use. But seeing this declaration of love, permanent and public, felt monumentally significant.

That weekend, Sierra sprawled across her living room floor in post-yoga bliss, Salem draped beside her like a furry shadow, while Thalia's voice filled the space through her phone speaker.

"You looked absolutely radiant in that picture." Thalia's warmth was clear even through the digital connection. "And that caption? Lauren is making a statement. How are you processing all this?"

Sierra exhaled slowly, watching dust dance in the afternoon light. "I love it, honestly. It makes me feel cherished, and I know how thoughtful Lauren is about what they share publicly. But it makes everything feel......officially real, you know? Like we've crossed into territory we can't uncross."

"Are you thinking about telling Mom and Dad?" The question hung in the air like smoke. Sierra could practically see her father's expression, could predict the careful way he'd choose his words while his discomfort radiated outward like heat from a furnace. Salem stretched, batting lazily at Sierra's ankle.

"I don't know," she admitted finally. "Part of me knows I should. It feels dishonest not to, but I'm not equipped to handle whatever reaction they've got chambered and ready to fire."

"That's fair, but you know I'm in your corner, always. Whatever you need."

Sierra's smile felt like sunshine. "Thanks, you beautiful nerd."

"Anytime, you marshmallow."

Their laughter mingled and faded, and Sierra was settling into the peaceful quiet when her doorbell rang. Salem shot upright, ears pricked, while Sierra groaned and hauled herself off the floor.

She opened the door to find Tobias standing on her doorstep, still in his work clothes but with that familiar lopsided grin that meant he was up to something. Her brother had an uncanny ability to show up exactly when she least expected it, and somehow always when she most needed it.

"Hey, stranger." He held up a bag from their favorite Thai place. "Thought you might be hungry. Also, we need to talk."

Sierra's stomach dropped even as the smell of pad thai made her mouth water. "About what?"

"Oh, you know." Tobias pushed past her into the apartment, Salem immediately winding around his legs in greeting. "Just saw something interesting on your social media profile. Someone I know looked absolutely smitten."

Heat flooded Sierra's cheeks as she closed the door. "To bias..."

"Relax, I come bearing spring rolls and zero judgment." He set the food on her kitchen counter and turned to face her, expression softening. "Though I've gotta admit, I'm a little hurt you didn't tell me you were seeing someone. We tell each other everything, remember?"

Sierra suddenly felt like she was fifteen again. "It's complicated." She sank onto her couch.

"How complicated can it be? You look happy. Like, disgustingly, radiantly happy." Tobias flopped down beside her, his lanky frame taking up half the couch. "Lauren seems to have a great smile, clearly adores you, and anyone who can make my sister glow like that gets my automatic approval."

"You don't understand."

"Then explain it to me. What's got you all twisted up?" His voice was gentle now, the teasing edge gone.

Sierra stared at her hands, trying to find the words. "Lauren is transgender. I checked with them. They're okay with my telling my siblings." She took a shaky breath. "Lauren prefers the pronouns they/them. But Mom and Dad..." She trailed off, the weight of unspoken fears settling between them.

Tobias was quiet for a long moment, and Sierra braced herself for awkwardness or confusion. Instead, he reached over and squeezed her shoulder.

"Okay. What else?"

"What else?"

"What's the problem? You're happy, they're clearly crazy about you, and from their posts they seem funny and kind and..." He paused, studying Sierra's face. "Oh. You're worried about Mom and Dad."

Sierra nodded miserably. "I can already see Dad's face. That polite, uncomfortable expression he gets when he doesn't know how to react to something, and Mom will probably start researching like it's a problem she needs to solve."

"Hey." Tobias turned to face her fully, his expression serious but warm. "Remember when I brought home that girlfriend who was training to be a circus performer? And she kept practicing her aerial routine in their living room?"

Despite her anxiety, Sierra snorted. "Mom made Dad move all the furniture."

"Exactly. They adapted. They always do, even when they need time to catch up." He bumped his shoulder against hers. "Besides, have you seen how Lauren looks at you in these photos? Anyone with functioning eyeballs can see they're head-over-heels. Mom and Dad want you happy more than anything else."

"But what if..."

"Nope." Tobias held up a hand. "No what-ifs. Look, I'm not gonna lie and say it'll be smooth sailing. They will need some time to adjust, ask some awkward questions, maybe say the wrong thing while they're figuring it out. But, Sierra, they love you. That doesn't change."

Sierra felt tears prick at her eyes. "When did you get so wise?"

"Duh, I've always been wise." He grinned sheepishly.

"You're such a dork." But Sierra was laughing now, the tight knot in her chest loosening.

"I'm your dork, and I'm team Sierra-and-Lauren all the way." He stood up and headed for the kitchen. "Now come on, let's eat this food before it gets cold, and you can tell me everything about how you two met. I want details. Did they sweep you off your feet? Was there dramatic eye contact? Please tell me there was dramatic eye contact."

As Sierra followed him into the kitchen, Salem purring around their ankles, she felt something shift inside her chest. Maybe telling her parents wouldn't be as terrifying as she'd imagined. And maybe, with her siblings in her corner, she was stronger than she'd given herself credit for.

Outside Sierra's window, the sky blushed deep rose, which felt like a promise of the days ahead.

Chapter 17

Lauren had always been incapable of keeping secrets and making surprises happen. Their social media bio declared them a "chronic over-sharer" for good reason. Subtlety had never been their strong suit, but their three-month anniversary demanded something different. Something that would catch Sierra off guard in the most beautiful way possible.

They opened their phone and fired off a message to the Inner Circle group chat, careful to exclude Sierra from the thread.

> **Lauren:** Emergency group chat moment. I want to surprise Sierra for our three-month anniversary, and I desperately need your collective genius.

Calliope: Omg yessss FINALLY. Spill every detail immediately.

Jett: Please tell me this involves glitter. Or fairy lights. Preferably both.

Raven: I'm already packing pillows. Just point me in the right direction.

Lauren couldn't help grinning at their screen. These people were ridiculous and perfect and exactly what they needed.

They laid out their vision: a surprise anniversary picnic beneath the same sprawling oak where they'd first collided into each other's lives. They'd lure Sierra there under the pretense of needing help with promotional shots for their makeup business, something about that soft amber light photographers love, framed as content creation, that would sound perfectly plausible. Sierra would arrive expecting work but find something infinitely more meaningful waiting instead.

They descended on the park like a well-orchestrated mission just as the afternoon light began its slow slide toward magic hour. Jett spread out a soft blanket in purple and pink beneath their tree, right where everything had started. Raven fussed with the pillows, fluffing and rearranging until the little patch of grass looked like someone's cozy living room. Calliope arrived with a bucket of ice, a bottle of champagne, and a box of tiny cupcakes that looked way too fancy for a picnic.

Calliope helped put it all on display. "Everything's better with frosting. That's not opinion. That's science."

Lauren focused on looping the fairy lights through the oak's lower branches, trying not to notice the faint shake in their hands. The playlist they'd obsessed over for three days, titled *This Feels Like Us,* drifted from a small speaker, each song chosen like it mattered.

The flush on their cheeks came from both the setting sun and the knot of anticipation they couldn't quite hide.

The crew left with wishes of good luck. Once it all looked perfect, they pulled out their phone, thumbs moving slower than they expected.

> **Lauren:** Hey babe, can you meet me at the park near the coffee truck? I need help shooting some promo content. bring your camera? Magic hour waits for no one.

Sierra's response was immediate.

> **Sierra:** On my way

Lauren's heart was doing backflips in their chest. When Sierra appeared at the edge of the clearing, camera bag over her shoulder, she looked completely confused. She looked from the cupcakes to the wine to the fairy lights starting to glow in the dim light, then at Lauren standing under their tree with a smile that felt too big for their face.

"This doesn't look like any work shoot I've ever seen." Her voice was soft and curious.

Lauren extended their hand, fingers slightly trembling. "That's because it's not work. It's for us."

Sierra's eyes went wide and glassy as she took in the full scene: the blanket spread like an invitation, the lights casting everything in warm amber, the bottle of champagne catching the last rays of sunlight. She let Lauren pull her down onto the pillows, settling close enough that their knees touched.

"Three months ago, you found me right here." Lauren began, their voice thick with emotion. "You saw me when I was lost and became my compass. You're the safest place I've ever known, Sierra. My home."

They pressed a small cream envelope into Sierra's hands, watching as she opened it with careful fingers. The handwritten note inside contained the same words, but seeing Sierra read them, watching her lips move silently as she absorbed each line, made them feel newly minted, precious.

Sierra clutched the paper to her chest, tears threatening to spill. "Lauren..."

But Lauren did not stop. They produced a small photo album, its cover decorated with pressed flowers they'd collected on various adventures. Inside, their three months together played out page by page: Sierra laughing so hard during movie night she could barely breathe, holding Salem like he was the most precious thing in the world, waving her hands around while she explained camera settings, a selfie of them both pressed cheek to cheek, laughing so hard the picture came out blurry.

The last page had a photo from just last week, the two of them curled up together on Sierra's couch, completely content. Lauren had written underneath: "real-life magic."

"There's one more thing." Lauren pulled out a small velvet box with shaking hands.

Inside was a simple silver keychain shaped like half a heart.

Sierra looked up with questioning eyes as Lauren revealed its match, the two pieces fitting together perfectly when held side by side.

"Now we match, and you have half of my heart." Lauren's voice was now barely above a whisper.

Sierra broke. No holding it back this time. Tears, laughter, everything all at once as she threw herself at Lauren. They went down together, landing in the pile of pillows with a graceless thud and a tangle of limbs.

"This is too much." Sierra swiped at her face and failed. "You surprised me. You can't stand keeping secrets."

Lauren's hands found her cheeks, thumbs brushing away the wetness. Their eyes were shining. "Guess you're worth the effort."

Sierra let out a half-sob, half-laugh. "I love you so much."

Lauren felt it hit them, warm and heavy, like the air before a storm. "I love you, too. Enough to pull this whole thing off instead of blurting it the second I felt it."

They laughed again, holding on to each other while the light shifted from gold, then pink, then the deep violet of early night. The fairy lights softened everything, as if the edges had been blurred.

Later, when they started gathering up the pillows and packing away the album, Sierra caught Lauren's wrist. "Come home with me?"

Lauren leaned in and kissed her, tasting the frosting on her lips. "Always."

They left the park together, hands linked, fairy lights behind them winking as if they knew. Lauren felt lighter than air, drunk on love and the success of their first genuine surprise.

"Hey, you've got frosting on your nose."

Sierra gasped in mock outrage and swatted at them. "That's incredibly rude to point out after such a romantic evening."

But she was laughing as she said it, and Lauren thought they could listen to that sound for the rest of their lives.

Chapter 18

Sierra had never freaked out this much about something that wasn't work. Her apartment looked like a Pinterest board threw up. Candles adorned every flat surface, fairy lights she'd spent an hour untangling, and a playlist Calliope helped her make called "For Every Version of You I've Loved" playing in the background.

"It's romantic but not spa-music weird," Calliope had promised when they picked out songs.

The rose petals had cost her forty dollars. Forty dollars for flower bits she was going to scatter on the floor like confetti. Lauren was worth every penny and then some. She'd made a trail from the door to her bedroom and covered the bed, then stood back wondering if it looked romantic or like a crime scene.

Wine was chilling. She assembled the cheeseboard. Candles were lit, and she was losing her mind. She grabbed her phone and made a quick group chat without Lauren.

Sierra: Help, is this too much??? What if they think I'm insane?

Raven: You're fine. stop spiraling

Jett: It's cute as hell

Calliope: Put on the black lace thing we bought and stop being a baby

Sierra sent back a row of kiss emojis and was reaching for her phone to text Lauren when it buzzed.

Lauren: Hey babe, can you meet me at the park near the coffee truck? I need help shooting some promo content. bring your camera? Magic hour waits for no one.

"Oh, come on." She stared at her phone. "Seriously?"

Salem was watching from his spot on the couch, tail twitching like he thought this was hilarious.

"Don't look at me like that. This timing is insane."

She blew out the candles, grabbed her camera, and ran out.

·♥·♥·♥·♥·♥·

Lauren's surprise had been perfect. The whole picnic thing with lights in the trees, the photo book, those little heart keychains. Sierra cried actual happy tears. They kissed under the fairy lights and walked home. Sierra felt like she might float away.

Now Lauren stood in her doorway looking stunned.

"Holy shit." Lauren took in the candles and rose petals. "You did all this?"

"I was about to text you when you texted me." Sierra was grinning so hard her cheeks hurt. "We're idiots."

"We planned the same thing on the same night?"

"Apparently we're that couple now."

"I love that we're that couple." Lauren kissed her cheek.

They ended up on the couch with wine. Sierra's hands were shaking when she handed over the letter.

You showed up in my life like something I didn't know I was looking for. That first coffee shop smile broke me open in the best way. With you, I laugh until my sides hurt and dream about things I never thought I wanted. I want to build something real and messy and beautiful with you. Thank you for seeing me, all of me, and sticking around anyway. Every day feels like we're just getting started. ~S

Lauren pressed the letter to their chest. "You're gonna make me cry."

"Good cry though, right?"

The drawing made them go quiet. Sierra had spent weeks on it. It was the two of them curled up on her couch with Salem draped between them like a furry blanket.

Lauren laced her fingers through hers. "This is us."

"This is how it feels. Like home."

They sat there sipping wine and talking in those soft voices you use when something feels sacred. Kissing slow and sweet. Then Lauren stood up with a look in their eyes and held out a hand.

"Come on."

The bedroom looked like a fairy tale with all the candles and scattered petals. Lauren stopped in the doorway.

"Sierra. This is..."

"Too much?"

"Perfect." They pulled her close. "You're perfect."

Salem meowed from the living room, offended they'd abandoned him.

"Sorry, buddy," Lauren replied. "Find somewhere else to hang out for a bit. You can't see what I'm about to do to your momma."

Sierra laughed, face hot from wine and nerves. "We don't have to—I mean, if you're not ready—"

"I'm ready. I don't want to wait anymore."

The first kiss was careful. The second one wasn't. They kissed as if they couldn't get close enough. Clothes came off slowly, every piece a question answered with a nod or a soft "yes."

Lauren's mouth found that spot on Sierra's neck, and she gasped. Sierra's hands got lost in Lauren's hair, holding them close as everything turned electric.

When Sierra eased Lauren back onto the bed, she kissed a trail across their skin, collarbone, chest, then throat. Every touch felt like a conversation they were having without words.

They moved together as if they'd been learning each other forever. Sierra's kisses traveled lower, reverent and slow, until Lauren's breath caught and they whispered her name like a prayer.

"Tell me if you want me to stop," Sierra said against their skin.

"Don't stop. Please." Lauren's fingers twisted in the sheets.

Sierra took her time, patient and devoted, until Lauren fell apart beneath her touch, calling her name into the flickering darkness.

Next, Lauren kissed her with a deep, hungry, and grateful kiss. "Your turn."

Lauren returned every tender kiss, every whispered devotion, until Sierra's back arched and her breath came in soft gasps, Lauren's name spilling from her lips.

Afterward, they lay tangled together, skin cooling in the breeze from the window. Lauren traced patterns on Sierra's shoulder while Sierra kissed whatever part of them she could reach.

"You're my everything, Sierra."

Sierra smiled against their collarbone. "... and you are mine."

Outside, the wind stirred the curtains like a lullaby, and for the first time in either of their lives, running away was the furthest thing from their minds.

Chapter 19

Sierra woke up slowly, awareness washing over her like warm water. Morning light was filtering through her curtains, all soft and golden. The first thing she noticed was Lauren's breathing next to her, steady and deep, the peaceful sleep that made Sierra's chest feel tight in the best way. Their bodies were still tangled together from last night, bare legs twisted under the sheets, skin warm and familiar against skin.

She was smiling before she had even opened her eyes. God, last night. The memory kept playing on repeat in her head. All those candles flickering everywhere, the way Lauren had said her name like it's sacred. The flower petals still scattered across her bedding, proving that it all happened and wasn't just some incredible dream.

Every part of her felt different this morning, like she was humming at a frequency she'd never reached before. Her body still carried the echo of Lauren's touch, and she never wanted that feeling to fade.

Lauren stirred beside her, eyelashes fluttering as they came back to the world. They blinked once, twice, then buried their face in the curve of Sierra's neck with a sleepy, satisfied sigh that made Sierra's heart do little flips.

"Noooooo, it can't be morning already." Lauren's voice was all gravelly and adorable.

Sierra pressed a kiss to the top of Lauren's head, breathing in that familiar scent of their shampoo mixed with the vanilla candles from last night. "Unfortunately, yeah, but I make killer waffles, so we're not doomed. You stay here."

Lauren's groan was dramatic, though muffled. "You're gonna annihilate me. I'll never recover from this level of perfection."

"That's the goal." Sierra kissed Lauren's forehead.

From down the hallway, Salem started his morning routine, loud, indignant meowing that echoed through the apartment as if their happiness offended him.

"Your son is having opinions about being ignored." Lauren laughed, and Sierra could feel the vibration against her throat.

Sierra withdrew from Lauren's embrace as if it was the most difficult thing she's ever done. She put on the silk robe from Thalia, the one that had been sitting unused since Christmas. She padded barefoot to the kitchen, began whisking the batter, and hummed. Humming... at this hour. She almost laughed at herself. She hated mornings, and she never hummed in them, but everything felt different today. Charged with this new domestic intimacy that made even making breakfast feel special.

She sliced fresh strawberries and arranged everything on her nicest tray. Golden waffles, fresh orange juice in actual glass glasses instead of her usual mismatched mugs, even a little sprig of mint from her windowsill herb garden, because why the hell not make this morning feel as magical as it was.

When Sierra went back into the bedroom, Lauren was leaning against the headboard with their hair askew and the white sheet draped over their chest. The sight made Sierra stop in the doorway for a second. Lauren looked like something out of an old painting, all soft in the golden morning light.

Lauren's entire face lit up when they saw the breakfast spread. "Okay, no offense to last night, which was absolutely mind-blowing, but this might be the sexiest thing you've ever done for me."

Sierra set the tray down and climbed back into bed, unable to stop grinning. "Just wait until you taste them."

They fell into a peaceful rhythm, feeding each other bites of waffle and laughing at nothing. Lauren got powdered sugar on their nose, and Sierra kissed it off. It was a moment of such perfection; it was almost unbearable.

Then, both of their phones started buzzing like crazy. The group chat was exploding with notifications.

> **Jett:** You're both very welcome. We're basically professional matchmakers at this point.

> **Raven:** Operation Double Surprise = MISSION ACCOMPLISHED

> **Calliope:** We accept payment in detailed gossip and bottomless mimosas

Sierra burst out laughing, nearly spilling orange juice everywhere. "Oh my God, they orchestrated the whole thing!" She typed back quickly.

> **Sierra:** We love you. You beautiful agents of chaos. No notes whatsoever.

Before she could put her phone down, it started ringing. Jonas' name flashed across the screen, and Sierra felt that familiar feeling of mild panic. Her boss never called this early unless something big was happening.

She gave Lauren an apologetic glance. "It's Jonas. Give me like two seconds?"

Lauren nodded, stealing another strawberry while Sierra answered.

"Morning, Jonas. What's happening?"

"Sierra, thank God you're awake. Hope I'm not interrupting anything important, but I've got an opportunity that fell into my lap."

She watched Lauren lick powdered sugar off their fingers and tried to keep her voice professional. "I'm listening."

"Last-minute travel gig. Hawaii. One week, lifestyle campaign for this luxury resort. Think beaches drenched in molten light, couples photography, that dreamy editorial style you're so good at. You'd be my second shooter, and I'm willing to pay rush rates because we leave in three days."

Sierra's heart did a little somersault thing. "That sounds incredible."

"There's one more piece; do you know if that makeup artist friend of yours is available? The client specifically wants a pro on set every day for hair and natural glam work, and Daphne isn't available. Beach goddess vibes, you know?"

Sierra's eyes met Lauren's curious gaze across the breakfast tray. "Let me check with them and get back to you ASAP."

"Perfect. I'll email you all the details. Thanks, Sierra."

After she hung up, Sierra stared at Lauren for a moment, hardly believing what she was about to ask. "So... how do you feel about going to Hawaii for work? Jonas needs a makeup artist, too."

Lauren blinked, as if they were processing the question in a foreign language. "I'm sorry. Is that a trick question? Did you ask me if I want to go to Hawaii with you?"

Sierra launched herself across the bed, barely managing not to knock over the breakfast tray. "We'd be working early morning and evening shoots when the lights at its best, but we'd have entire afternoons free to explore. Lauren, we would be in Hawaii. Together. Getting paid to create beautiful things in paradise. We'd leave in three days."

Lauren's squeal was so pure and joyful that Salem came running down the hall to see what was happening. They grabbed their phone, fingers flying across the screen. "Hold on, let me message my clients about rescheduling. Yes. Yes, yes, yes, absolutely yes!"

Sierra was already dialing Thalia before Lauren finished typing. "Hey, are you free to cat-sit for a week? I desperately need the world's best cat-sitter, so Lauren and I can go to Hawaii to work! I leave in three days."

Thalia didn't even hesitate. "For my nephew Salem? Always! But you're buying me dinner when you get back and spilling every single detail."

"Deal." Sierra laughed and gave Lauren a thumbs up.

Lauren clapped their hands together like an excited kid. "This is happening! We're going to Hawaii! Together! For work that we both love."

Sierra felt like her chest might explode from pure happiness. "This feels like some kind of dream."

They kissed with syrup-sweet lips, their excitement bubbling between them like champagne. Sierra could already taste the future — salt air, sunset shoots, lazy afternoon swims, and evening walks on the beach. Everything felt wide open, like the horizon was stretching out in front of them, full of waves, possibilities, and whatever this beautiful, messy, magical thing between them was still becoming.

Outside, the morning sun kept climbing higher, but neither of them felt any rush to leave this perfect little cocoon of rumpled sheets and shared dreams they'd built together. The day could wait a little longer.

Chapter 20

Jonas' voice came through Sierra's phone speaker, crackling with that slightly fuzzy quality.

"Oh, one thing. The resort's pretty packed right now, and the client booked everything last minute. The only room they had left has a king bed. Is that going to work for the two of you?"

Sierra glanced over at Lauren, who immediately gave her the most obvious wink in human history and mouthed "please" with exaggerated lip movements that made Sierra want to laugh out loud.

"We can share." She tried to keep her voice professional while Lauren made ridiculous faces behind the phone. "No problem at all."

"Perfect. See you both bright and early Monday morning."

· ♥ · ♥ · ♥ · ♥ · ♥ ·

Lauren was a wreck getting through security. They kept pulling out their boarding pass as if it might change between checkpoints, and by the time they reached the gate their leg was bouncing so hard Sierra half-expected the chair to rattle apart.

Sierra buckled herself into the seat. "Alright, be honest. This is your first flight, isn't it?"

Lauren latched onto her hand as if it was the only solid thing on the plane. "I just don't trust metal tubes shooting through the sky faster than cars are even allowed to go."

Sierra tried not to laugh, gave their fingers a squeeze, and shook her head. "You trust GPS to guide us through the middle of nowhere, but you don't trust actual trained pilots?"

Lauren shot her a look that was half panic, half indignation. "At least GPS doesn't drop you from thirty thousand feet if it has a bad day."

"Fair point. But GPS also doesn't come with tiny bags of pretzels and ginger ale. Plus, we can't drive to Hawaii."

"That's not a terrible argument."

Sierra laced their fingers together more tightly. "Hey. You're safe, and when we land, we're gonna be in actual paradise."

Lauren took a few shaky breaths, but by the time they were airborne and cruising, Sierra caught them staring out the window like they were watching pure magic happen. The endless blue sky reflected in their eyes, and their entire face had this expression of wonder that made Sierra's chest feel warm and tight.

"You're so beautiful," Sierra said softly, not meaning to say it out loud.

Lauren turned to her with raised eyebrows. "What?"

"Nothing." She grinned. "Just... I love your face."

Lauren's smile could have powered the entire airplane.

·♥·♥·♥·♥·♥·

The moment they stepped off the plane, warm island air hit them like a hug, and someone immediately draped flower leis around their necks. The petals were soft against Sierra's skin and smelled like heaven.

"Well, looks like we're getting lei'd right off the plane." Lauren tried to keep a straight face.

Sierra groaned so hard it hurt. "Oh, my God. I bet they've literally never heard that joke before."

The resort was like stepping into a tropical fairy tale. Palm trees swayed everywhere, ferns the size of small trees created natural canopies, and flowering vines twisted around every surface. Their room had an incredible panoramic view of the beach, a full kitchen that was way nicer than Sierra's actual apartment, a balcony that overlooked the ocean, and...

"One bed," Sierra announced, grinning as if she'd won the lottery.

"What a complete tragedy." Lauren deadpanned, then launched onto the mattress like a kid in a hotel for the first time.

Sierra didn't hesitate to dive right after them. They bounced on the plush mattress, laughing and being ridiculous until Lauren grabbed Sierra's shoulders.

"Wait. Hold up. We're in Hawaii." Lauren's eyes went wide as if they were just now processing it.

"We're in Hawaii!" Sierra shrieked.

They screamed and tore out of the room barefoot, not even thinking... through the resort, straight to the beach. The sand was scorching, soft, sticking between their toes. They didn't stop running until the waves caught their ankles.

Both of them doubled over, laughing too hard to breathe.

"I can't believe this is actually happening." Sierra stared at the water rolling in.

Lauren pulled out their phone, snapped a shot of their feet side by side in the sand like proof it was real. Then they used their finger to draw a heart around them in the wet sand. "Now it's real."

They took about fifteen selfies, including one where Sierra was kissing Lauren's cheek while Lauren grinned at the camera. Lauren posted it with the caption: *Found paradise. Found everything.*

The grocery store run felt surreal, like they were playing house in the most beautiful place on earth. They grabbed tropical fruit, local snacks Sierra had never heard of, a bottle of wine, and basic supplies. Lauren insisted on taking a picture of Sierra holding a fresh pineapple above her head like some kind of tropical trophy. Then they made a store employee take one of them in front of the produce section, which they tagged *domestic life in paradise unlocked.*

Back in their room, they spread everything out on the bed and ate like they were having the world's most exotic picnic. Jetlag hit them both like a truck around seven PM. They put on a random movie, but neither of them was watching. They just curled into each other on top of the covers, legs tangled together, breathing evening out into sleep.

The alarm went off at four-thirty in the morning, which felt like actual violence.

Lauren made a noise that wasn't quite human. "Someone needs to delete the sun."

Sierra rolled over and buried her face in the pillow. "You first."

They shuffled into the bathroom together, took one look at their combined bedhead situation in the mirror, and burst into laughter.

Lauren tried to brush their teeth with one hand while attempting to tame their hair with the other. "Wow. We are absolutely beach glam ready."

Breakfast wasn't possible, so they grabbed coffee and bagels from the lobby, packed up all their equipment, and met Jonas and the models down on the beach as the sky turned that perfect golden color.

Sierra fell into work mode, moving around the shoot with her camera as if she were dancing. Lauren was in their element, too, touching up makeup and adjusting hair while the ocean breeze tried to undo all their work. They moved around each other as if they'd been working together for years, occasionally brushing shoulders or stealing glances when they thought no one was looking.

By noon, they were done and exhausted but happy.

Lauren stretched their arms above their head. "Okay, new rule. We didn't fly all this way to work and sleep. Let's explore."

They wandered through this incredible outdoor market, taking in all the colors and smells. The energy was incredible. Street vendors were selling everything from hand-carved jewelry to fresh coconut water. Lauren stopped dead in their tracks when they spotted a small sign advertising free hula lessons.

"Oh my God, Sierra. We have to do this!"

Sierra backed away. "Are you joking? Me hula? I can barely walk in a straight line. I can twerk a little, and that's literally it."

"That's complete bullshit!" Lauren grabbed her hand and started dragging her toward the instructor. "Come on, it'll be fun!"

The lesson was a beautiful disaster. Sierra tripped over her own feet multiple times. A hip-shimmy by Lauren nearly resulted in a face-plant against a tiki statue. The instructor, this sweet older woman with flowers in her hair, gave them the most polite pity claps Sierra had ever witnessed.

They thanked her way too many times and continued wandering, eventually stopping at a food stand to try poi for the first time.

"It's very... earthy." Lauren was trying to be diplomatic, though their face screamed otherwise.

Sierra made a face. "You mean it tastes like someone mixed sand with disappointment."

They both tried hard not to offend the sweet lady who kept offering them more samples.

Back at the resort, they had enough time to shower off the beach sand and change into fresh clothes before the evening shoot. Lauren touched up their makeup kit while Sierra transferred the morning's photos onto her laptop. As if they had always done this, they moved around the room with a gentle rhythm.

Just before the light turned golden, they returned to the beach with their things.

The second shoot went even better than the morning one. Sierra expertly captured every perfect moment as Lauren flawlessly blended bronzer on sun-kissed skin. In between setting things up, they'd share smiles, eye contact, and light touches.

By the time they wrapped, the first stars appeared in the darkening sky. They were both sun-drunk, salty, and ridiculously happy.

Back in their room, they had every intention of recreating some of the romance from their last night together. They began showering together, rinsing away the salt and sand, until Lauren yawned mid-kiss and Sierra almost dozed off.

They toweled off, changed into soft pajamas, and fell into bed, utterly spent.

Sierra's face planted into her pillow. "Tomorrow."

Lauren curled up against her side. "Definitely tomorrow."

And they were both asleep before either of them could say another word.

Chapter 21

The alarm went off like an air-raid siren at four-thirty again.

Lauren made a noise that sounded like a dying whale and pressed their face deeper into the pillow. "Remind me why we're voluntarily torturing ourselves at this ungodly hour?"

"Because they're paying us stupid amounts of money." Sierra forced herself to sit up even though her entire body was protesting.

"Ugh. Okay, that's a brilliant point."

They stumbled through their now-familiar morning routine. Coffee that was too hot, equipment that felt heavier each day, and the sleepy fumbling around that somehow still got them out the door on time. The morning shoot went off without a hitch, but by the time they finished packing up all the gear, they looked at each other with matching expressions of pure exhaustion.

Sierra looked at Lauren. "We're dead."

"So incredibly dead."

They both started laughing, which probably looked insane to anyone watching, but they were too tired to care.

No touristy adventures today. They couldn't handle anything more intense than a slow walk along the beach, bare feet in the warm sand, hands intertwined while the salty breeze cooled their overheated skin. The rhythm of the waves was better than any meditation app Sierra had ever tried.

Lauren stopped every few minutes to take photos, some for their social media, some for potential brand content, but mostly because they couldn't seem to help themselves. They caught Sierra staring out at the endless ocean, the afternoon sun creating a perfect halo effect in her hair. Then they got a windblown selfie of them both, sleepy grins and salt-tangled hair on full display, which they posted right away with the caption: *soft days with my softest person.*

They returned to their room and collapsed onto the bed as if someone had shot them, intending to nap for about an hour before their late afternoon session. Sierra was drifting off when her phone started buzzing insistently on the nightstand.

Jonas. Of course.

She groaned but forced herself to answer. "Hey, what's happening?"

"Quick update about tomorrow's shoot. We're stepping it up a notch. I reserved a yacht for us for the next two days. Sunrise to sunset. Get ready for serious luxury vibes and a lot of sea breeze messing with everyone's hair."

As soon as she hung up, Sierra turned to Lauren with wide eyes. "Guess what we're doing tomorrow?"

Lauren raised an eyebrow, clearly too tired for guessing games.

"Yacht."

Their eyes went wide simultaneously.

"Oh shit, we're gonna die fancy." They both burst into slightly hysterical laughter.

Back in their room, they got undressed after the evening shoot. They both were too tired to talk. Sierra started the shower, and the room quickly became steamy. After a long day in the sun, hot water was pure bliss.

Lauren stepped under the spray first, and when Sierra joined them, they shared one of those looks that seemed to communicate entire conversations. The look that made Sierra's chest feel tight and warm and perfect.

"It's tomorrow." Lauren repeated what Sierra had teased them with the day before.

Sierra grinned and reached for the shampoo. She worked it into Lauren's hair with slow, gentle fingers, rubbing at their scalp until their eyes slipped shut. Lauren let out a soft, content sound that made her chest warm.

The water carried the suds away, along with the weight of the day. Sierra lingered, taking her time, because this was simple and close and hers.

She grabbed the body wash next, rubbing it between her palms before smoothing it over Lauren's shoulders. Slow circles, steady pressure, kneading at muscles that had hauled camera gear and makeup bags for hours. Her hands moved over every curve and angle, down their back, massaging their legs and working their way back up over their hips. When Lauren turned around to face her, Sierra traced every line and freckle she could find, until they were both breathing harder.

Then it was Lauren's turn. They shampooed Sierra's hair with the same careful attention, fingers working through the tangles that salt air and wind had created. Rinsing it clean, then reaching for the body wash with hands that were gentle but sure.

When Lauren's touch moved between Sierra's thighs, the gasp that escaped echoed off the shower walls. Sierra's hands found Lauren's shoulders, holding on when her knees nearly gave out. Lauren kept her steady, their touch slow, circling, careful. Sierra's breath hitched, broke, and turned ragged. And then it hit her all at once, pleasure flooding through, drowning out everything, even the water still pouring down around them.

Before she could even catch her breath properly, Sierra's hands found Lauren's hips. She pressed her mouth to their shoulder, tasting water and skin, then slowly moved lower. Her hands wrapped around Lauren's length, stroking in rhythm with the sound of water falling around them. Lauren cried out, head falling back against the shower wall as release took over.

They stood there afterward, pressed close together, hearts pounding against each other's chests.

Lauren kissed her temple. "Bedtime?"

Sierra agreed, and they quickly dried off, climbed into bed still warm, and immediately cuddled up together, as if it were the most natural thing. Clean, loved, and perfectly exhausted.

As they both started drifting toward sleep, Sierra murmured against Lauren's shoulder. "I love shower days."

Lauren smiled into her hair. "I love you."

Later, wrapped in towels on the balcony, Lauren went quiet. Sierra was scrolling through the day's photos when she noticed.

"What's wrong?"

Lauren hesitated. "That model today. The one with the green eyes."

"What about her?"

"She kept looking at you. Like, really looking."

Sierra set down her phone. "Lauren..."

"I know. I'm being stupid." They laughed, but it didn't reach their eyes. "It's just... sometimes I look at you and I can't believe you chose me. That you keep choosing me."

Sierra cupped their face. "Every single day. That's not going to change."

Lauren kissed her palm. "I know. Sorry. I'm just... really happy. And sometimes that's scarier than being sad."

And that was the last thing either of them remembered before sleep took over.

Chapter 22

The sun stretched across the water as they stepped onto the yacht, golden light rippling over the waves like liquid magic. Sierra let out a low whistle as her feet hit the gleaming deck. This thing was massive, all polished wood and chrome railings that probably cost more than her parent's house.

Sierra slung her camera back over her shoulder. "Okay, real question. Why don't we do this every day?"

"Because we're not millionaires yet." Lauren put on these oversized sunglasses, way too dramatic for the moment, and somehow pulled them off. Movie star. No question.

The yacht was chaos... equipment everywhere, crew running in circles, papers flapping. Sierra went through the motions, but her focus was gone. Lauren looked unreal this morning. Sunlight from yesterday had stained their skin golden, as if it refused to leave. She wanted to sketch them. Not the models. Forget the models. She wanted to capture only Lauren.

They kept things mostly professional. Mostly.

During setup, Sierra grabbed a piece of mango from the elaborate fruit spread the yacht had provided and held it out to Lauren, but instead of taking it normally like a reasonable person, Lauren leaned forward and pretended to bite Sierra's fingers, too. Sierra yelped and dropped the mango, which went rolling across the deck, and they both dissolved into laughter that definitely drew some curious looks from Jonas.

"Focus, lovebirds." Jonas tried not to smile.

Later, on a break, they dropped into two lounge chairs at the back of the boat. Pinkies brushed, hooked, like it was second nature. Legs stretched out toward the sun. No rush. Just quiet and warm and easy.

Lauren tilted their face to the light, those ridiculous oversized sunglasses covering half their expression. "I could seriously get used to this lifestyle."

"Same. Maybe we should become yacht people."

"Do yacht people have to wear white pants all the time? Because that seems like a lot of pressure."

The morning shoot was like something out of a dream. Models posed at the edge of the yacht while Sierra moved around them with her camera, capturing the way the ocean breeze played with fabric and hair. Lauren worked their magic with lighting, reflectors, and touch-ups. They made everything look effortless, even when the wind was determined to mess with everyone's carefully planned styling. The salt air clung to their skin like the most expensive body glitter money could buy.

When they broke for lunch, Lauren caught a pic of Sierra mid-laugh, cheeks flushed from sun and pure joy. Then both of them in frame, their feet side by side near the helm with endless ocean stretching out behind them.

"Keep taking photos like that and I might actually stop hating the camera," Lauren said, half-smiling.

A little later, one of the models passed by. Tall. Gorgeous. Straight off a Vogue cover. She didn't even hide it. She looked them both up and down before stopping.

"You two together?" She smirked as if she already knew the answer.

Sierra and Lauren glanced at each other, both caught mid-bite of the bananas they'd been sharing.

Lauren tilted their head with exaggerated confusion. "Us? Whatever gave you that idea?"

The model laughed. "Right. Okay." She walked away with a knowing smile.

As soon as she was out of earshot, they both cracked up.

"I mean, she's not exactly wrong." Sierra nudged Lauren's foot with hers.

"Not even a little bit."

The boat rocked as the afternoon shoot picked up again. Sierra crouched, shifting her camera to catch how the light scattered over the water. Lauren's hand brushed hers, just for a quick squeeze, but it shot straight through her, leaving her unsteady.

She glanced over. Lauren was already watching, smiling like they'd just seen something impossible. And then, because the day wasn't already perfect enough... dolphins. The first gray shape cut through the waves, and before Sierra could even process it, Lauren let out a shriek so full of joy it made her laugh out loud.

"DOLPHINS! Oh my God, actual dolphins!"

Sierra turned just in time, camera up, and caught Lauren's face. Wide-eyed, amazed, lit up with pure joy. The look made Sierra's chest ache, made her realize she was falling even harder than she meant to.

The rest of the afternoon slipped past in pieces: snapshots, quick smiles, brief moments she knew she'd hold on to. Shots that felt right, glances that said more than words. A day too good to be true, almost unreal.

As the sun started sinking lower and the yacht began its journey back toward shore, Lauren leaned into Sierra's side and whispered, "Yacht day number one: absolute perfection."

Sierra looked out over the horizon, then down at Lauren's face, golden in the late afternoon light.

"Yeah, but honestly? I think tomorrow might be even better."

Chapter 23

Lauren didn't think the ocean could top yesterday. Somehow, it did.

The second morning on the yacht came with salt in the air and coffee strong enough to jolt the dead awake. The crew dragged their feet a little, hair messy, movements slower after yesterday's long hours in the sun and wind. Lauren felt wired and alive, though.

Being out here with Sierra, surrounded by endless wind and sun and wild open space, felt like breathing properly for the first time in their life. It was still work, though, and Lauren was damn good at it.

They unpacked their kit without even thinking, years of habit guiding their hands. Brushes lined up in neat rows on a scrap of linen, ready to go. They hummed quietly while they started on the first model, brushing on bronzer over skin already kissed by yesterday's sun, blending until the light caught just right.

Their fingers moved with rhythmic confidence... tap, swirl, sweep, each movement pure muscle memory at this point.

"I swear you always make me look like I got eight hours of sleep," one model said, eyes closed as Lauren worked concealer magic under her eyes.

Lauren grinned. "I'm basically a magician, but don't test how far the powers go."

The second look of the day leaned into beach goddess territory... sleek ponytails that moved with the wind, cheeks kissed just enough to look natural, skin glowing like it had its own light. Lauren gave a final mist of setting spray and stepped back, checking their work.

Out of the corner of their eye, Sierra moved past with her camera, already chasing her next shot.

They caught Sierra glancing over, watching them work with an expression that made heat rise under Lauren's collar and spread down through their chest.

Later, while the models posed up front, Lauren slipped below deck to the little corner they'd turned into a touch-up station. Quick fixes... dusting shimmer along collarbones, smoothing lipstick, misting SPF setting spray so nothing melted in the heat.

Every time their hands moved, they felt the weight of this moment, not just because they genuinely loved what they did for work, but because they loved this version of their life. This exact moment, this incredible ocean, this amazing girl waiting for them outside.

Around midday, Sierra appeared with two perfectly cut slices of watermelon, holding one out with that smirk that always made Lauren's stomach flip.

"Hydration break. Doctor's orders."

Lauren took a big bite, then leaned forward and kissed Sierra's cheek with sticky-sweet lips. "Thanks, Mom."

Sierra rolled her eyes, big and exaggerated, but she didn't pull away. Lauren counted that as a victory. On the next break, they wound up on the upper deck again, stretched out in the sun. Sierra's head rested in Lauren's lap while the boat rocked steadily beneath them. Lauren idly combed fingers through Sierra's salt-tangled hair, completely content.

Lauren uploaded a few photos from that morning: one was a sun-drenched shot of the blue ocean, a candid photo showed a model laughing with her hair blowing in the wind, and another captured Sierra smiling barefoot, with the golden light washing over her.

They typed out a caption: *This one? She steals hearts for fun. Don't say I didn't warn you.*

Sierra peeked up at the screen, read it, and immediately turned pink. "You're such a complete sap."

"Accurate."

Back at the front of the boat, Lauren worked quickly even as the yacht shifted with the waves. The motion didn't throw them off at all, not when they were in the zone like this. They knelt beside the model and ran a fan brush along her cheekbone. "Close your eyes for me." They carefully lined them with a waterproof shimmer that would photograph beautifully.

As Sierra adjusted a light reflector nearby, she brushed against Lauren's shoulder. Lauren steadied themselves with one hand on the yacht's railing and the other gripping their makeup palette, pretending they hadn't noticed the little thrill that shot through them at the contact.

When the model opened her eyes, Lauren smiled with satisfaction. "Go slay them."

The model winked back. "Girl, your hands feel like actual silk. Keep this up, and I'm never leaving your makeup chair."

Lauren shrugged. "Many years of practice, and an ungodly amount of coffee. Mostly the coffee."

While everyone gathered for a group photo, Sierra slipped her hand into Lauren's. Hooked pinkies, like yesterday. Their little ritual.

One model leaned over and whispered conspiratorially, "You two are seriously soulmates. It's disgusting how cute you are."

They both grinned but let it drop there, fingers tightening together in a quiet squeeze.

With the equipment packed and everyone else already moving toward the dock, they lingered at the back of the boat.

The sun was sliding down, turning the water gold, orange, too beautiful to seem real.

Sierra's eyes were on the waves. "Do you realize we did a two-day shoot on a yacht, saw actual dolphins, learned hula, and still managed to flirt our way through the whole thing?"

Lauren grinned, stepping closer. "You make it sound like some kind of incredible dream."

Sierra looked out at the endless blue stretching to the horizon. "Maybe it is."

Lauren stepped behind her, sliding their arms around Sierra's waist and pulling her back against their chest. "Then promise me we won't wake up yet."

Sierra leaned into them, content. "Not a chance."

Chapter 24

Jonas' text came through right before their alarm went off, and Sierra could practically hear the relief in his voice even through the phone screen:

No shoot today. Resetting for the next location. Enjoy the day off.

Sierra let out a squeal that probably woke up half the resort and could've launched a seagull into orbit. Lauren did this ridiculous victory spin in the middle of their room like they'd won the actual lottery.

They made coffee that was way too strong and loaded up a plate with tropical fruit and these incredible flaky croissants from the resort's breakfast spread. Sierra popped a grape into Lauren's mouth and got a strawberry in return. Their sweet little trade-off made them both dissolve into giggles.

Sierra twisted her hair into the messiest bun known to humanity. "Okay, real question. What the hell are we gonna do with a whole free day? We could beach-hop around the island, or get matching tattoos that we'll definitely regret."

Lauren's eyes lit up like Christmas morning. "Oh! We could take one of those fire hula hooping classes. or, hear me out, rent mopeds and zip around until we get lost."

"I don't think Jonas would survive getting a call from the hospital saying we crashed into a palm tree."

Lauren chewed thoughtfully on another strawberry. "We could build the most outrageous sandcastle this beach has ever seen. Like one that needs actual zoning permits."

"Okay, tiny criminal mastermind."

Lauren suddenly had that focused look they got when they had a real idea. "Or, I saw this brochure yesterday about a waterfall hike through an actual jungle forest, ending at this waterfall you can swim in."

Sierra raised an eyebrow. "You seriously want to go hiking on our one day off? When we could lie on the beach and do absolutely nothing?"

Lauren's eyes were sparkling. "We have to. It's been on my bucket list forever. Plus, if I'm willing to wear a bathing suit in public, you know I'm serious."

Sierra groaned loudly and theatrically. "God, I hate how much I love you sometimes."

Lauren's grin spread like victory. "So that's a yes."

They over-packed for what was supposed to be a simple hike—snacks, way too much water, towels, sunscreen, and an emergency chocolate bar that Lauren swore was essential. Swimsuits under their clothes, sneakers that weren't built for this, and enough SPF for an entire army.

Lauren reached the trailhead and looked at Sierra. "It's only three miles."

"I'm gonna die."

The trail was unreal. Green everywhere. Vines hanging low, trees blocking out most of the sky. The sun kept breaking through the trees in wild bursts that made everything shimmer. Birds wouldn't shut up overhead. Sierra swore they were mocking her for huffing and puffing on what was supposed to be an "easy" hike. Everything smelled amazing though, like the earth after it rains mixed with something sweet. Maybe mangoes?

The sound of the water got increasingly louder until they rounded a bend and the trees just stopped. And there it was, this insane waterfall crashing down over moss-covered rocks into a pool so crystal clear it looked fake. Like someone had Photoshopped nature.

Sierra gazed up, awestruck. "Is this for real?"

"I know." Lauren's voice was low, their eyes shining like the view was too much to hold.

The sunlight was flashing across the water in ripples. Lauren looked around, relieved that no one else was there. They adjusted their top and swim skirt. "I'm still not comfortable in a swimsuit."

"You look phenomenal." Sierra gave them a passionate look.

They stepped in together, fingers still locked. The first touch of the cool water stole their breath, then turned exhilarating. They both went under, then came up laughing and flinging water like kids.

Sierra swam over and wrapped her arms around Lauren's neck, feeling Lauren's hands settle around her waist beneath the water. The current was gentle but constant, holding them together.

Their laughter faded into a breathless quiet. Their foreheads touched, water droplets catching the filtered sunlight. Then came the kiss... slow and lingering and the kind you could drown in if you weren't careful.

Sierra pulled back. "I could stay exactly like this forever."

In response, Lauren's kiss deepened, which was honestly the perfect answer.

They pushed in closer to the falls. Kissed again. Hands sliding down each other's backs. Fingers caught in wet hair.

The waterfall was deafening. Sierra couldn't think straight with all that noise, couldn't focus on anything except Lauren's lips and the way their heart was hammering against her chest.

Lauren broke the kiss first, practically panting. That smile, though. That smile could've powered the whole island. "We seriously need to stop, or I'm gonna do something that gets us arrested in paradise."

They made their way back to their towels, laughing and holding hands.

For lunch, they made a spread of assorted cheeses and crackers. Afterward, they lay on their backs while sunlight danced through the leaves above them.

Lauren stared up at the canopy above. "Okay, hear me out. We just move to Hawaii. Permanently."

Sierra snorted. "We're broke as hell, babe."

"Counterpoint: endless sunshine, gorgeous beaches, and we could probably get away with never wearing pants again."

"Counter-counterpoint: Salem would never forgive us for abandoning him."

Lauren sighed dramatically. "Fine. Vacation dreams only. For now."

As they descended the trail, exhausted and content, they passed a little tiki bar glowing with string lights and the sound of laughter spilling out into the evening air.

Sierra pointed. "That looks like it could be fun."

Lauren peeked through the doorway and grinned. "Oh my God, it's karaoke night."

Sierra stopped dead in her tracks. "Nope. Abort mission immediately."

Lauren grabbed her arm and started dragging her inside. "Oh, we are absolutely doing this!"

After a round of Mai Tais that were way stronger than they looked, Sierra finally agreed to a duet. They stumbled around on the tiny stage, belting out lyrics and cracking up every time one of them hit a wrong note. The entire bar was cheering them on, probably more entertained by the disaster than the actual song.

Then Sierra, buzzing from those ridiculously strong Mai Tais, did something she'd never done sober... grabbed the mic and told everyone this song was for Lauren. Initially, her voice wavered, but then she found her rhythm. The drinks may have been the reason, or she finally let herself feel all her pent-up emotions.

Lauren never moved. Just stood there getting teary-eyed, staring at Sierra like she was watching magic happen.

For Lauren's turn, they picked a softer, more intimate song. Their voice trembled but stayed clear and true, and Sierra watched with her jaw hanging open, heart thundering like the beat's bass line.

When the last note faded, Sierra stepped forward, wrapped her arms around Lauren, and kissed them right there on stage.

Sierra pulled back and smiled. "That's my person."

The entire crowd erupted. Someone yelled, "Relationship goals!" Another voice screamed, "Just get married already!"

They left the bar giddy, Sierra a little tipsy and leaning on Lauren as they made their way back through the resort's winding paths.

Back in their room, Lauren helped Sierra out of her shoes, pulled the covers over both of them, and kissed her forehead like a promise she intended to keep forever.

Sierra yawned and curled into Lauren's warmth. "Best day ever."

Lauren kissed her temple. "Tomorrow, we're gonna top it."

Chapter 25

The alarm went off at the crack of dawn again, and Lauren made a noise that sounded like they were being personally victimized by time itself.

"One more four-thirty wake-up, and I'm throwing this phone straight into the ocean."

Sierra chuckled, rubbing sleep out of her eyes. "We should've just passed out on the sand last night. Skip the whole 'pretending to be human' thing."

They'd gotten their morning disaster routine down pat by now. Stumble around in the dark trying to find clothes. Grab whatever snacks were within reach. Stuff camera gear into bags as if they were packing for the apocalypse. Then shuffle out looking like extras from a zombie movie.

The shoot that morning was pretty stunning. Gray clouds hung low over the water, making everything look soft and dreamy. The models floated around in these flowy dresses that caught the breeze just right.

Lauren set up next to her, all business. Sierra kept getting distracted watching them work. The way they dabbed highlighter onto a cheekbone with this tiny brush. How they'd blend eyeshadow in these perfect little circles, tongue sticking out when they concentrated.

Lauren would tuck their hair behind their ear without even realizing it. Sierra probably stared too much.

Lauren glanced over at her. "Keep that up, and I'll charge admission for the show!"

Sierra didn't even pretend to be embarrassed. "Worth every penny."

By mid-morning, the light had gotten too harsh, and Jonas called it. He gave them a break until late afternoon, and Lauren practically vibrated with excitement when he suggested they kill time by going snorkeling.

"YES. FINALLY. Mask me up right now, I'm ready."

They grabbed snorkel gear from the rental place and found a perfect little cove where the water was crazy clear. They could see straight down to the bottom.

Sierra was still figuring out her mask when Lauren tried walking into the waves wearing flippers. Big mistake. Immediate face-plant into the surf, arms flailing like some kind of sand-bound sea turtle.

Sierra stifled a laugh. "Graceful."

Once they got underwater, it was like swimming inside an aquarium. These tiny yellow fish kept zipping past in perfect formation. The coral was so beautiful, all swaying and colorful.

Sierra paddled next to Lauren, and when their fingers brushed, she got this stupid grin going even with the snorkel in her mouth. Lauren's eyes crinkled above their mask like they were smiling, too.

When they finally surfaced, Lauren yanked off their gear and let out a victory yell, which probably scared every fish in a mile radius.

"Did you see that fish that looked like someone had attacked it with every highlighter in existence? It was more colorful than a rainbow threw up on a unicorn."

Sierra beamed, watching Lauren's face still glowing with pure joy. "You looked so happy down there. Like your whole soul was lighting up."

Lauren shrugged. "Maybe I was a mermaid or something in another life."

"Start singing to seagulls, and I'm leaving you here."

They flopped onto their towels after that, totally exhausted. The sun felt amazing on their salt-crusted skin. Sierra dozed off for a bit while Lauren polished off most of a water bottle.

They'd grabbed these ridiculous macadamia cookies from some shop earlier. Lauren ate like half the bag before Sierra even got one.

"Save some for me, you cookie monster."

Back at the hotel, they had to rush through showers. There was no time to mess around. The evening shoot was starting soon, and they still looked like drowned rats.

The sunset shoot turned out pretty good though. Models in these bright tropical colors, palm trees everywhere. Sierra ran around getting shots while Lauren touched up makeup between takes. Everyone looked decent by the end, which was a miracle considering how fried they all were.

"Is it fair that we're both this talented and this hot?" Lauren asked as they finished wrapping up equipment.

Sierra wiped sweat from her forehead. "Speak for yourself. I've been a complete sweaty disaster all day."

"Yeah, but like, a sexy sweaty disaster."

As they went back to their room, they laughed, sighing with relief after the day.

Sierra flopped face-first onto the bed. "My shoulders are officially staging a full rebellion against me."

Lauren tossed her a playful look. "Want me to do something about that?"

Sierra raised an eyebrow. "Are you gonna make it worse?"

"Trust the process."

Sierra flipped over onto her stomach. Lauren climbed on, settling carefully across her thighs. They grabbed the coconut oil and rubbed it between their palms first.

The second Lauren's hands hit her shoulders, Sierra let out a sound somewhere between a purr and a dying walrus.

"Oh my God! I'm proposing to you immediately."

Lauren chuckled. "Marriage talk can wait until after I work on these knots first."

They got to work, really digging into all the tight spots. Their thumbs found every sore muscle in Sierra's neck and shoulders. When they started working down her spine in slow circles, Sierra practically melted into the bed.

"Your turn," she said when Lauren was done.

Sierra worked her fingers into the base of Lauren's neck where they always got tense and continued down their back. When she finished, she planted a soft kiss on each shoulder blade.

"Feel better?"

Lauren was a puddle at this point. "I think you turned me into jello. I have no bones left."

They passed out tangled up together, all loose-limbed and content. Tomorrow could bring whatever; they were ready.

Chapter 26

The alarm went off way too early again, but it felt different this time. Sierra slid her hand under the covers until she found Lauren's. "Last one."

Lauren pressed their lips to Sierra's hand. "We're saving the best for last." Even half-conscious, that little kiss made Sierra's stomach flip.

The morning shoot was pretty chill. Just a few quick shots, nothing fancy. Lauren barely had to touch anyone up. Everybody was already glowing from a week of sun. Sierra snapped away while the models laughed about something, the whole thing feeling natural for once.

The crew was running on fumes, excitement, and that weird energy you get when something's ending.

Jonas found them at lunch, smacking them both on the shoulders like a proud dad. "You two absolutely killed it this week. You've more than earned the rest of the day off."

They thanked him, probably a little too enthusiastically, then practically skipped back to their room like kids getting out of school early.

Sierra did a little spin. "We have the entire afternoon and evening. I don't even know what to do with that much free time?"

Lauren leaned against the doorframe, arms crossed, watching Sierra with a soft expression that made her chest feel warm. "Actually, I might have an idea."

They had the entire afternoon to themselves. No schedule, no rush. Just them. They grabbed some towels and headed down to the beach, holding hands as they walked along the water. Lauren kept pulling out their phone to take pictures. Some would end up on Instagram, but most were just for them. Sierra squinted adorably at the bright sun. Their shadows tangled together in the sand. The way the light caught in Sierra's hair.

They bought ridiculously expensive fruit smoothies from a roadside stand and shared them, Sierra stealing Lauren's last sip and then offering her own as compensation. They found a spot to watch the waves crash and laughed at the tourists who were way braver than either of them when it came to trying paddle boarding.

While Sierra crashed for a nap, Lauren snuck around packing stuff into a beach bag. They moved like a ninja so they wouldn't wake her up.

When the sun started getting low, Lauren shook Sierra's shoulder. "Come on, sleepyhead. I want to show you something."

Sierra followed without asking questions, just kept shooting Lauren these curious looks as they walked down some random path she'd never noticed before.

Then they hit this little hidden beach, and Sierra's jaw dropped. Paper lanterns were everywhere. Several of them were just sitting there waiting to be lit.

Lauren looked bashful. "So I maybe traded those cookies we bought for some help from housekeeping."

Music was playing from somewhere. Lauren had hidden a speaker behind one of the tiki torches. The whole place smelled of flowers and the ocean. The sky was already turning pink and orange.

Sierra was awestruck. "You did all this for me?"

"I wanted to say thank you. For this entire week. All of it. For you." They handed Sierra a lantern and a piece of paper. "You can write your wish on the paper and send it up with the lantern, and your wish will come true."

They each wrote their wishes on the delicate paper. Lauren's read, *Let us always find our way back to each other, no matter what.* Sierra's was simpler but just as heartfelt: *More of this. More of us. Forever.*

They lit their lanterns and watched them rise, golden orbs floating higher into the darkening sky like tiny prayers being carried away.

And then, as if the universe was listening and decided to show off, fireworks suddenly exploded in the distance, bright blooms of color silhouetted against the palm trees.

Sierra gasped. "Was that part of your elaborate plan, too?"

Lauren grinned. "I wish I was that good. Pure luck." They turned, brushed a strand of hair from Sierra's face. "You look radiant."

Her cheeks went pink, not from the sun. "Probably just the sunscreen."

Lauren answered with a kiss, soft and steady, as if silence had finally settled over the world.

Back in their room, the shower steamed up around them. No teasing this time, no rush. Just unhurried touches, every movement deliberate. Lauren's fingers traced along Sierra's skin as if trying to memorize every line.

With the doors cracked open to feel the ocean breeze in and the sound of waves rolling outside, they made love again. Slower. More intentional. As if time had stretched out for them alone.

"I love you," Sierra whispered against their ear.

Lauren said it back, quiet as a breath, but it landed heavy, deeper than anything they'd ever spoken before.

Afterward they lay tangled up in the sheets, skin damp, hearts racing, foreheads pressed close in the dark.

"I don't want this to end," Sierra said quietly, and there was something vulnerable in her voice that made Lauren's chest tighten.

Lauren kissed her temple. "Then we won't let it."

Chapter 27

The flight home was somber, unlike the excitement of the flight out. It was quieter, and there was a hint of sadness, like the end of something beautiful.

Lauren conked out on Sierra's shoulder pretty much right after takeoff, their fingers still locked together. Every time they hit a bump, Lauren would make tiny snoring sounds. Sierra grinned like an idiot every single time and kissed the top of their head.

Let people stare. She was so happy she didn't care.

When they finally landed, Sierra's phone lit up with the group chat exploding in welcome-back memes and messages from The Inner Circle. She responded with a sleepy selfie of her and Lauren holding hands across their airport coffee table, captioning it: *Jet lag, but make it cute.*

At baggage claim, they kissed goodbye, just a quick but lingering thing that somehow conveyed everything they were feeling. A promise of "text me the second you get home" and

Lauren's soft "I miss you already" was passed between them as they waved and headed toward their separate cars.

Sierra went straight to Thalia's to pick up Salem. The second she walked through the door, he launched into this whole guilt trip routine, yowling as if she'd abandoned him forever instead of just a week.

His tail was going crazy, whipping back and forth in typical dramatic Salem fashion.

Sierra scooped up his chunky black cuteness. "Okay, okay. I missed you, too, you absolute drama king."

Thalia leaned against the doorframe with a knowing smirk. "So... did you two survive your romantic getaway without killing each other?"

Sierra rolled her eyes and followed her sister inside. "Barely. We worked our asses off. But also... yeah. It was pretty much pure magic."

She collapsed onto Thalia's couch while Salem claimed her lap like he hadn't spent the entire week pointedly ignoring her FaceTime attempts.

Thalia brought her a glass of cold lemonade and raised an expectant eyebrow. "Alright. I want the full recap. Every detail."

Sierra took a sip and grinned. "Okay, so day one was this whole adventure with Lauren's first flight. They were so nervous, it was adorable. Then we got lei'd the second we stepped off the plane..."

"You got what now?"

"Not like that, you pervert. Hawaiian flower necklaces."

They both cracked up, and Sierra launched into the high-lights: snorkeling adventures, professional photo shoots on yachts, wish lanterns floating into the sunset, late-night swims, terrible karaoke performances, couples massages, and waterfall hikes that nearly killed them both.

"We kind of... fell even harder for each other. It wasn't just vacation fun. It felt real and deep. We talked about everything. We even said 'I love you.'"

Thalia's smile shifted into something gentler. "Yeah, I kind of figured that part out. It's written all over your face."

Sierra stared into her lemonade, face getting warm. "It's just so easy with them, you know? Even when we're both dead tired and everything's falling apart, it still feels right."

Thalia got quiet for a second. Then she asked, "You gonna tell Mom and Dad about this?"

Sierra started drawing little circles in the water droplets on her glass. "I need to tell them about me first. Before I can even begin to explain more."

Thalia nodded with understanding. "Well, family dinner's tomorrow night. Are you thinking about coming out then?"

Sierra's heart started racing, but she forced herself to nod. "Maybe. Yeah."

Thalia reached over and placed her hand over Sierra's. "Whatever you decide to do, I've got your back. Always have, always will. You know Tobias will, too."

Sierra met her sister's eyes and felt some of her anxiety ease. "Okay. Tomorrow it is."

· ❤ · ❤ · ❤ · ❤ · ❤ ·

That night, Sierra finally unpacked and took the world's longest shower to get all the travel grime off. She flopped into bed with Salem, who immediately claimed his spot like he owned the place.

She grabbed her phone and FaceTimed Lauren.

Lauren picked up right away, already in bed with their hair back and no makeup on. They still looked tanned as hell from the week they'd just had, but also soft and sleepy. "Hey there, beautiful."

"Hey yourself. Missing me yet?"

Lauren scoffed. "I was missing you before I even made it out of the airport parking lot."

Salem suddenly popped his head into the frame and let out the loudest, most indignant meow possible, like he had something very important to communicate.

Lauren burst into laughter. "There's my favorite furry man! Has he forgiven you for abandoning him yet?"

Sierra scratched behind Salem's ears. "Barely. He's definitely keeping a grudge scorecard."

They talked for a few more minutes, drowsy voices, and gentle smiles, sharing little details about their separate trips home, before Lauren said, "You should come over tomorrow night. I was thinking I could make that creamy mushroom pasta you love so much. We could eat out on my balcony, maybe string up some fairy lights."

Sierra's smile faltered. "I would absolutely love that, but I've got family dinner tomorrow. I think I'm going to tell them I'm pansexual."

There was a pause. Lauren's expression softened with concern. "Is this because of me? Because of us?"

Sierra shook her head. "No. This is about me. I should've done this forever ago, honestly. I want them to know who I actually am. And maybe if they don't completely freak out, then I can tell them about you."

Lauren blinked a few times, visibly moved. "I'm so proud of you."

"Hold on to that pasta idea for another night though, okay?"

Lauren smiled warmly. "It's definitely a date."

They made kissy faces at the phone screen like a couple of teenagers and said goodnight. After Sierra hung up, she just lay there in the dark with Salem rumbling like a tiny motor against her side. Her heart was racing, adrenaline keeping her awake. Tomorrow, she was really going to do this.

The next morning, Sierra was messing around with her camera stuff for like the millionth time when someone knocked. She opened the door to find Jett holding two coffees and wearing his *we need to have a serious talk* face.

Sierra opened the door. "Okay, what's wrong?" Salem immediately wound around his legs in greeting.

"Is it that obvious?" Jett flopped onto her couch with a dramatic flair that didn't quite mask his tension.

"You brought me the expensive coffee. You only do that when something's eating at you." Sierra settled beside him, tucking her legs under her. "Spill."

Jett was quiet for a moment, absently scratching Salem's ears. "My mom called last night. She's been asking about my dating life again, wanting to know if I've met anyone special."

"That's good, right? She's always been supportive of you being gay."

"Yeah, she has been. She's amazing about that part." Jett's smile was complicated. "But, Sierra... I haven't told her about Ellis."

Sierra's eyebrows drew together. "Why not? You're crazy about him. You light up every time someone mentions his name."

"Because Ellis is white." The words came out flat, matter-of-fact. "And my mom has very strong feelings about her Black son dating white men."

Understanding dawned. Sierra reached over and squeezed his hand. "Oh, Jett."

"She's got this whole thing about how white men fetishize Black bodies, how they'll never truly understand our experience, how they'll leave when things get real." Jett's voice was getting smaller. "And I get it, I do. She's seen what happened to her friends, to our family. But Ellis isn't like that. He's not some tourist in my life."

"Have you tried talking to her about him specifically? Not as 'some white guy' but as Ellis?"

Jett shook his head. "You don't understand. My mom grew up in the Dominican Republic. She's seen what happens when white men treat Black and Brown women like experiments. She moved here to give me better opportunities, and in her mind, dating a white guy is asking to be someone's learning experience. I'm scared, Sierra. What if I tell her how happy he makes me, and she can't see past his skin color? What if I have to choose between my family and the person I love?"

Sierra felt her chest tighten with recognition. "I know that fear. I've been carrying it around for months."

"With Lauren? But your parents seem like they're trying to understand."

"That's it, though; my parents haven't seen it. They don't even know they exist. I keep making excuses, pushing it off, terrified they'll look at me differently. I haven't even told them I'm pansexual yet. Terrified they'll think this is a phase or that I'm throwing away my chance at a 'normal' life. You know how they are. Dad still thinks living together before marriage is scandalous, and Mom keeps asking when I'm going to settle down with 'a nice boy' and give them grandchildren the proper way."

They sat in comfortable silence for a moment, both lost in their respective worries.

Jett squeezed her hand. "Your parents might surprise you and be more accepting than you think. My mom definitely loves me, but I know exactly what her reaction will be."

"But what if you're mistaken? What if you tell her about Ellis and she sees how good he is for you?"

Jett gave her a look. "What if you tell your parents about Lauren and they see how happy you are?"

Sierra laughed despite everything. "God, we're a mess, aren't we? Both of us hiding the most important parts of our lives because we're scared."

"Maybe that's exactly why we need to stop hiding." Jett shifted to face her fully. "Listen, babe, I can't promise my mom will come around to Ellis. But I can't keep pretending he doesn't exist just because it's easier. And you... Sierra, you're glowing when you talk about Lauren. Your parents would have to be blind not to see that."

"You think we should do it? Both of us?"

"I think we should stop letting fear make our choices for us." Jett stood up and pulled Sierra to her feet. "Besides, if our families can't handle our happiness, at least we know we've got each other. The Chaos Coven stands together, right?"

Sierra hugged him fiercely. "Right. So when are you going to tell your mom about Ellis?"

"When are you going to tell your parents about Lauren?"

They looked at each other and both grinned with the kind of nervous energy that comes before jumping off a cliff.

"I'm doing it tonight at our family dinner. Thalia and I already talked about it."

Jett nodded. "I'm in, and whatever happens, we debrief immediately after."

"Deal. And, Jett? For what it's worth, Ellis looks at you like you hung the moon. If your mom can't see that he makes you happy, that's her loss."

"Same goes for Lauren and your parents. They'd be crazy not to love someone who loves you that well."

"You know what's crazy? I can see how much Ellis has changed you. In the best way. You've completely hung up your... well, let's call it your 'social butterfly' lifestyle."

Jett let out a surprised laugh. "Yeah, he really has. I never thought I'd be the settling-down type, you know? I used to think variety was the spice of life and all that."

"And now?"

"Now I can't imagine wanting anyone else. Ellis makes me so happy that the idea of being with other people just... doesn't appeal anymore. Never thought that would happen to me, but here we are."

After Jett left, Sierra stood in her kitchen staring out the window. The conversation with Jett had crystallized something for her. She was tired of hiding, tired of letting fear dictate her choices.

It was time to trust that love was stronger than fear.

Chapter 28

Sierra kept walking back and forth in the hallway, her feet making weird squeaky sounds on the tile. Thalia's enchiladas smelled amazing, but Sierra's stomach was doing backflips.

Thalia hung out nearby, not hovering but close enough if Sierra needed backup. "You can do this. It's not like you're asking for anything crazy. You're just telling them who you are."

Sierra steadied herself and walked into the dining room before she chickened out.

Her parents were already eating, talking to Tobias about something boring and work-related. Dad spotted her first, mid-bite. "There she is. Come eat before it gets cold."

Sierra sat down in her usual spot, hands clamped together under the table so no one would see them shaking. Mom passed her the enchiladas with the same smile she'd had since Sierra was five.

"You okay, honey? You look kind of freaked out."

"I am freaked out." Sierra's voice came out way quieter than she meant it to.

Thalia caught her eye and nodded, like, go for it.

Sierra took another deep breath. "I need to tell you guys something. Something I should've said forever ago."

Everyone stopped eating. Mom's hand just hung there, reaching for the salad. Dad put his fork down.

"I'm pansexual."

Dead silence. As in one could hear the clock ticking in the kitchen silent.

Then Tobias just shrugged and kept eating. "Of course you are. I mean, I distinctly remember you having posters of both Jensen Ackles and Emma Watson up in your room during middle school. Wasn't exactly hard to connect the dots. I thought you were bi, but pan is like... bi with an even bigger heart, right?"

Her mom let out a slow, careful breath, clearly trying to process everything. Dad looked like someone had just told him aliens were real. "Pansexual? What in God's name does that even mean? Is this some new internet thing?"

Sierra's neck got all hot, but she pushed through it. "It means gender doesn't matter to me. I can fall for people. If there's a connection, if we understand each other, that's what counts. Not their body parts."

Dad leaned way back, shaking his head. "But you've always been such a normal girl. You dated Josh in high school. What happened to wanting a traditional family? Marriage? Kids?"

Mom's voice was strained. "Sweetheart, I just... in my day, people were either one thing or the other. This is all so confusing. What will people think? What do we tell the neighbors?"

Thalia straightened up, getting that look she used to get when kids picked on Sierra in middle school. "Mom, Dad, she didn't catch this like a cold. It's not something that happens to you. And who cares what the neighbors think?"

Sierra put her hand out on the table, palm up. Her mom stared at it for a long moment before slowly, carefully taking it.

"I didn't always have the right words for it, but meeting Lauren helped me finally understand myself better. I've always known I was different somehow. But now I understand why, and I'm done hiding who I am."

Mom squeezed her hand, but her face was tight with worry. Dad kept staring at his enchiladas like they might provide answers.

Mom suddenly looked between Sierra and Thalia with growing alarm. "Wait... who's Lauren?"

Sierra paused for like half a second, then her face just broke into this huge smile even though everyone was still being weird about everything.

"Lauren is really important to me. They're amazing and hilarious, and they actually get me, you know? We met a few months ago and got really close. They helped me feel brave enough to tell you this, but it's not like they turned me pansexual or anything. I just stopped pretending around them. Around everyone."

Her dad's face went red. "They? You mean... like multiple people? Sierra, what kind of situation have you gotten yourself into?"

Sierra shook her head, her voice staying calm but getting firmer. "No, Dad. Lauren prefers they and them as pronouns."

Dad threw his napkin down. "Oh, for crying out loud! Now there are special pronouns? I can't keep track of all this modern nonsense."

Mom was clearly struggling, wringing her hands. She kept opening her mouth as if she were going to say something, then closing it and opening it again. Finally, she got it out. "I'm sorry, Sierra. I just don't understand any of this. We raised you in the church. We taught you right from wrong. This feels like... like you're throwing your whole future away."

"Mom—"

"What about grandchildren? A proper wedding? I had such dreams for you, sweetheart."

Sierra felt tears threatening. "I know, Mom. I'm not expecting you to understand everything all at once. What I'm asking for is that you try. Lauren isn't a phase or rebellious statement. They're someone who makes me incredibly happy."

Her dad finally looked up at her, and his eyes were harder than she'd ever seen them. "I'm not mad, Sierra. But I am disappointed. This world is cruel enough without you making it harder on yourself. You've always wanted a family someday, kids. Normal kids need a mother and a father."

"I still want all of those things, and they're all still possible. Just maybe not exactly the way you always pictured it in your head."

Mom's voice cracked. "But what will the pastor say? What will your aunt Margaret think? We can't just pretend this is normal."

Thalia jumped in, her voice warm but fierce. "She's still exactly the same Sierra. Still your daughter. Still the same big-hearted, brilliant woman who makes everyone around her better by existing. The only thing that's changed is that she's being honest with you."

Mom's eyes got all watery. "I just... I love you, baby. But this scares me. I don't know how to handle this."

"I know. But I'm done hiding."

Dad went quiet for a long moment, just looking at her. When he finally spoke again, his voice was heavy. "I need time to process this. I can't promise I'll understand it, and I can't promise I'll like it. But... you're still my daughter."

Sierra felt her throat get tight. "That's all I can ask for right now."

Tobias cleared his throat awkwardly. "So... can we maybe eat before the food gets completely cold? This is still Sierra. She still puts hot sauce on everything and cries at animal videos."

Mom managed a watery smile. "You *do* cry at those ridiculous videos."

Dad picked up his fork again, though his movements were stiff. "We'll... we'll figure this out. Somehow."

They finished dinner in relative quiet, the conversation stilted but not hostile. Sierra's stomach finally stopped doing backflips, though the tension in the room was thick enough to cut with a knife.

As she was leaving, Dad stopped her at the door. "Sierra. I meant what I said. You're still my daughter. Always will be. This Lauren person... they better treat you right."

Sierra hugged him tight. "They do, Dad. They really do."

It wasn't perfect. It wasn't the acceptance she'd dreamed of. But it was a start.

Her hands were still shaking from the adrenaline of saying the words out loud to her parents. Sierra was about to call Jett on her way home before she decided to just go see him. She needed to see him in person.

After everything they'd talked about, after promising to debrief immediately, a phone call didn't feel like enough. She needed a hug from someone who understood exactly what she'd just been through.

The drive to Jett's apartment was a blur of streetlights and nervous energy. She pulled into his complex and hurried up the stairs, her heart still racing from dinner.

As she approached his door, she heard what sounded like... groaning? And a thud against the wall.

Sierra's blood ran cold. Was Jett hurt? Was someone attacking him?

She pressed her ear to the door and heard more sounds. They were definitely distressed noises, maybe struggling. Without thinking, she reached for the spare key Jett kept hidden under the fake rock by his door (the world's most obvious hiding spot, which they'd all teased him about).

"Jett?" she called as she unlocked the door. "Are you okay? I heard—"

Sierra froze in the doorway.

Jett was very much not hurt. In fact, he was very much occupied with Ellis against the living room wall, both of them completely naked and very obviously in the middle of something intense and passionate.

"Oh my GOD!" she squeaked, immediately spinning around and covering her eyes. "I'm so sorry! I thought you were hurt. I heard noises and I just—"

"SIERRA!" Jett's voice was strangled with a mixture of mortification and breathlessness.

"I'm leaving! I'm leaving right now! Pretend this never happened!" Sierra practically ran out of the apartment, slamming the door behind her.

She sat in her car for a full five minutes, face burning with embarrassment, before her phone rang.

"Before you say anything," Jett's wry voice came through the speaker, "Ellis is never going to look me in the eye again."

"I am SO sorry! I heard what sounded like someone getting hurt, and I panicked. I should have knocked louder or called first or literally anything other than barging in with a spare key."

"It's fine. I mean, it's mortifying, but it's fine. How did the dinner go? Please tell me it went better than this did."

"Well, I didn't accidentally walk in on any family members having sex, so yes."

"Details. I need details to distract me from my shame."

"I did it. I did it." Sierra settled back in her car seat. "I told them everything. About being pansexual, about Lauren, all of it."

"Wow! How did it go?"

"It was rough. Really rough. They're struggling with it. Mom's worried about what everyone will think — from family, the neighbors, to church. Dad feels like I'm making my life harder for no reason. They need time to process, and I can tell they're disappointed." Her voice cracked a little. "But they said they love me, even if they don't understand. It's not the reaction I wanted, but at least they're still talking to me. How did it go with your mom?"

There was a long pause. "Not great."

Sierra's heart sank. "Oh, Jett."

"She hung up on me." His voice sounded flat. "I told her about Ellis, how awesome he is, how he treats me. And she goes, *'You're being stupid! That white boy's just messing around with you; he's gonna break your heart'.*"

"God, Jett. That must have been awful."

"The thing that kills me is I could tell she was scared, you know? It comes from a place of love. She's just trying to protect me. Under all that anger, she's just terrified someone's gonna hurt me. But she wouldn't listen when I tried to explain that Ellis isn't that guy."

Sierra's eyes started burning. "So what now?"

"I don't know. Maybe give her space. Keep being happy and hope she comes around. But I'm glad I told her, and I'm really glad you told your parents, too. We did the scary thing."

"We absolutely did the scary thing, and whatever happens next, we've got each other."

"Damn right we do. Now tell me everything about dinner. Did Thalia have to physically restrain your dad from asking inappropriate questions?"

Despite everything, Sierra laughed. "She basically did! She jumped in when Dad started getting confused about the whole pansexual thing. And then she backed me up when I told them about Lauren. I don't think I could have done it without her there. Tobias, too."

"Thalia's always been your secret weapon."

"I wish your mom's reaction was different." Her voice grew softer. "And I'm sorry again about... walking in on you and Ellis."

"Remember how I said I can't imagine wanting anyone else? I still feel that way. Which makes what my mom said hurt even more, because this isn't just some fling for me."

"She'll come around. She has to. Anyone who sees you two together can tell this is real."

"I hope so. And, Sierra? Even though tonight sucked for me, I'm happy for you. You deserved to have parents who see how amazing you are."

Sierra could feel tears welling. "I love you, you know that?"

"I love you, too. And hey, next family dinner, you're bringing Lauren and I'm bringing Ellis. We'll show them what happy looks like."

"Deal. But I'm making sure Thalia and Tobias will be there for moral support. Maybe Calliope and Raven, too."

"Obviously. The Chaos Coven provides backup for all major family events. It's in our charter. And, Sierra? Next time you think I'm in mortal danger, maybe try calling first?"

"Noted. Though in my defense, you two were being very loud."

"I'm hanging up now."

"Tell Ellis I said hi and that I'll never make eye contact with him again!"

After they hung up, Sierra sat in her car outside Jett's apartment, drained but oddly peaceful. One scary conversation down, one mortifying walk-in she'd never live down, but still, authenticity for a lifetime lay ahead of her.

Chapter 29

When Sierra got to Lauren's place, it smelled incredible. Like someone had gone overboard with garlic, which was exactly what Sierra needed right now. Lauren was bouncing around their cramped kitchen in bike shorts and a ridiculous oversized shirt that said, "Allergic to Mediocrity." They had their game face on, stirring whatever was in that pot as if their life depended on it.

"Fair warning. I'm feeling emotional today, so there's a decent chance I might cry over this pasta sauce. Or literally nothing at all."

Sierra grinned and slipped her arms around Lauren's waist from behind, pressing a kiss to their shoulder. "Noted and prepared for all emotional possibilities. Speaking of emotional things, family dinner went okay."

Lauren turned in their arms, eyebrow slightly raised. "Just okay? That doesn't sound super encouraging."

"Honestly? They're disappointed. They made it pretty clear they think I'm making a mistake, that this isn't what they wanted for me. But Dad said I'm still his daughter, even if he needs time to process it. It's not acceptance, but it's not total rejection either."

Lauren's face saddened. "Did you tell them about me?"

"I told them I met someone named Lauren who makes me ridiculously happy. That's about it."

Lauren hesitated, and something unreadable flickered across their face. "Did they ask questions about me specifically?"

Sierra shook her head immediately and firmly. "No. I wouldn't have given them more if they did. Your story is not mine to tell. It's nobody's business but yours."

Lauren exhaled and leaned their forehead against Sierra's. "Thank you. Seriously. That means everything to me."

The rest of the evening was cozy but oddly quiet. Lauren was still affectionate, still Lauren, but their usual bright energy seemed dimmed somehow. Sierra noticed the change, but she didn't want to push. Instead, she offered gentle kisses and soft touches.

As they were getting ready to leave, she asked, "Do you want to come back to my place tonight?"

Lauren nodded without hesitation. "Yeah. I missed Salem."

Sierra raised an eyebrow with exaggerated offense. "That's it?"

Lauren smirked; some of their spark returned. "Obviously not."

They walked hand in hand back to Sierra's apartment, and Salem gave Lauren exactly thirty seconds of cold-shoulder treatment before dramatically collapsing onto their lap on the couch and demanding immediate attention. Lauren obliged, scratching under his chin with exaggerated devotion.

"You're very demanding."

Sierra headed to the bedroom to change, and the sound of her phone buzzing broke the silence. A new text from Thalia arrived, causing the screen to light up, and Lauren instinctively looked down at the display.

> **Thalia:** I know that wasn't the reaction you deserved. I'm proud of you for telling them, and I hope you and Lauren are okay.

Lauren's lower lip trembled, and tears welled in their eyes as she looked away, the message's words echoing in the silence.

Sierra returned, and they went to bed and cuddled, but Lauren remained silent and kept to herself, only the hollow echo of Lauren's unspoken pain.

Sierra brushed her thumb gently along Lauren's cheek. "You sure you're okay?"

Lauren nodded, but it didn't quite reach their eyes. "Just being emotional makes everything feel bigger than it is. I'll be better after some sleep."

Sierra kissed their forehead softly. "I'm here for you right now. We'll figure out the rest later."

They drifted off to sleep, their bodies touching, the warmth of their skin a comfort as their breaths melded into one.

Sierra had a shoot scheduled at the park the following day. Mid-afternoon, straightforward stuff. Just some engagement photos for this couple. As she was putting her camera away, someone called out from across the lawn.

"Sierra? Oh my God, is that you?

She looked up startled. "Josh?!"

They both laughed and went straight into an enormous hug. The kind you give someone you hold in high regard. He paused, his hands lingering on her shoulders as he took in her appearance, and then he enveloped her in another hug.

"Wow, it is you. You look absolutely amazing." Josh grinned with the same easy smile she remembered.

Sierra felt her own smile spreading across her face. "I'm technically still working, but we're basically done here. Give me like ten more minutes?"

"Yeah, absolutely. I'll wait. Want to grab lunch after and catch up properly?"

"Sounds good to me."

Ten minutes later they were at a cafe with drinks getting watery and sandwiches they kept forgetting to eat. Josh filled her in on his life: graduated college, got a job at a startup, been with his girlfriend for like a year and change.

"Things are good." She knew he truly meant it.

"That's so awesome. I'm happy, too. I actually met someone I'm totally crazy about."

Josh's eyebrows went up.

"Lauren is incredible. We've been together a few months, and it just feels so right, you know? I've always been more into the person than what gender they are, if that makes sense. Then they appeared, and everything just seemed to fall into place."

Josh's expression grew softer and genuinely pleased. "That's amazing, Sierra. I'm so glad you found someone who gets you."

He paused, then added with a self-deprecating grin, "My girlfriend's kind of like you, now that I think about it. Full of personality, funny as hell, and super into art and photography. I think I accidentally replaced you without even realizing it."

Sierra laughed out loud. "You always did have excellent taste."

They ended up talking for like an hour, catching up on people they both knew and swapping work horror stories. When they finally had to go, Sierra walked home feeling happy but also a little weird about the whole thing.

She hadn't mentioned Josh to Lauren yet. It wasn't as if she was hiding anything. They were over years ago. Today was totally innocent, but it felt like something Lauren should probably know about.

Chapter 30

Classes were starting back up at the community center after the summer break. Sierra felt jittery walking over there. It was good jittery, but still jittery.

She unlocked the art room and hit the lights. The fluorescent bulbs always took forever to stop flickering. While she waited, she started putting out supplies for everyone. Charcoal sticks, oil pastels, all the usual stuff. The familiar routine helped calm her nerves a little.

Her students started trickling in, already talking and laughing before they even sat down.

"Miss Sierra, you're so tan!" one of the younger girls exclaimed.

"Okay, spill. Where have you been all summer?" asked another with a knowing smirk.

Sierra couldn't help grinning. "Hawaii. Work assignment, but also a little vacation thrown in."

She let their comments and questions wash over her like warm water, their laughter and gentle teasing providing a comforting soundtrack as they dove into today's lesson. They focused on sketching, expressive line work, and light studies that had everyone's hands stained with charcoal by the end. After days of feeling down, Sierra felt a little lighter.

After the last student packed up and left, she wiped down the counters and pulled out her phone to text Lauren:

> **Sierra:** Just finished teaching. Are you feeling up for some company tonight?

No reply.

Sierra gathered her supplies and walked the familiar route home, phone clutched in her palm. Every few blocks, she checked the screen. Still nothing.

Just as she reached her front door, her phone finally lit up.

> **Lauren:** Not feeling great today. I just wanna be alone right now.

A cold sweat prickled Sierra's skin, and the floor seemed to tilt beneath her feet.

She typed back quickly:

> **Sierra:** Let me bring you something. Soup, medicine, whatever you need. I want to help.

Lauren's response came a few minutes later.

> **Lauren:** I'll be okay. I'm gonna try to sleep this off. I might feel better tomorrow.

Inside her apartment, Salem wound himself around her legs, meowing with obvious concern. She scooped up his chunky black form and pressed her face into his fur.

"Our Lauren's not feeling well, buddy, and I don't know what to do."

He meowed again, a softer sound this time, and he just melted into her arms, as if he understood her perfectly.

"I know. I wish we could fix everything for them too."

She tried watching TV, flipping through channels, watching nothing. Eventually, she gave up and started scrolling through her phone instead, getting lost in her camera roll from Hawaii. Ocean sunrises. The two of them in silly flower crowns. Lauren passed out on the couch with Salem curled under their arm like a spoiled stuffed animal. Sierra smiled before it slipped away.

She opened Lauren's socials, scrolling slowly. Each post is bursting with color and light. Her heart ached, remembering the joy of just days ago.

The apartment felt way too quiet. Too empty. She cleaned the counters. Then cleaned them again. Dusted shelves she barely noticed most days.

After a while, she gave up. The silence was too much. She went to bed early, holding the half-heart keychain in her palm until her fingers ached.

By morning, she was at the counter with a mug of coffee gone cold, phone in hand, typing out another text.

Sierra: Hope you're feeling better today. My bed feels empty without you. I love you.

Still nothing.

She tried to shake off the heavy feeling as she walked into the photo studio for work.

Jonas glanced up from adjusting a camera lens. "You doing alright? You look a little rough."

"Yeah, I'm just really tired." Sierra forced herself to focus on setting up her equipment.

"Relationship troubles?"

She shook her head, and then immediately reconsidered. "Lauren isn't feeling well. I don't know how to help. They won't let me."

Jonas tweaked a studio light, looking thoughtful. "Sometimes people have to be ready to accept help before they can let anyone in. Even the people they love most."

Sierra nodded, but the pain in her chest didn't go away. There was still no response to her messages after the workday.

Worried that something had happened, Sierra decided to go to Lauren's apartment. She knocked and knocked, calling their name through the door. No answer. She finally sank down to sit on the floor with her back against the door, feeling helpless.

A couple walking by stopped and looked at her with gentle concern. "You okay, sweetheart?"

"Just waiting for someone," Sierra managed.

"Oh, we saw them leave about an hour ago," the woman said kindly.

Sierra blinked, her breath catching in her throat. She stood up quickly and called Lauren's phone. Straight to voicemail.

She practically ran home, hoping maybe Lauren had gone there. There were no signs of them anywhere.

Feeling desperate and out of options, she opened her phone and scrolled to find a group chat she hadn't used in a while. Not The Inner Circle, that one included Lauren. She found The Chaos Coven instead with one new addition. She added Thalia to their group chat.

> **Sierra:** Something's going on with Lauren and I don't know what to do.

The replies came immediately.

> **Raven:** On my way over right now.

> **Jett:** Be there in ten minutes.

> **Calliope:** Already grabbed wine and emergency snacks. Hang tight.

> **Thalia:** Leaving right now.

When they arrived at her apartment like a small army of concerned friends, Sierra told them everything: how she said she'd been feeling emotional, the increasing distance, the empty apartment, the unanswered calls.

Jett frowned, processing. "You said they weren't acting like themselves the last night you saw them?"

Sierra nodded miserably. "They were quiet and withdrawn. They said they were just feeling emotional. I get it. I have those moments, too, but now I'm wondering if something else is going on." Tears welled up in her eyes. "I just need to know they're okay. I don't even know if I did something wrong."

Raven pulled her into a fierce hug. "You didn't do anything wrong. Even if something's happening with them, it's not because you failed them somehow."

"Want to watch a terrible horror movie as a distraction?" Calliope offered gently.

Sierra's face crumpled. "Those were Lauren's favorites. We used to watch them together all the time."

Jett pulled out his phone with determination. "I'm texting them."

"No." Sierra reached for his phone. "Please don't. I don't want them to think I'm sending people after them."

"Relax, I'll be totally casual about it." He typed quickly:

> **Jett:** Sup, beautiful. Lunch tomorrow? We need a proper catch-up.

They stared at his phone. Waited. Nothing.

By the time Sierra sank into the couch, she felt wrung out. Raven offered to crash on her couch, but she shook her head.

When the apartment was quiet again, she sat with the half-heart keychain in her hand, reading Lauren's anniversary note until the lines swam.

In the dark, with no one there to see, she finally let it hit her. Sleep came, but it was thin and full of empty spaces.

Chapter 31

Lauren left the studio early with a takeout bag swinging at their side, the kind of comfort food Sierra loved when she was wiped after a shoot. The evening had a soft blue light that made everything look kinder. They pictured the surprise; the easy grin Sierra always gave them before she reached for a kiss. It felt simple. It felt like safety.

On the corner by the warehouse, Lauren slowed. Sierra stood near the loading dock with a man Lauren didn't recognize. Clean-cut, easy smile, the sort of guy parents liked. Sierra laughed at something he said and leaned in for a hug, long enough for him to lift her a little off her feet. When she stepped back, she touched his forearm, casual and familiar, and they started down the block side by side.

The street sounds dropped out of Lauren's head. Heat roared in their ears. All at once they were sixteen again on a different sidewalk, the night they learned the door could lock behind you forever. They told themself to breathe, to walk forward, to trust what they knew about Sierra. Their body would not move. They watched until the two figures turned the corner and disappeared.

Maybe it was nothing. Maybe it meant everything. The thoughts stacked fast and crooked. Sierra's parents had been polite and distant. Sierra had said she was working on it, that she needed time. Time could turn into distance. Distance could turn into doors closing. The man had looked simple in a way Lauren could not be. Explainable. Safe.

Lauren's fingers tightened on the paper bag until the grease bled through. They placed it down on the steps and sat hard. They could call, they could ask, they could choose trust, the way Sierra always asked them to. The muscles in their chest felt locked. Words would not come. Instead, a thousand old alarms went off at once, a chorus of, *leave first, end it before it ends you, make it clean so it hurts less.* A lie that had kept them alive.

They walked home without remembering the blocks in between. Their phone buzzed in their pocket. Sierra's name lit the screen. Lauren stared at it until the call went to voice-mail. A new text. Another call. The phone kept lighting, then going dark, the room flashing and dimming as if they were underwater.

In the bathroom mirror, their face looked strange. Too pale. Eyes too wide. They gripped the sink and tried to slow their breathing. It did not slow. They slid down the wall, pressed their forehead to their knees, and told themself that love was supposed to be easier than this. Sierra would be happier with someone who did not bring a storm into every room.

They drafted a message and deleted it. Typed another and deleted that, too. Words kept breaking apart in their hands. When the last call went to voicemail again, the sound of Sierra's voice pulled something loose and aching in Lauren's chest. They set the phone face down on the counter and let the silence fill the apartment until it pressed on their ribs.

End it clean, the old voice said. *Save her from the part of you that ruins good things. Make it simple so she doesn't fight for you and make it harder.*

They picked up the phone, found the few sentences that felt like armor, and held on to them like a ledge.

Sierra stared at her screen until her eyes stung. The little delivered checkmarks lined up like a row of closed doors. She told herself a dozen reasonable stories and did not believe any of them. The quiet in her apartment pressed in from every side, so she put on shoes and walked.

She walked to the park where Lauren had first kissed her under the oak tree, where the air had smelled like cut grass and heat. Then walked to Bean & Bloom and bought a chai she did not drink. She sat by the window and watched the evening slide down the glass, telling herself that any minute now the bell would jingle and Lauren would wander in with that crooked smile and say, "Sorry, the day got away from me, I'm here."

Her phone stayed still on the table, face up like a dare.

By the time the sky tipped toward violet, she called Thalia. "I can't do this! I feel like I'm losing my mind."

"I know, sis. Breathe if you can. Give them a little time. They'll come back to you when they can say it out loud."

It made sense. None of it helped. She went home and lay on the rug with Salem sprawled on her ribs like a weighted blanket with opinions. When she closed her eyes, every version of Lauren's face flickered behind her lids. Laughing. Concentrating. Sleepy. Gone.

Two days later, her phone lit up with Lauren's name. Relief hit so hard she had to grab the counter to steady herself.

"Oh my God, Lauren! Are you okay? I've been so scared something happened to you. I thought maybe you were hurt or—"

"I'm okay." The voice on the other end sounded thin, like it had been pulled through wire. "I just wanted to tell you it's over."

The words did not fit in her ear. "What?"

"It's over. We're done."

"Why?" She heard her own voice go small and hated it. "Just tell me why. I love you so much. If I messed something up, I can fix it. Whatever it is, I can fix it."

A pause opened. Sierra could hear them breathing. Not steady. Not calm. Like someone holding their shoulders too tight.

"I saw the text from Thalia that said, *'I know that wasn't the reaction you deserved. I'm proud of you for telling them, and I hope you and Lauren are okay'.*"

"I told you how they reacted. It's not fair to us, but they'll come around. If they don't, I'll always choose you."

"Your parents are already disappointed in you because of me. You shouldn't have to choose between your family and someone like me. I'm only going to keep hurting you. Your family will never accept me, and I can't watch you lose them because of me."

"No," she said, louder than she meant to. "No, I would not. I want you."

"I also saw you." The words scraped. "With that guy. You hugged him. You left together."

"Josh?" The name landed like a dropped plate. "He's from my high school. I ran into him after a shoot. We grabbed lunch. He has a girlfriend he won't shut up about. I told him I was in love with someone."

"This is getting too messy." Their voice tightened. "Too complicated. You need someone like Josh. Someone your family can accept."

"I need you! Only you."

"I love you too much to let you throw your life away for me." Lauren's voice cracked on the words.

Another stretch of silence. For a second she thought she heard a sound that might have been a swallowed sob. She reached for it like a rope.

"Lauren, please come over. Let's talk where we can see each other. If you're scared, say you're scared. I can handle scared. I can handle messy. I'm right here."

"Please don't call me again," they said, and the words were careful in a way that felt like a slap. "Please respect my wishes."

The line clicked. The call screen disappeared. Sierra stood very still, phone hot in her hand. Then her knees gave, and the tile came up too fast. The phone skittered across the floor. She folded in on herself, palms pressed to her sternum like she could keep her heart from falling out.

For a moment, there was nothing. No air. No sound. Then her body remembered how to cry and it tore through her, loud and helpless. Salem hovered, uncertain, then pushed his head against her shoulder, a small, steady weight insisting she still existed.

She stayed on the kitchen floor until the light changed color on the cabinets. When the sobs finally thinned, the quiet did not feel like calm. It felt like a cliff. She crawled to her phone, stared at Lauren's name in the recent calls, and did not press it.

She pulled herself up by the counter, wiped her face with the heel of her hand, and whispered to the empty room, "I don't accept this. I don't accept that this is all there is."

The apartment did not answer. The refrigerator hummed. Somewhere outside, a siren wailed and faded. She picked up Salem and carried him to bed like he was the last soft thing left in the world. She lay there with his purr vibrating against her ribs and let the dark come, certain of only one thing.

Morning would happen anyway. And when it did, she would still love Lauren. She did not know what to do with that. She only knew it was true.

Chapter 32

The days after that phone call just ran together like spilled paint. Everything turned into an awful gray blur where nothing mattered.

She kept moving around, technically doing things, but it was like watching someone else live her life. She breathed, but never deeply enough. Even the air itself seemed to hurt.

The next morning, she woke up clutching her phone. Dead screen, cold as ice against her palm. She pressed it to her chest, where Lauren used to be, and felt absolutely nothing.

Everything was too quiet. She couldn't deal with coffee. Didn't shower. Didn't even get dressed. She just sat on her bedroom floor with Salem pressed against her side, watching dust float in the sunlight coming through her blinds.

At some point, she reached for her camera out of habit. She lifted it, aimed at the shifting light, tried to focus on Salem's whiskers. Her finger hovered on the shutter button, but she couldn't bring herself to press it. The weight of the camera grew unbearable, so she set it back down as if it were something fragile that might shatter her if she touched it wrong.

Hours passed like this. The day moved on without her permission. The next one did, too.

Thalia called repeatedly. The phone buzzed and buzzed, its sound rattling through the silence. Sierra stared at it until the screen went dark again. She couldn't even make her arm move to answer.

Four days later, she finally grabbed it. When she spoke, her voice sounded like sandpaper.

"Hey," Thalia said immediately. "Thank God. You don't have to say anything, okay? I just needed to know you were breathing. I'll just stay on with you."

And she did. For twenty-three silent minutes, Sierra sat on her bed, Salem tucked under her chin, listening only to her sister's steady breathing on the other end.

Jonas texted.

> **Jonas:** If you need some time off work, take it.

Sierra stared at the words for nearly an hour before her fingers finally managed to type back.

> **Sierra:** No, that's the last thing I need.

If she stopped moving, she might never start again.

So she went to work. She photographed families, couples, graduates. She lifted her camera, adjusted her lens, and gave directions in a voice that sounded distant even to her own ears. A little boy in one family stared straight at her between takes and whispered, *"Are you sad?"* His mom hushed him gently, embarrassed, and Sierra forced a smile that made her face ache. She clicked the shutter and kept going, but the question stayed lodged under her skin.

She showed up for every appointment, but she wasn't really present. Everything felt like watching life through thick glass.

The Chaos Coven texted her every single day. Jett offered to come sit with her. Raven left a container of soup on her doorstep. Sierra reheated it one night, stood over the stove, and stared at the steam until it faded. She dumped the untouched bowl down the sink. Calliope texted that she was going to burn down Lauren's studio "just to be a bitch about it." Sierra almost smiled at that. Almost.

Two weeks later, her parents guilt-tripped her into dinner. She showed up because lying about being busy felt like too much work.

Tobias was bouncing around as usual, launching into some comic book rant about Batman and explosions. Normally she'd argue, but tonight she just pushed food around her plate. Even he couldn't snap her out of whatever zombie state she was stuck in.

The doorbell rang.

Her mom bustled to answer, too cheerful, like she'd been hiding a secret prize. "Sierra, sweetie, we invited someone over."

It was a clean-cut, conventionally attractive, painfully polite man. He handed her flowers and a box of dessert from a bakery downtown. He grinned too much, asking questions about photography that sounded like they'd been ripped from a Google search.

Sierra lasted five minutes before she excused herself to the bathroom. She gripped the sink until her knuckles went white. Hollow eyes stared back at her from the mirror. She wanted to throw up.

She came back out, mumbled a goodbye, and hugged Tobias so hard he wheezed. Then she left without explanation.

Her mom texted later.

> **Mom:** I tried to understand this whole pansexual thing. I just can't. I thought since you and Lauren broke up, you needed someone who could give you a real future, sweetheart.

Sierra turned her phone off.

Later that night she stood in her bathroom again, staring at the stranger in the mirror who used to be her. Eyes permanently exhausted. Mouth locked in a line that felt carved there.

Almost without realizing it, she reached for her camera again. This time she pressed the shutter. Once. Twice. Again. Not selfies. She couldn't bear her own face, but pieces of her grief. Her hands hung useless. The sketchbook filled with drawings of Lauren she couldn't look at anymore. The empty side of her bed.

She printed them all and taped them to her wall in a jagged collage. At the top, in uneven handwriting, she scrawled *Missing*. It wasn't just Lauren who was gone. She'd lost herself, too.

"I don't know who I am without you."

Salem made a soft little sound and rubbed against her leg. His warm body was the only thing that didn't hurt.

She was bracing herself for another sleepless night when her phone rang. Tobias.

She answered, her voice barely above a whisper. "Hey."

"Don't hang up," he blurted out. "I can't stop thinking about dinner. That setup with Random Dude? Total bullshit. I already chewed Mom and Dad out."

Her throat closed. "Tobias..."

"Don't. Just listen for a second. You're dying inside and pretending everything's fine. Cut that shit out. Not with me."

The words cracked her. She started crying again.

"You were in love with Lauren. It was obvious every time you said their name. That doesn't just disappear because Mom and Dad are uncomfortable." His voice was low, but fierce.

"I have no idea how to do this. How do I even exist without them?"

"You don't need to have it figured out tonight. Just breathe. And when that feels too hard, call me. Anytime. I'll answer."

"What if I never feel normal again?"

"Then we'll figure out a new normal. Together. You're my sister, and I love you, broken heart and all."

That made her sob harder, but it felt different—like something tight inside her finally cracked open.

"Thank you," she whispered.

"Always. Now get some sleep if you can. Tomorrow doesn't have to be good. Just show up."

When they hung up, Sierra lay in the dark with Salem purring against her shoulder. The emptiness still pressed in heavy, but now there was a thin seam of light running through it. She cried until there was nothing left, and somehow morning happened anyway.

Chapter 33

The first month was survival mode. Sierra taught her classes on autopilot, smiled at the right moments, came home to Salem and tried not to look at the empty spaces Lauren had left behind. Thalia brought groceries. The Chaos Coven texted daily. Some days she forgot to eat until Calliope showed up with takeout.

By month two, the sharp edges had dulled to a constant ache. She started journaling again. It was angry scrawls at first. The pages were messy with feeling, words spilling out faster than she could control. Anger that didn't fit inside her. Hurt that felt endless. Love with nowhere left to go. Some entries fell apart into charcoal sketches in the margins—an eye she knew too well, hands she couldn't forget, the outline of a jaw that belonged to someone who didn't want remembering.

Jonas gave her extra work, probably recognizing she needed the distraction. She began sleeping through the night again, most nights.

One particularly rough Thursday, Thalia physically dragged her to a therapist's office on Fifth Street. Dr. Lowe had kind eyes and didn't push when Sierra spent the first ten minutes just staring at the tissue box.

"I keep thinking I should be over it by now. It's been months. People break up all the time."

"Grief doesn't follow a schedule, and this wasn't just any breakup. You lost someone you'd built a life with."

"But they left me. They chose to leave." The words came out bitter, sharp.

"They did, and it hurt you deeply. But their leaving doesn't mean you weren't worth staying for."

Sierra's throat closed up. She grabbed a tissue she didn't need just to have something to do with her hands. "Then why does it feel like it does?"

"That's the work we're here to do."

Month three brought small victories: laughing at one of Jett's terrible jokes without feeling guilty, buying coffee without automatically ordering Lauren's drink, too, taking photos for herself instead of just for clients.

The grief was still there, but different. Not easier, exactly. More like a bruise that had faded but still hurt when she poked at it. And she kept poking at it, like an idiot.

She'd finally stopped obsessively checking her phone every five minutes, stopped getting her hopes up every time it rang. But her heart still did this stupid little twist whenever she saw a blocked number or heard a song that reminded her of listening to music at night with Lauren, sharing earbuds.

Work became her escape. She said yes to every shoot, stayed up way too late editing photos until her eyes felt like sandpaper. At the community center, she taught about light and shadows while trying to pretend she wasn't drowning in her own darkness.

Everyone was worried about her, but at least she wasn't actively drowning anymore. More like floating in this strange liminal space between okay and not okay.

Still, she dragged herself to the community center every week. Without fail. Even on the mornings when getting out of bed felt like more than she could manage. Even when her voice cracked halfway through explaining color theory and she had to collect herself. The students never asked invasive questions, but a few started staying after class to talk about nothing important, or sometimes to sit beside her in comfortable silence. It helped more than she'd ever be able to admit out loud.

One evening, she finally worked up the courage to log into social media after months of complete digital silence. The memories hit her like a physical wave — selfies from Hawaii with flower crowns and sun-drunk grins, late-night movie marathon photos, candid shots of her laughing into Lauren's shoulder while Salem photo bombed in the background. She didn't scroll for long, but she also didn't cry, which felt like some kind of minor victory.

Thalia had been gently but persistently pushing her to do something, anything, for herself. "Go paint outside in the park. Try street photography. Hell, take a pole dancing class if you want. Just feel something other than this, sis. Anything else."

Sierra didn't sign up for any dance classes, but she started carrying her camera around again like she used to. One afternoon, she discovered this incredible alleyway downtown where murals exploded with color and life, layer upon layer of street art creating a visual symphony. She wandered for hours with her camera. Close shots of chipped paint, sunlight breaking between fire escapes, kids flying by on scooters with streamers trailing behind them. Little things, ordinary things, and finally after months, she felt awake. Present.

That night she lit her sandalwood candle and wrote in her journal, hand steady for once: *Today I remembered who I am without her.*

Not the same as before. But still me.

Her friends had never given up, even when she went quiet, even when she canceled at the last minute. They kept showing up. Jett appeared with bubble tea and aggressively dumb memes that made her laugh despite herself. Raven physically dragged her to the farmers' market on Saturday mornings, even when Sierra sulked and complained the entire time about crowds and sunshine. Calliope started crashing on her couch regularly, usually falling asleep with Salem sprawled across her chest like a furry heating pad. They never asked her to be okay or to put on a brave face. They asked her to exist, and somehow that felt manageable.

By month four, the seasons had shifted in a subtle way that creeps up on you. Her apartment smelled like sandalwood and fresh air again instead of stale sadness. Not all of her plants were dead. She'd watered them a few times, enough that some leaves still looked alive, and when a stranger smiled at her in the coffee line, she didn't flinch or drop her eyes right away.

She wasn't healed. Not even close. The Lauren-shaped hole in her chest was still there, maybe always would be. But she was surviving, not just drifting through the motions. On the better days, that was enough.

Some mornings she even woke up wondering, just a little, what the day might bring. Not excitement, but more like curiosity. It wasn't happiness. Not yet, but it was something lighter than the crushing weight she'd been carrying.

It was a tiny glimmer of hope, a fragile seed in the darkness. Small and delicate, but present nonetheless.

Chapter 34

Five months in, winter was creeping into the city. All the leaves had finally given up and died, covering the sidewalks in a crunchy carpet of brown and yellow. The air got that cold bite which made Sierra zip up her jacket, but she didn't hate it anymore.

She'd stopped flinching every time her alarm went off, though she still had this stupid habit of checking her phone first thing in the morning. Just in case. There never was.

But there were these brief moments now. Glimmers of something that might eventually become okay.

She'd been working on this photography thing for Jonas. He kept bugging her to put together a gallery show. She spent forever arranging prints all over her living room floor like some crazy person, staying up too late editing until her eyes wanted to fall out of her head.

The last photo she picked was from Hawaii. She and Lauren on that perfect beach, laughing at something stupid, all golden and happy. To most people, it probably just looked like a nice vacation photo. But to Sierra it was everything. It was tucked away in the middle of all these other ocean shots and random portraits like a secret.

She didn't tell anyone the actual story behind that photograph. Didn't need to. Some things belonged only to the heart that held them.

At the opening, Sierra put on her lucky black jumpsuit, the one that always made her feel like she had her life together, and nursed a glass of prosecco while trying not to stare at the Hawaii photo.

People drifted around making those art gallery sounds, you know, "mmm, such interesting use of light," and taking Instagram selfies in front of her stuff. Some woman with expensive glasses called her "an artist with a soul that truly sees," and Sierra smiled politely while internally rolling her eyes. But then this guy in a ridiculous hipster beanie made a terrible pun about one of her blurry sunset shots, something about "romantic smog pollution," and she laughed. Genuine laughter that came from somewhere deep in her chest.

It shocked her. The sound felt so weird coming out of her mouth after months of nothing, and then she felt guilty for laughing when Lauren wasn't there to hear it. But when she laughed again a few minutes later at something else equally stupid, it came easier, and it didn't feel like betrayal anymore.

It felt surprisingly good. Maybe she could still find things funny, even when her heart was still healing.

Her parents showed up halfway through, looking out of place but genuinely proud. Her mom immediately started taking photos of Sierra standing next to her pieces, fumbling slightly with her phone.

Mom started angling for a better shot. "Smile, sweetheart, I want to get you with that beautiful sunset piece."

Her mom's phone suddenly went dark. The screen had timed out. As she pressed the power button to wake it back up, Sierra caught a glimpse of the lock screen before her mom entered her passcode. She saw the rainbow PFLAG logo bright against a simple background.

Her throat went tight. Her mom had been learning, quietly and on her own, trying to understand this part of Sierra's world.

"Mom." Sierra's eyes suddenly misty.

Her mom looked up from her phone, concerned. "What's wrong, honey? Did I miss the shot?"

Instead of answering, Sierra stepped closer and wrapped her arm around her mom's shoulders. "Take a selfie with me?"

Mom's whole face just lit up. She held out her phone, and they both smiled as it clicked. In the picture, Sierra's eyes were all watery, and Mom looked so happy and proud, clueless that she'd just made Sierra's entire week with one stupid little gesture.

· ♥ · ♥ · ♥ · ♥ · ♥ ·

That night, Sierra flopped on the couch, and Salem made himself at home on her lap. He did that annoying kneading thing on her leg for like five minutes before finally turning into a furry black blob.

She scratched behind his ears. "I miss them too, buddy."

His tail twitched once, as if to say, "Yeah, but I'm always right here". Typical Salem, always reminding her that some love sticks around even when people bail.

The windows were getting all foggy from the heat being cranked up, and she could still smell her chamomile tea from earlier. She pulled her favorite blanket up to her chin and watched it snow outside. The flakes looked like tiny stars under the streetlight.

These brief moments didn't fix everything. Not even close. She still had a Lauren-sized hole in her chest that probably wasn't going anywhere, but at least she remembered that life kept happening around her, and she was still part of it somehow.

Still breathing. Still capable of random laughter and feeling okay sometimes, even when she didn't see it coming.

Chapter 35

Month six arrived with the icy rain that made everything look gray and muted, but Sierra found herself oddly comforted by its steady rhythm against her windows. Her daily routine had become second nature by now... work, clean the apartment, teach her classes, exist in whatever way felt manageable that day. She wasn't anywhere close to whole yet, but she was genuinely present in her own life again. Most days, that felt like a pretty significant victory.

The community center manager approached her after one of her regular classes with a request. Would she maybe give a little talk about using art to heal?

Sierra's gut reaction was absolutely not. Standing up in front of a bunch of strangers talking about her feelings? Her stomach tied itself in knots just thinking about it, but then she looked around at her students packing up their stuff. These people dragged themselves here every week even when they were falling apart. She could see their pain in every messy charcoal sketch, every wonky painting they worked on. They were all carrying heavy trauma, just like her.

"Okay. Yeah, I'll do it."

On the day of the talk, she threw on her jeans and a huge sweater that felt like a hug. No makeup. She wasn't trying to impress anyone. She didn't need armor today, just complete honesty.

She began, her voice surprisingly steady as she looked over the small audience. "The thing about creating when you feel broken is that sometimes the actual act of making something becomes the mending itself."

She clicked through slides showing student artwork... raw, imperfect, beautiful in its vulnerability. Then she shared some of her own pieces from what she privately called "the grief months." Not the beach photo with Lauren, definitely not that one, but other work from those dark days: messy, bold strokes that were strangely vibrant despite being born from pain.

She glanced down at her hands briefly before meeting their eyes. "I fell hard in love last year. The kind of love that makes absolutely everything louder and brighter and more intense, and then I lost them."

A few people made soft sounds, as if they were connecting with what she was saying. Sierra took a steady breath.

"For a while I thought I was done making art. Like, permanently. I couldn't even look at a blank page without feeling hollow, but when I finally picked up my camera again, I realized something. The pictures that meant the most to me weren't the flawless ones. They were the ones with a crack in the smile, or a shadow I didn't mean to catch, or a little blur around the edges. The mistakes that made it real."

She stopped for a second, felt something loosen up in her chest, then actually smiled for real.

"That's when I figured out you don't have to throw your broken pieces away. You can still make something out of them. Maybe even something worth keeping. Healing isn't about pretending the cracks aren't there. It's about letting them belong in the frame."

Nobody said anything, but it wasn't an awkward silence. It was the kind where everyone's actually listening. Sierra didn't notice the woman in the third row discreetly recording on her phone.

Later that week, Jett tagged her in a video with about fifteen exclamation points. It was her talk, filmed by someone in the audience and already reposted dozens of times across different platforms. Someone had slapped a caption on it: *When heartbreak meets healing. This will give you chills.*

Sierra just stared at her phone forever, pulse jumping like crazy. Finally, she got brave enough to watch herself up there talking about the worst time in her life like she had her life together. Just a few blocks away, Lauren was hitting play on the same video.

Chapter 36

The icy rain hadn't let up since morning, streaking down every surface in jagged, unforgiving lines. It was the kind of bone-deep chill that made you seriously question every life choice that required actually leaving your apartment. Sierra adjusted the strap of her heavy camera bag as she pushed through the entrance of the converted warehouse where to-day's shoot was happening. The building was massive, all soaring ceilings and exposed brick walls that had been trans-formed into this moody winter set with hanging Edison bulbs casting warm pools of light and rich velvet backdrops in deep jewel tones.

She spotted Jonas across the space and walked over, im-mediately suspicious of how pleased with himself he looked. "What's the vibe we're going for today?" she asked, setting down her equipment.

"Warm but edgy, editorial with a romantic undertone," he said, then added with studied casualness, "Oh, and I had to call in a last-minute makeup artist. They should be here any second now."

Sierra narrowed her eyes at him, but before she could press him about why that felt like suspiciously important information, a voice she knew better than her own heartbeat reached her from across the warehouse.

"Hey Jonas, where do you want me to set up my station?"

Her entire chest clenched as if someone had reached inside and squeezed her heart with a fist. Lauren.

They emerged from behind a rolling rack of clothes, setting down their familiar, well-worn makeup kit on a side table near the main lights. Their hair was shorter now, still damp from the rain and tousled in that effortless way that had always made Sierra's stomach flutter. They wore this thick cable-knit sweater over dark jeans and those combat boots Sierra had always loved. They looked stunning, and completely unaware that she was even there until their eyes suddenly met across the space.

Both of them froze. One heartbeat passed. Then another. Time seemed to stretch like taffy.

Jonas, obviously pretending not to notice the tension so thick you could practically cut it with a knife, clapped his hands together enthusiastically. "Alright everyone! Let's make some absolute magic today!"

They didn't speak. Not at first. Sierra forced herself to focus on setting up her camera gear with shaking hands. Lauren unpacked makeup brushes with a mechanical precision that suggested they were also trying very hard not to look in her direction. They moved around each other like wounded animals, hyperaware of each other's presence but desperate to avoid direct contact.

Throughout the entire shoot, their paths kept crossing in ways that felt both accidental and inevitable. Sierra would adjust lighting equipment right next to Lauren's makeup station. Lauren would touch up a model's powder while standing just close enough that Sierra could smell their familiar perfume. Everything was professional, distant, careful. When their eyes accidentally met across the set, Sierra looked away immediately, her chest tightening with old hurt. Lauren's gaze would linger for a split second before they forced themselves to focus on their brushes.

Sierra found excuses to work at the far end of the set, her stomach churning every time she heard Lauren's laugh with the models.

When the shoot finally wrapped, the crew started packing up their equipment with the usual efficient bustle. Sierra was coiling cables with unnecessary focus when Lauren approached, their voice barely above a whisper.

"I saw the video from your class."

Sierra's breath caught in her throat. "You did?"

Lauren nodded, their expression soft but unreadable. "It was really beautiful and brave."

A pause settled between them, heavy but not uncomfortable. Just filled with everything they weren't saying.

"I didn't know you'd be here today," Sierra managed.

"Jonas didn't tell me either," Lauren replied, then gave a small, knowing smile that made Sierra's heart skip. "But I'm thinking he might have been hoping for exactly this."

Sierra looked away quickly, blinking hard against the sudden threat of tears.

Lauren hesitated for a moment, then took a small step closer. "Would you maybe want to talk? We could grab coffee somewhere."

Sierra searched their face, looking for any sign of what this meant. "I still have some of your things at my place. We could talk there, and I can return them to you?"

Lauren's smile was cautious but genuine. "Yeah. I'd really like that."

Chapter 37

They walked the last few blocks to Sierra's apartment in complete silence, the kind that felt heavy with everything they couldn't say. The icy rain had turned the sidewalks into a treacherous skating rink, and Lauren's cheeks were bright pink from the biting cold, their breath coming out in visible puffs like ghosts of words they weren't ready to say yet.

When they finally stepped inside the warm apartment, Salem immediately let out his most dramatic meow and launched himself toward Lauren like a furry missile. But when Lauren crouched down to greet him the way they always used to, the cat sniffed once, gave a low, deeply judgmental trill, and turned away with his tail held high in obvious disdain.

"Holding a grudge, huh, buddy? I don't blame you. It's my fault." Lauren watched him stalk away.

Sierra stood awkwardly by the kitchen counter, unsure what to do with her hands. The familiar apartment felt strange with Lauren in it again, like a song played in the wrong key. "So..." she started, then stopped. "I guess we should talk."

Lauren opened their mouth as if to speak, then closed it. Started again. "I don't even know where to begin."

The silence stretched between them, not comfortable like it used to be, but loaded with six months of hurt. Sierra wrapped her arms around herself. "You said you wanted to talk."

"I did. I do." Lauren ran a hand through their hair, the gesture achingly familiar. "Sierra, I need to apologize for how I ended things between us. I was hurt and terrified, and I handled it in the worst possible way."

They took a shaky breath. "I thought if I pushed you away before you inevitably left on your own, it wouldn't destroy me completely. I genuinely thought I was doing you some kind of favor, giving you a shot at a simpler life without me there to complicate everything. I was so afraid that loving me would cost you your family the same way it cost me mine."

Sierra stared at them, something sharp and protective rising in her chest. "Six months, Lauren. Six months of nothing, and now you want to explain?" Her voice was steady, but there was steel underneath.

Lauren flinched. "I know how it sounds—"

"Do you?" Her voice cracked slightly. "Because it sounds like you made a decision for both of us and then disappeared. You didn't give me a choice."

"Then I saw you with him, and I thought maybe you'd be better off with someone easier. Someone your family could accept without question." Their voice grew smaller.

Sierra felt tears threatening, but anger was stronger. "Josh meant nothing to me. Less than nothing. I should've mentioned running into him, but I didn't think it mattered because to me, it genuinely didn't. You didn't even give me a chance to explain."

"I know. I was wrong about everything." Lauren stepped closer, then stopped when they saw Sierra tense.

"I think I understand now where your reaction came from. All that pain, all the abandonment you've carried. But understanding doesn't fix what you did."

Lauren's shoulders sagged. "I thought if I gave you a clean break, you could move on and be happy."

"But we were torn apart by things that could've been talked through and fixed. If you'd let me in instead of shutting me out." Sierra wiped her eyes angrily. "I would've chosen you, Lauren. Every time. But you didn't trust me enough to let me."

"You're absolutely right. I was a coward."

Sierra's voice went quiet, dangerous. "I haven't stopped loving you. But I can't go backward. If you left once, you could do it again, and I couldn't survive that twice. I barely survived it the first time."

Lauren set down their barely touched coffee and moved toward the door. "Maybe this was a mistake. I should go. I'm just hurting you more—"

"Wait." The word escaped before Sierra could stop it. Lauren froze with their hand on their coat.

Sierra closed her eyes, fighting with herself. "Don't just leave again. Not like this."

Lauren turned slowly. "What do you want from me, Sierra?"

"I don't know." Her voice broke. "I don't know what I want. I'm terrified of you, but I also..."

"Also what?"

"I missed you. Every single day. And I hate that I missed you."

Lauren's eyes filled with tears. "I missed you, too. More than I thought was possible to miss another person."

They stood there in the horrible space between wanting and not trusting, love and self-preservation.

"Maybe we could try starting over as friends?" Lauren's voice was barely audible. "I want to prove to you that I can stay when things get hard."

Sierra hesitated for a long moment, every self-protective instinct screaming warnings. "I don't know if I can do this. Trust doesn't just come back because you apologized."

"I know. I wouldn't expect anything from you. But maybe... maybe we could try? Just try?"

Sierra stared at them for what felt like forever. Finally, she gave one careful, reluctant nod. "Friends. That's all. And if you disappear on me again—"

"I won't. I swear to you, I won't."

Lauren's smile was tentative, like they were afraid it might break something. "Well, as your friend, I have to point out that your cat still absolutely hates me."

From his perch on the windowsill, Salem's tail gave one particularly dramatic flick, as if he'd been listening to every word and found their entire conversation lacking.

Sierra let out a laugh that was more tears than humor. "He'll come around eventually. Maybe."

They ended up sitting on opposite ends of the couch, a careful distance between them. Two people who weren't quite whole yet, weren't entirely broken anymore either, trying to figure out if they could build something new from whatever pieces were left behind.

Chapter 38

The morning after Lauren came over, Sierra found herself curled up on her couch with Salem sprawled across her legs like the world's most judgmental weighted blanket. Her thoughts had been spinning all night—anger, hope, terror, and love all crashing into each other like waves in a storm. One minute she felt like she could trust Lauren again, the next she wanted to scream at herself for being so stupid.

She'd barely slept. Every time she closed her eyes, she saw Lauren's face when they'd almost left, heard their voice breaking when they said they missed her. But then she'd remember the six months of silence, the way her heart had shattered, and fury would rise up so fast it made her dizzy.

She grabbed her phone and typed into the group chat with shaking hands.

Sierra: Emergency friend council needed. Can we meet up? I need to talk through some stuff.

Thalia, Raven, Jett, and Calliope all responded within literal seconds. They agreed to meet at Bean & Bloom, which had been redecorated with mismatched vintage chairs. The plants had taken over the entire front window, but their lavender lattes were still to die for.

By the time Sierra arrived, they'd already claimed their usual corner booth and ordered her drink. But instead of the warm welcome she expected, there was tension in the air. Thalia's smile was tight, Calliope's arms were crossed, and even Jett looked wary.

Thalia scooted over to make room, but her hug felt protective rather than comforting. "Alright. Tell us everything. And don't you dare sugarcoat it."

Sierra took a shaky sip of her latte. "Lauren and I hashed it out last night. It was incredibly heavy. But we talked, really talked this time instead of hurting each other. They apologized for how they ended things. I got to say everything I'd been carrying around for months."

"And how do you feel about the apology?" Raven asked, but there was an edge to her voice.

"It felt real. They explained where their head was at, and I think I understand the fear that made them run, but—"

"Love, are we just ignoring the fact that you were completely shattered? Like, couldn't-function-for-weeks destroyed? And now they show up with an apology and suddenly we're considering forgiveness?"

Sierra flinched. "I'm not."

"Sierra." Thalia's voice was gentle but firm. "I saw what losing them did to you. I held you while you cried for months. So forgive me if I'm not ready to welcome them back with open arms just because they finally decided to apologize."

"But you don't understand," Sierra's voice cracked. "When I saw them yesterday, it all came flooding back. Not just the hurt, but everything good, too. And I—" She stopped, pressing her hands to her face. "I don't know what I'm doing."

Jett leaned forward, his usual playfulness replaced by fierce protectiveness. "Gorgeous, you're feeling everything and thinking nothing. I get it, but last time your heart made the decisions? Six months of devastation."

"What am I supposed to do?!" Sierra's voice rose slightly, drawing glances from other customers. "Pretend I don't still love them? Pretend seeing them didn't turn my whole world upside down again?"

"Love them all you want. Doesn't mean they won't bail again," Raven replied.

Sierra stared into her latte, tears threatening. "They want to be friends. They said they want to prove they can stay when things get hard."

The table went quiet for a long moment.

"And what do you want?" Thalia asked softly.

"I don't know!" Sierra's voice broke. "Part of me wants to text them right now, to say forget the friendship thing, let's try again. The other part wants to change my number and pretend yesterday never happened. I'm a mess."

Calliope's expression softened slightly. "Being a mess is normal. But, Sierra, you've worked so hard to put yourself back together. Don't let them break you again."

"What if they don't?" Sierra whispered. "What if they really have changed?"

"Then they'll prove it," Jett said firmly. "Over time. With actions, not words. But you don't owe them anything. Not friendship, not forgiveness, nothing."

Thalia squeezed Sierra's hand. "Whatever you decide, we've got your back. Always. But promise me you won't rush into anything. Your heart can't take another hit like that."

Sierra nodded, though she wasn't sure she believed her own promise.

Later that afternoon, Sierra marched into Jonas' office with her hands planted firmly on her hips and fire in her eyes.

"You absolutely KNEW Lauren would be at that shoot yesterday!"

Jonas looked up from his computer with the most sheepish expression she'd ever seen on his face. "I needed a makeup artist on short notice, and maybe I thought seeing each other again might help both of you get some closure. Did it work?"

Sierra stared at him for a long moment, trying to decide if she wanted to throttle him or thank him. "I don't know yet. Ask me in six months."

"That's fair," he answered carefully. "Are you okay?"

"No," she said honestly. "But I will be. Probably."

That evening, Sierra sat at her kitchen table with Salem supervising from his perch on the windowsill. She pulled out a fresh journal, not the grief-stained one from the past few months, but something clean and new. She opened it to the first page and stared at the blank lines.

She wanted to make lists, ground rules, some kind of plan that would make sense of the chaos in her head. But every time she put pen to paper, the words felt wrong. Too neat. Too hopeful. Too scared.

Sierra stared at the blank journal page, pen hovering. She had no idea what came next, and for the first time in months, she wasn't sure if that terrified or excited her.

What she did know was that tomorrow, she'd have to decide whether to text Lauren back. Whether to take the first step on whatever path they were building. Whether to risk her heart again on someone who'd already broken it once.

The thought made her stomach clench, but it also made her feel alive in a way she'd forgotten was possible.

Salem meowed softly, as if sensing her turmoil, and she reached over to scratch his ears.

"What do you think, buddy? Am I completely insane?"

Salem blinked slowly and settled into a loaf position, which Sierra chose to interpret as "proceed with caution, but proceed."

She closed the journal and headed to bed, still no closer to answers but somehow okay with the uncertainty. Tomorrow would bring whatever it brought. Tonight, she just had to survive the wanting.

Chapter 39

Life kept moving forward, though Sierra felt like she was still treading water rather than floating. The volatility from seeing Lauren again had settled into a different kind of unease, not the sharp pain of before, but a constant low-grade anxiety about what came next.

Sierra filled her days with photography gigs that excited her again, community center classes where her students were showing real artistic growth, and this tentative search for the inner calm that used to come naturally before everything got complicated.

She'd said everything she needed to say to Lauren that afternoon in her apartment. She didn't regret any of it — not the boundaries, the honesty, or even agreeing to try friendship. But that didn't mean that missing had magically disappeared. Some mornings she still woke up reaching for the empty space, still caught herself wanting to text them about something funny Salem had done.

On a particularly gray Tuesday morning a couple of weeks later, Sierra pushed through the door of Bean & Bloom. The bell above the door gave its familiar jingle, and the rich smell of espresso and fresh cinnamon rolls wrapped around her like the world's most caffeinated hug.

She was standing in line, scrolling through her phone and trying to decide between her usual latte or something more adventurous, when she looked up and froze. There was Lauren.

They were sitting at the small round table by the front window, hair slightly tousled like they'd been running their fingers through it, hands wrapped around a ceramic mug. The second their eyes met, Lauren's went wide with something that looked like panic mixed with hope.

Sierra's stomach did an immediate somersault, but she kept her expression neutral. After ordering her drink, she walked over with what she hoped looked like casual confidence.

"Hey."

"Hey." Lauren half-stood as if they weren't sure what the proper etiquette was for this situation.

Sierra glanced at the empty chair across from them. "I can sit. If you don't mind the company."

"I'd like that. I mean, if you want to. No pressure."

They sat in this careful arrangement, both holding their drinks like shields. They didn't talk much that first time. Sierra scrolled through social media while Lauren stared out the window at pedestrians hurrying past in the drizzle. But it wasn't the awful, heavy silence she'd expected. It was quiet. Almost familiar in a way that made her chest ache.

When Sierra finally had to leave for a client meeting, Lauren looked up with hopeful eyes.

"Same time next Tuesday?" They immediately looked embarrassed. "I mean, if you happen to be here. No big deal if not."

Sierra considered this for a moment. "Yeah. Maybe I'll see you here."

The following Tuesday, it happened again. Sierra arrived at nine, and Lauren was already there at the same table, looking like they'd been waiting but trying to appear casual about it. This time they managed actual conversation, nothing deep or relationship-related, just safe topics like work and the weather and whether the new barista was too heavy-handed with the foam art.

And the Tuesday after that.

It became an unspoken ritual. That little round table by the window, two people carefully navigating the space between friendship and something undefined. Sometimes they talked about Sierra's photography projects or Lauren's latest make-up techniques. Sometimes they sat in comfortable silence, Lauren sketching in a small notebook while Sierra edited photos on her laptop.

Each week, Sierra noticed slight changes in Lauren, but she remained guarded, analyzing every interaction for signs they might disappear again. They'd started making gentle jokes again, the self-deprecating humor that used to make Sierra laugh until her sides hurt. Their relationship was not discussed, and they never pushed for more than these careful Tuesday mornings. They consistently showed up, and Sierra found herself looking forward to it in a way that both comforted and terrified her.

"How are the coffee dates going?" Thalia asked one evening while they cooked dinner together, her tone carefully neutral.

"They're not dates. They're... I don't know what they are. We drink coffee. Sometimes we talk. It's nice."

Thalia raised an eyebrow but didn't push. "And how do you feel about it?"

Sierra paused, considering. "Honestly? I enjoy having them back in my life, even in this small way, but I'm also scared as hell I'm setting myself up to get hurt again."

"That's fair." Thalia squeezed her shoulder. "Just remember you get to set the pace here. Don't let anyone, including yourself, rush you into anything you're not ready for."

Meanwhile, the Chaos Coven had their own opinions about the situation.

"I still don't trust them." Calliope declared during a group dinner at Jett's apartment. "Coffee shop meetings are cute and all, but showing up for lattes is not the same as showing up when life gets messy."

"But they are showing up." Raven pointed out gently. "Every week, consistently. That's not nothing."

Jett nodded. "It's something, but I'm with Calliope. I need to see them handle actual adversity before I'm convinced they won't bolt again."

"What does Sierra say about all this?" Thalia asked.

"I'm taking it day by day." Sierra ran her fingers through her hair.

Calliope grabbed Sierra's hand. "Which I respect, but I'm still prepared to activate full chaos mode if they hurt you again."

Back at the coffee shop the following Tuesday, Lauren looked up from their sketchbook as Sierra settled into her chair with her usual latte.

"Can I ask you something?" Lauren's voice was hesitant.

Sierra nodded, though her shoulders tensed slightly.

"Do you think..." Lauren paused, clearly choosing their words carefully. "Do you think there's any chance we could be real friends again? Not just these careful coffee shop interactions, but actual friends? I don't want to push or pressure you, and I'm not going anywhere, even if the answer is no."

Sierra studied their face, looking for any sign of ulterior motives or hidden expectations. All she saw was genuine hope mixed with vulnerability.

"I think that friendship is something you build, not something you declare. So far, these Tuesday mornings have been good. Let's see where it goes from here."

Lauren's smile was small but radiant. "I can work with that."

As Sierra walked home, she realized something had shifted. She didn't know what it meant yet, but the future felt like something other than survival. Maybe even something like possibility, which terrified her but also made her happy.

Chapter 40

Sierra's hands were trembling as she arranged supplies around the art room at the community center. The idea for this new class had been growing in her mind ever since her viral talk, a dedicated space for healing through creativity, where grief, loss, heartbreak, and trauma could be translated into color and form and whatever shape they needed to take. She arranged each paintbrush with almost ritualistic care, as if she were preparing for something sacred.

Her regular students started filtering in first, offering warm smiles and comfortable small talk as they claimed their usual spots. But there were several new faces, too, people who'd obviously heard about the class through word of mouth or social media. They entered more tentatively, scanning the room with the careful wariness of people who weren't sure what they were signing up for but knew they needed something. The turnout was better than she'd dared to hope for, and Sierra felt her chest swell with a cautious, fragile kind of pride.

She was walking toward the door to close it and officially begin when she suddenly froze mid-step.

Lauren stood in the doorway, bundled up in a thick cable-knit sweater that made them look smaller somehow, their cheeks pink from the cold. When they spoke, their voice trembled.

"I hope this is okay. I think I could genuinely benefit from the class."

Sierra's heart did this stuttering little skip, and she stared for a beat too long before forcing herself to step aside and open the door wider. Lauren walked in quietly, and Sierra noticed some of her regular students exchanging knowing glances. They recognized the person whose absence had been written all over Sierra's art for months.

Trying to keep her voice steady and professional, Sierra addressed the full room.

"We all carry pain." Her eyes avoided Lauren's section of the room. "Sometimes it's fresh and raw and feels like it might kill us. Sometimes it's been with us so long it feels like part of our basic anatomy. But that pain has to go somewhere, right? It can't live inside us forever without destroying us, and art gives it a safe place to land."

She paused, letting her words settle, then continued. "I want you to think about one of the hardest moments in your life. You don't need to draw a literal scene or a recognizable face. Just try to capture the feeling itself. Let it come through however it needs to... abstract, realistic, whatever feels right."

The room filled with the sounds of pencils scratching against paper and brushes moving across canvas. Sierra walked among her students, offering gentle guidance here and there. One woman was sketching what looked like a cemetery under storm clouds. A young man was drawing a cracked photograph with precise lines. Some sat motionless, staring at blank pages with obvious frustration.

"Don't overthink it. Just draw what you feel. It doesn't have to make sense to anyone else."

She deliberately avoided Lauren's table, staying mostly at the front of the room where she felt safer.

After about forty-five minutes, Sierra called for attention. "Would anyone feel comfortable sharing what they created? No pressure at all, but sometimes talking about our art can be part of the healing process."

An older woman with silver hair raised her hand tentatively. "I drew my heart." She stood and held up her paper so others could see. "There's this piece missing right here. My mom passed away from cancer last year, and I still don't know how to fill the empty space where she used to be."

Sierra swallowed past the sudden lump in her throat. "That's incredibly beautiful and honest. Thank you for sharing that with us."

Lauren stood up before Sierra could prepare herself.

"This is me." They held up a jagged drawing of a lone figure hunched on concrete steps beneath a sky that seemed to collapse in on itself. Their voice wavered. "I was sixteen years old. My parents kicked me out of the house because they couldn't accept that I wasn't the son they thought they'd raised. I didn't even know who I was yet, just that it wasn't him."

A tear slid down Lauren's cheek, but they kept going. "I buried all that pain so deep I convinced myself it was gone. I used it as fuel to prove I was untouchable. But it never left. That terrified kid still shows up—in how I love, in how I... run, when it gets hard."

Then they looked at Sierra. Directly.

"I'm trying to learn how to stay."

The words hit Sierra like a fist to the chest. For a heartbeat, the room seemed to tilt. She wasn't just hearing Lauren's confession—she was watching her students witness it, too. Every raw piece of their history, laid bare in the space she'd carved as her sanctuary. Pride swelled in her chest, tangled with fear and something dangerously close to love.

She forced herself to breathe, fingers tightening around the dry-erase marker she'd been holding as if it could anchor her. When she spoke, her voice came out steadier than she felt.

"That took so much courage. Thank you for trusting us with it."

Lauren pressed their lips together, blinking hard, and sat back down.

Across the room, a ripple of emotion moved through the students. One woman murmured that her cousin had gone through something similar. A young man walked over to Lauren's table and whispered, "Me, too."

Sierra stayed at the front, her heartbeat still unsteady, her body taut with the effort of holding professional composure while every part of her wanted to cross the room, touch Lauren's hand, and tell them she'd heard every word.

Eventually, the room emptied until it was just Sierra and Lauren, surrounded by art supplies and the lingering emotional weight of what had happened.

"I didn't tell you I was coming because I wasn't sure I'd go through with it." Lauren's eyes didn't quite meet Sierra's. "I didn't want to upset you or make this about us, but I knew I needed to be here. I hope it's okay if I keep coming. I don't know of any other program like it, and I truly need it."

Sierra felt something shift in her chest as she really looked at Lauren, maybe for the first time since they'd walked back into her life. She could see the scared sixteen-year-old in their posture, the adult trying so hard to heal, the person she'd fallen in love with, still learning how to stay in one place when things got difficult.

She reached out and touched Lauren's arm. "Of course you can stay. This class is for anyone who needs it."

They walked out of the community center side by side, not saying much but connected in a way that felt different from their careful Tuesday morning coffee dates. Both of them were healing; both of them were learning. Neither was running away.

Chapter 41

Tuesday rolled around again, and Sierra found herself walking toward the coffee shop despite every rational voice in her head telling her this was a mistake. The coffee shop buzzed with its usual morning energy, but Sierra felt anything but settled. She'd claimed a corner table. Not their old one, she wasn't ready for that level of familiarity—and sat nursing her latte while pretending to read Aperture magazine. Her eyes kept drifting to the door, a habit she both craved and resented. Part of her hoped Lauren wouldn't show up, would spare her this weekly emotional minefield. The other part feared they wouldn't come, and that fear scared her more than anything.

When Lauren finally walked in, their eyes met instantly across the crowded space. No awkward pause this time, no careful navigation of whether they should acknowledge each other. Just this soft, familiar smile that made Sierra's chest feel warm in a way that had nothing to do with the coffee.

Lauren slid into the booth, already peeling off thick wool gloves and unwrapping the oversized scarf that had been protecting them from the wind. There was something steadier about them today, something that made Sierra's chest unclench.

Lauren began without preamble. "Ever since that Hawaii shoot brought me into Jonas' orbit, I've been absolutely booked solid. Like, more work than I know what to do with. I actually have almost enough saved to have top surgery if I want it, but I don't know if I do. I'm a little terrified of the thought; I can't forget what happened to my mom. There's so many things that can go wrong."

Sierra's eyebrows lifted with genuine concern. "That sounds terrifying, but you don't have to figure it out alone. Ask every question you can. Make sure you feel safe with whatever choice you make."

"It's surreal, having a financial goal for once in my life and actually reaching it. Hard to believe I was homeless not that long ago. Meeting you and Jonas gave me a way forward I didn't think I'd find." Lauren paused, then tilted their head with a mischievous expression Sierra remembered from their early days together. "But can I ask you something? Jonas was in a bind when he called me for that shoot, wasn't he? But he also chose me specifically on purpose?"

Sierra couldn't help the grin that tugged at the corners of her mouth. "Oh, he absolutely did. He gave me this whole spiel about being desperate for a makeup artist, but I could see right through him. He knew exactly what he was doing, and he admitted it."

Lauren leaned forward. "You didn't murder him, did you?"

Sierra burst out laughing, the sound bubbling up from somewhere deep in her chest. "I considered it. Actually, I marched into his office and confronted him, but I ended up giving him the evil eye and then hugging him."

"That sounds about right." Lauren chuckled, and they both smiled at each other, with a gentle, unspoken understanding hanging in the air between them.

The barista called out someone's complicated order, breaking the spell. Sierra glanced at her phone, realizing she needed to leave soon.

She grabbed her camera bag. "Speaking of Jonas and his schemes, I've got to run to do a shoot with him. Some kind of editorial thing for a local magazine. Will I see you at class tomorrow night?"

Lauren nodded. "Absolutely. I wouldn't miss it. It's the first time I've had somewhere safe to let this out instead of carrying it around alone." They hesitated, then went on. "Actually, I've been seeing a therapist for a few months. Dr. Martinez at the clinic pointed me her way. She's the one who told me about your healing-through-art class. Said it might give me a safe place to work through things. She also got me journaling, which I swore I'd hate, but I don't. She's helped me see my abandonment patterns and taught me how to sit with the feeling instead of running from it. She also connected me to a support group. Just other trans folks talking about life stuff. It's all been really helpful."

Sierra felt her face soften; her smile reached all the way to her eyes. "That's wonderful, Lauren. I'm proud of you for doing that work."

Her hand twitched before she even realized what she was doing, the impulse stronger than the voice in her head telling her not to. She reached across the small table and let her fingers rest over Lauren's knuckles, warm and gentle and so unexpected that both of them froze, eyes locked on the point of contact.

The moment stretched between them, heavy with careful hope. But almost immediately, Sierra's chest tightened with panic. This was exactly what she'd promised herself she wouldn't do. Her pulse jumped in her throat, not with romance but with alarm. She was crossing the line she'd drawn, falling back into old patterns that had destroyed her once before.

"I'm sorry!" She jerked her hand back as if she'd been burned. "I shouldn't have—that wasn't—" She stood abruptly, nearly knocking over her chair. "I should go."

Lauren's face fell, but they nodded with understanding. "Sierra, wait. It's okay. We don't have to—"

"No, it's not okay." Sierra's voice was tight with self-recrimination. "I said friends. I meant friends. I can't keep doing this to myself. I should head out."

Lauren's expression was understanding but disappointed. "Sierra, it's okay. We don't have to define anything. I'm sorry if I made you uncomfortable."

"You didn't," Sierra said quickly, then shook her head. "Yes, you did. Not intentionally, but... I can't keep doing this dance with you. One minute I think I can handle being friends, the next I'm..." She gestured helplessly at the table. "This is exactly what I was afraid would happen."

As Sierra walked toward the door, she could feel Lauren watching her leave, but this time it didn't thrill her. It made her feel exposed, vulnerable. For the first time since their coffee shop meetings began, she was questioning whether she could actually do this. Whether seeing Lauren every week was healing or just another way of torturing herself.

Outside, the cold air stung her cheeks, and she realized her hands were shaking. Not from the temperature, but from the effort of walking away when every instinct screamed at her to go back inside. She pulled out her phone to text Thalia, then stopped. She already knew what her sister would say: that she was playing with fire and eventually she'd get burned again. Maybe it was time to admit Thalia was right.

Walking home, Sierra wondered if she was being unfair to Lauren, or if she was finally learning to protect herself. She couldn't tell the difference anymore.

Chapter 42

Movie night at Sierra's apartment continued as it always did, the ritual so familiar it could have played on autopilot. But without Lauren, it was never quite the same. The empty space on the couch felt like its own character, heavy and insistent, pulling Sierra's eyes back to it no matter how hard she tried to stay focused on the ridiculous action flick Jett had picked.

She laughed at her friends' sarcastic commentary, chimed in with the occasional snarky remark, but her heart wasn't in it. Every time she glanced at the cushion beside her, the ache sharpened. Thalia had been joining them more often lately, which helped ease the quiet, but not the specific absence of someone who used to belong there.

During an especially absurd chase scene, Calliope grabbed the remote and froze the screen. She turned toward Sierra with the kind of pointed look that meant she'd been holding back for a while.

"Okay. How are things with Lauren? Really."

The sudden attention made Sierra's pulse skip. She toyed with the corner of the throw pillow in her lap, words coming out slower than she wanted. "We're friends. They come to my class every week, and sometimes we run into each other at the coffee shop. It's... slow. Careful."

Calliope raised her brows. "But are you two going to get back together? Because it feels like there's this giant elephant on the couch that we're all politely ignoring."

Sierra went quiet, the question catching her square in the chest. Weeks ago, she would've had a definite answer, but now? She stared down at her hands before lifting her gaze again. "A few weeks ago, I'd have said no. But they've been showing me they're trying—therapy, real growth, not just words. I'm not making any declarations. I just... I can't say never anymore."

The group exchanged looks, their expressions a mix of caution and hope.

Thalia leaned in, voice gentle but steady. "Be careful with your heart. But don't lock it away either. You deserve to be happy, however that ends up looking."

Emotion burned behind Sierra's eyes, and she clutched the pillow tighter. "I love you guys. Thank you for always being on my side, even when you think I'm making questionable choices."

"Always," Raven said firmly.

"Always," the others echoed in their own ways, the word weaving itself into the air like a promise.

·♥·♥·♥·♥·♥·

The following week at the community center, Sierra stood at the front of her classroom, every supply carefully arranged on the table—charcoal sticks lined up, watercolor trays gleaming, stacks of paper fanned neatly. She'd been thinking about tonight's theme for days, the one that wouldn't leave her alone.

Her chest tightened as she faced the room, eyes skimming across familiar faces and new ones alike. She could feel Lauren sitting somewhere behind those expectant gazes, and the weight of that fact pressed hard against her ribs.

"Tonight's prompt is: *What I Couldn't Say.*"

The room went still, the silence thick and heavy. Her voice wavered, but held. "Interpret it however you need. Words you never spoke. Things you wish you'd heard. Feelings that have been trapped too long. Whatever it is—let it out. In whatever form feels right."

As students dispersed to gather supplies, the room filled with the quiet sounds of creation: pencils scratching, brushes swishing, the occasional sigh of frustration. Sierra moved among them, offering encouragement, her teacher's smile fixed in place even as her mind churned.

She paused by a woman who'd painted a red thread tangled around the silhouette of a mouth. Another student sketched a gravestone surrounded by half-formed sentences. Sierra praised them softly, though her own throat felt tight.

Then she reached Lauren's table.

Her breath caught.

The piece was raw and messy, bleeding with emotion. A figure walked away on one side of the page, its shape dissolving into streaks of gray. On the other side stood another figure, stark and still, chest ripped open—blue and red ink spilling like something vital torn loose.

And tucked within the shadows, Sierra saw words written in Lauren's neat handwriting: *I'm sorry I let go without letting you reach for me.*

Her vision blurred. Every instinct screamed to demand an explanation, to collapse under the weight of it, but she forced herself to turn, to walk calmly out into the hallway. The cool wall pressed against her back as she dragged in a shaky breath, steadying herself. She was the teacher here. She couldn't break down in front of the class.

After what felt like forever, she reentered the room, voice carefully even. "Wonderful work tonight, everyone. Let's wrap up a little early."

Confusion flickered across a few faces. They still had twenty minutes, but no one questioned her. Chairs scraped, bags zipped, and one by one, the room emptied.

Except for Lauren.

They sat still, eyes on their drawing, shoulders hunched. When they finally spoke, their voice was raw. "I'm sorry. I didn't mean to make things harder for you. Maybe I shouldn't come back."

Sierra's pulse pounded, but she shook her head. "No. If we're going to be friends, real friends, we'll hit rough patches. Walking away isn't the answer."

Lauren's eyes shone, their jaw tight. They packed up slowly, pausing at the doorway. "Thank you. You could've shut me out so many times. I don't deserve your friendship, but I'm grateful you're letting me try."

The door closed softly behind them, leaving Sierra alone among the scattered brushes and damp paper. She stood still, the air heavy with everything unsaid. Her chest ached with equal parts fear and hope, the edges of both cutting sharp as she whispered to the empty room, "Neither of us is running anymore."

Chapter 43

The art class ended in a hush that felt heavier than usual. Brushes clattered into jars, chairs scraped across linoleum, but few people spoke as they packed up. Sierra moved slowly, rag in hand, wiping down tables that didn't need wiping, her eyes flicking again and again to Lauren.

They slipped toward the door, shoulders tense, gaze fixed on the floor. Before Sierra could say a word, the heavy door thudded shut behind them.

She froze, rag still in her hand. Part of her wanted to chase after them, to close the distance with a word or a touch. But she stayed rooted, heart thumping with a quiet, familiar ache. If Lauren needed space, Sierra wouldn't force her way in. Not anymore.

When she bent to collect a stray sketchpad near the front row, something caught the light under a chair leg. A silver bracelet, slightly tarnished, one she recognized instantly from

Lauren's wrist. She turned it over in her palm, thumb brushing the familiar curve of metal.

She slipped it into her pocket, intending to hand it back next week. But the thought nagged at her. Lauren never forgot things like this. Not unless something was seriously wrong.

By Sunday afternoon, Sierra couldn't shake the image of Lauren's hunched shoulders disappearing into the stairwell. The bracelet sat on her kitchen counter like an accusation, its silence louder than anything she could ignore.

Finally, she gave in. She drove across town with it clutched in her hand, telling herself it was just an errand. Just returning something. But deep down, she knew it was more than that.

Every rational voice told her to just text about the bracelet, but seeing Lauren so unlike themselves in class had triggered something protective she thought she'd buried. She hated that she still cared this much.

When the door opened, her first thought wasn't the pallor on Lauren's face but the shirt they were wearing—her old Razor Braids tour tee. It hung loose on their frame, collar stretched, black faded to gray from too many washes. For a second, her breath caught in her chest.

Then she really looked at them. The washed-out color of their skin. The slackness around their mouth. The way their shoulders sagged as though every ounce of energy had been wrung out.

Sierra lifted the bracelet between them. "Hey. You left this in the classroom. Thought you might want it back."

Lauren blinked, like they'd forgotten it existed. "Oh. Thanks." Their voice was hoarse, weaker than she'd expected. Their hand shook as they reached for it.

Sierra frowned. "You don't look okay."

"I'm fine," Lauren said too quickly. Their hand brushed across their stomach before disappearing into their pocket. "Probably just stress. I've had this ache all day, but I'm sure it's nothing. Just tired or maybe a bug."

"Lauren..." Sierra started, but they cut her off with a thin, uneven laugh.

"I promise, it's not a big deal. I just need sleep."

Every instinct in her screamed to push harder, but their expression stopped her cold. The same walls she'd seen before were back in place, fragile but impenetrable. She held out the bracelet instead. "Okay. But if it gets worse, you have to promise you'll call me."

"I promise."

She lingered another second, memorizing the way the shirt hung on them, the shadows carved under their eyes, the way their voice faltered on simple words. Everything about them radiated wrongness. Still, she forced herself to step back, let them close the door, and walked slowly to her car with unease pressing against her ribs like a stone.

That night, Sierra curled up on the couch with Salem sprawled across her legs, tail flicking against her ribs. The muted glow of the TV lit the room, but she couldn't follow the movie. Her thoughts kept circling back to Lauren. They were too pale, too quiet, wrapped in their shirt like armor.

The phone buzzed just after nine.

> **Lauren:** Thanks for coming by. Sorry I was weird. I'm fine. Just need rest.

> **Sierra:** Okay. Please take care of yourself.

She set the phone on the coffee table. Salem purred against her, steady and grounding, but even with the cat's warmth anchoring her, she couldn't shake the image of Lauren leaning in the doorway, pale and exhausted, insisting it was nothing.

Hours later, the credits had long since rolled, but Sierra was still awake. She lay in the dark with Salem curled at her feet, phone face-up on the cushion beside her. Every time she closed her eyes, she saw Lauren's trembling hands, heard that too-quick laugh.

She told herself she was overreacting. People got tired, caught colds, had off days. But the memory of that gray pallor wouldn't let her rest. Her chest ached with the heavy certainty that something was wrong, even if she couldn't name it.

She rolled over, stared at the silent phone, and whispered to the ceiling, "Please call me if it gets worse."

But the room stayed still. The cat stretched. The phone stayed dark.

And dread settled heavier and heavier in her chest, keeping her awake until the first light of morning.

Chapter 44

Monday dawned gray and brittle, rain streaking her windows in uneven lines. Sierra tried to focus on her lesson prep, pencil tapping against her sketchbook, but her eyes kept sliding to her phone. No new messages.

She gave in and typed:

Sierra: How are you feeling today?

Ten long minutes passed before the bubbles appeared.

Lauren: Rough. Not coming to class. Sorry.

Her stomach dropped. She hit call before she could talk herself out of it. Lauren picked up on the second ring, their voice thin and papery.

"Hey. You're up early."

"You sound awful." Sierra tried to smooth the panic out of her tone. "Let me come over. I'll make tea or soup. Class can wait."

A small laugh that didn't sound like them. "I'll be fine. Just a bug. Please go to class. Promise me you won't worry."

"I am going to worry no matter what. If it doesn't get better, you have to call me or at least get checked out at the clinic."

"I will."

The word landed flimsy, and then the line went quiet.

The day moved like wet concrete. Sierra taught on autopilot, corrected charcoal lines that didn't need correcting, smiled at the right moments without feeling any of it. Every buzz of her phone hit like a jolt. Student questions. Thalia's memes. Nothing from Lauren.

By late afternoon, she sat at her kitchen table with her sketchbook open and blank. The rain had thinned to a fine mist that turned the streetlights into halos. She stared at her phone until her eyes ached.

It rang with an unfamiliar number.

"Is this Sierra Turner?" a calm voice asked.

"Yes."

"This is University Hospital. You are listed as the emergency contact for Lauren Reeves. I'm calling to let you know they have just come out of surgery. Their appendix ruptured. The procedure went well, and they are stable."

The words made little sense at first. Then her pulse launched into her throat so fast she nearly dropped the phone. "I'm on my way."

She was already jamming on shoes and snatching her keys from the bowl. "Please be okay," she whispered to the empty apartment, to Salem blinking slow from the couch, to anyone listening.

The hospital smelled of antiseptic and coffee. It was too bright and too quiet at the same time. Sierra nearly ran to the front desk, blurting out Lauren's name before the receptionist even finished asking how she could help.

"They are in recovery," the woman said gently, eyes kind. "Give us a few minutes. I'll let the nurse know you're here."

Minutes stretched thin as wire. Sierra sat on a stiff plastic chair that dug into her spine, torn between pacing and staying perfectly still. Her leg bounced until the floor trembled. She pressed her palms together until they hurt, then forced them apart, then pressed them back together again.

Her phone lay heavy in her lap. She unlocked it and reread the last message Lauren had sent the night before. The words blurred from repetition. She locked the screen and set it face down, palm flattening over it like pressure might keep her from shattering.

The waiting room hummed faintly with vending machines and distant overhead announcements. A man in scrubs tapped on his tablet across from her. Someone coughed behind a partition. Sierra barely heard any of it. Her body sat in the chair, but her mind was unspooling everywhere else.

Memory offered itself in sharp fragments: Lauren in the park, black hair catching the sun while they laughed at something Sierra couldn't hear. That cautious smile at the café, like a door cracking open. Salt wind in Hawaii, wish lanterns lifting over black water. The quiet of her living room when one hand found another with no words at all.

Her throat burned. If she lost them now, she didn't know who she would be. Salem would wait at the door for footsteps that never came. Thalia would hold her in silence, because there would be nothing to say. Her parents would offer practical advice that landed like weather reports.

Her heart felt like a dam about to burst, every second straining harder against the weight behind it.

She inhaled slowly. Exhaled even slower. "Hold on. Please just hold on."

"Sierra Turner?" a voice called.

She stood so fast the chair skidded back. "Yes."

A nurse with kind eyes gestured down the corridor. "You can come back now."

The walk felt endless. Doors, curtains, monitors, the quiet thrum of machines. When the nurse drew the curtain aside, Sierra's breath caught.

Lauren lay propped against white pillows, skin pale and damp, an IV snaking from their arm. The monitor beside them kept a steady beat that sounded like a lifeline. Their lips were cracked. Their eyelashes stuck together at the tips.

Sierra's hand flew to her mouth. "Thank God!"

Their eyelids fluttered. They found her through a fog of anesthesia and managed a faint smile. "What are you doing here?"

"I could ask you the same." She sank into the chair and took their hand, fingers fitting like they always had. "You scared the life out of me."

"They took it out," Lauren whispered. "My appendix. It ruptured."

Sierra brushed damp hair back from their forehead. "That is terrifying. I'm so glad you're okay."

Their eyes filled, but the drugs tugged them under before any tears could fall. The monitor kept time. The nurse smiled at Sierra in a way that felt like mercy.

Sierra sat with their hand in hers and let her own breath even out. The room hummed with soft machine sounds and the distant roll of a cart. For the first time all day, the panic let go of her throat.

She pulled out her phone with shaking fingers and opened the group chat.

> **Sierra:** Lauren's appendix ruptured. They are stable now. Thalia, can you get Salem, please?

Responses arrived in a quick flicker. Shock. Hearts. Promises to be there the minute visiting hours are allowed. Thalia said she was already in the car to get Salem.

Sierra set the phone face down again. She turned back to Lauren, watched the slow, uneven breaths, the way their chest rose and fell like a tide. The hospital lights bleached everything pale, but the sight of Lauren breathing steadily was vivid enough to outshine it all. Alive felt like a miracle.

She leaned forward until her forehead rested against their joined hands. Her voice came out as a rough whisper. "You are not doing this without me. Not again. Not ever. Boundaries can wait. I just need you alive."

Lauren stirred faintly but didn't wake. The words fell into the quiet like a vow only the walls would keep.

Sierra let the tears come. She didn't try to swallow them or pretend they were anything else. They slid warm over her cheeks and into the space between their hands. She closed her eyes and pictured the frame of their life widening again, imperfect and real, the image strong enough to hold.

Chapter 45

The first thing Sierra registered was the weight of a hand tangled with hers. Her neck ached from the awkward angle of the chair, but when she blinked awake, she realized Lauren's eyes were open, watching her through the fog of morning light.

"You stayed," they whispered, voice rasping.

Relief punched through her chest so hard it almost hurt. "Of course I did."

A nurse swept in, brisk and efficient, tugging at wires and checking monitors. Sierra's grip tightened instinctively on Lauren's hand until the nurse smiled. "They're doing well. Once we get your discharge papers sorted, you'll be able to go home. Rest is key. No lifting, no exertion."

Sierra leaned forward before Lauren could speak. "They're not going to be alone. I'll stay with them until they're healed."

Lauren's protest came out hoarse. "Sierra, you don't have to—"

"I do," she cut in, firm. "Thalia's got Salem, so don't even argue. I'm not taking no for an answer."

By the time they reached Lauren's apartment later that afternoon, Sierra had orchestrated everything: water by the bed, meds within reach, a stack of books, and their journal with a fresh pack of pens. She even tucked a blanket around them before heading to the kitchen. Soon, the smell of simmering broth filled the air, and she returned with a steaming bowl of soup.

Lauren sipped slowly, warmth sliding down their throat, and Sierra pulled out her phone to update The Chaos Coven group chat:

> **Sierra:** Lauren's home, appendix gone, currently bossing soup around like it owes them rent.

Hearts and laughing emojis poured in, making Lauren chuckle weakly. Then their smile faltered. "I don't deserve you."

Sierra set the phone aside, eyes steady. "You don't get to decide that. I'm not leaving you alone right after surgery. End of discussion."

That night, she stretched out on the couch, insisting Lauren needed the bed to themselves. She listened to the quiet creak of the springs as Lauren shifted, comforted by the simple fact that they were under the same roof again.

The next morning, Sierra tiptoed into the bedroom. Lauren was still asleep, their face soft in a way she hadn't seen in months. Something on the nightstand caught her eye: an open journal, slightly askew, as if abandoned mid-thought.

At the top of the page, in Lauren's unmistakable handwriting, she saw: *Sierra, if you find this...*

Her chest tightened. She knew she should close it. She knew. Reading it would cross every boundary she'd fought to maintain. But her hand hovered anyway, and before she could stop herself, her eyes skimmed the page.

It spilled with confessions of raw love, deep regret, gratitude so fierce it made her throat ache. Lauren's words painted her as light, as compass, as the reason they believed they were worth saving.

The words blurred as tears filled her eyes. She'd built walls, yes. Careful boundaries to protect what was left of her heart. But Lauren's handwriting—*you make me believe I'm worth saving*—tore through them like they were made of paper. She pressed the journal to her chest, trembling. She had never stopped loving them. Not for a single day.

Sierra placed the journal back exactly as it had been and fled to the shower, letting the hot water mask the sound of her sobs. Maybe when Lauren healed, they could talk about it. For now, she had to focus on helping them recover.

When she emerged, Lauren was propped against the pillows, sleepy but more alert.

"How are you feeling?" she asked, easing into the chair beside the bed.

"Like I got hit by a truck. But a smaller truck than yesterday," Lauren said with a faint grin. Their gaze softened. "Are you okay? You look like you've been crying."

Sierra waved it off. "Just emotional about everything that happened. I'm fine."

They sat in silence, broken only by the soft clink of Lauren sipping the tea she'd made. Sierra pretended to read a magazine but mostly just watched them, cataloging every flicker of discomfort.

The days blurred together after the surgery. A full week passed with Sierra camped out at Lauren's apartment, making sure every meal was eaten, every pill swallowed, every restless night soothed. By the end of it, the doctor cleared Lauren. The color had returned to their cheeks, and though they still tired easily, they were stronger.

Finally, Sierra cleared her throat. "If you're stable enough, I think I should head home today. Salem's probably staging a feline coup by now."

Lauren nodded, though disappointment flickered across their face. "Makes sense. You've already done more than enough."

"I've been thinking of getting a cat," they added after a beat. "I miss having Salem around."

Sierra's heart skipped. "That's not a bad idea. Cats make great recovery companions. But you know you can visit Salem anytime. He'd love the attention."

When it came time to leave, she hugged Lauren goodbye at the door. It was supposed to be quick. It wasn't. The embrace lingered, both of them clutching tight, unwilling to let go. Sierra felt Lauren's heartbeat, steady and strong against her chest.

"Thank you. For everything," Lauren whispered.

Her voice cracked before she could stop it. "You don't need to thank me. This is what people do when they love each other."

The words hung between them like a live wire, too raw to touch. Sierra pulled back slowly, cheeks flushed, and left before she could make it worse.

Driving home, the ache returned, but softer this time, and it was laced with something like hope. And that hope terrified her more than anything.

At her apartment window, Sierra stood with Salem twining around her legs, staring out at the night. Her chest still hummed with the memory of Lauren's heartbeat against her own.

Chapter 46

Sierra and Lauren had drifted back into their own apartments and routines, but something fundamental had shifted since the hospital. Lauren was moving without the careful slowness that had marked those first days home. They'd even joked that they were "Never having surgery again, not if they could help it." Sierra smiled, heart tightening with relief.

Their weekly coffee meetings had become something Sierra both looked forward to and dreaded. Some days the conversation flowed easily, others were stilted with the weight of everything unspoken.

When Lauren appeared at movie night, Calliope's smile was polite but cool. Jett made space on the couch but didn't engage them in conversation. The group was civil, but Sierra could feel their protective energy. They texted often, sometimes called just to talk about nothing. It wasn't romance, not yet, but something tender was growing in the space between.

Hope could be terrifying when you'd already lost everything once.

The community center buzzed with its usual pre-class energy as people filtered in with their sketchbooks and rattling pastel boxes. Sierra adjusted the sleeves of her favorite cardigan while scanning the room.

Lauren lingered by the doorway, tugging at the strap of their art bag like they were working up courage.

"Hey there," they called out.

Sierra looked up, and her face lit up the way it always did when she saw them unexpectedly. "Hey, you made it!"

Lauren shifted their weight, almost shy. "So, I have a proposition. Razor Braids announced a last-minute show Saturday night. I thought maybe... just as friends... we could go together? I still owe you that T-shirt. We could make it a group thing, but if it's too much like a date, I totally understand."

Sierra hesitated, not because she didn't want to go but because of what saying yes might mean. Lauren's words tumbled faster.

"Maybe it's too soon. I totally get it if you're not ready. I just didn't know when they'd be back."

Her smile was genuine. "That sounds fun. I'm sure everyone would be up for it."

Relief softened their whole posture. "Great. Perfect. I'll text you details later."

The moment lingered between them, longer than casual friendship allowed, until Sierra clapped her hands to gather attention.

"Alright, everyone. Tonight's prompt is a little different. I want you to think about the first time you felt genuinely misunderstood. Not ignored or dismissed — but misunderstood by someone who mattered to you. Don't draw facts or literal scenes. Capture the feeling. Colors, shapes, movement. It doesn't need to make sense to anyone but you."

The room settled into that sacred creative silence — markers squeaking, charcoal smudging, papers shifting.

From the front of the room, Sierra caught Lauren gripping their pencil so tightly their knuckles went pale. They stared at the blank page for a long time, frozen. When their hand finally moved, it was with a kind of urgency that made Sierra's chest ache. She couldn't see the details from here, but she noticed the fierce pressure of the strokes, the way the pencil snapped under their hand.

By the time she called for everyone to wrap up, Lauren was still frozen at their seat, the broken pencil tip lying forgotten. Other students packed up and trickled out.

Sierra crossed the room and lowered herself into the chair beside them. "Hey. You doing okay?"

Lauren blinked like someone surfacing from deep water. Without answering, they folded the drawing once, then again, until it was a tight square tucked into their bag.

"I didn't think it would hit me that hard," they admitted.

"Do you want to talk about it?"

A long pause. Then a nod.

· ♥ · ♥ · ♥ · ♥ · ♥ ·

They walked out to the courtyard behind the center, settling on a concrete bench. The evening smelled faintly of lavender from the flower beds, mixed with the lingering tang of charcoal still on their fingers.

Lauren kept their gaze forward. "I always had this soft quality that other kids could sense. Even before I had words for what I was feeling, they knew. My dad started calling me 'sissy' before I even understood the word." Their voice cracked. "He'd say I needed to toughen up, that the world would eat me alive, and it did. Kids can smell difference, and the words they used... Sometimes those cut deeper than fists."

Sierra's throat burned. She placed her palm open on the bench, an invitation.

Lauren stared at it for a long moment before threading their fingers through hers. Their hand trembled.

"My mom didn't stop it," they went on quietly. "Sometimes she'd say maybe if I tried harder to act normal, things would be easier. Like it was my fault for not being the son they ordered."

Sierra squeezed their hand, tears stinging her eyes.

"I used to think if I could just perform well enough, I'd earn their love. But nothing I did was ever enough."

Her voice shook, but it was steady with conviction. "It was never your fault, Lauren. You didn't deserve any of it."

Tears slipped free on both their faces, not loud sobs, just a quiet release. Lauren gave a watery laugh. "Not what I thought would come out of tonight's prompt."

Sierra smiled through her own tears. "You created something true. That's exactly the point."

They looked at her then, eyes shining. "You always know how to make space for people."

She shook her head softly. "You made space for me first. You showed me it was safe to be seen."

They sat until the sky turned from gold to lavender to the deep purple of night. Sierra held on to their hand, her heart aching with equal parts grief and hope.

Chapter 47

The next morning, Sierra pulled out her phone and typed into the Chaos Coven group chat:

Sierra: Lauren invited all of us to see Razor Braids this Saturday night. Is anyone interested?

Raven: Wait, WHAT?! I did not know they were coming to town!

Sierra: Lauren said it was a last-minute addition to their tour.

Calliope: More importantly... do you *want* to go? And do you want us there, or are you just being polite?

Sierra: I'm a little nervous about how the whole evening will play out, but I'm going. You're all welcome to join us. I'd love to have you there, but I understand if it feels too weird or complicated.

Jett: I'm in. I'm always there for you, plus it's freaking Razor Braids. Obviously, I'll bring Ellis so you can all finally meet him.

Sierra's heart swelled reading their responses. Her friends were her anchor, her safety net, her chosen family in every way that mattered.

But as she set her phone down, a quiet pang twisted through her chest. Lauren didn't have this kind of support system. No family to call when things got hard. No parents who were awkwardly, stubbornly trying to understand them anyway. Sierra knew her own parents had only softened because of time, persistence, and maybe some behind-the-scenes nudging from Thalia and Tobias.

She looked down at her hands, still able to feel the warmth of Lauren's fingers intertwined with hers from the night before, and whispered into the empty apartment, "I just wanted them to be my person. I still want them to be my person."

A few tears slipped down her cheeks — for everything they'd lost, for everything they might still rebuild, for the beautiful, complicated mess of loving someone who'd been through so much pain.

Hope bloomed in her chest anyway, fragile but undeniable.

The Chaos Coven descended on Sierra's apartment for pre-concert prep, turning her living room into a glitter-streaked war zone of glam sessions, clinking glasses, and Razor Braids music blasting at a volume that probably violated her lease. Raven declared herself head makeup artist, smudging dramatic eyeliner on anyone who got within arm's reach. Calliope had already started dancing like she was in the pit, spinning so hard she nearly collided with the coffee table.

Thalia, somehow inducted as an honorary Coven member, had crammed lyrics in only three days but belted them with such conviction you'd think she'd been following the band for a decade.

By the time the doorbell rang, the energy was peaking. Jett bounded over to answer and returned with a man who made everyone blink twice.

Ellis was tall and broad-shouldered, with the kind of easy charm that seemed unfair. His smile was so confident it bordered on cinematic.

"Everyone, this is Ellis." Jett was practically glowing. "Ellis, this is my chosen family of magnificent weirdos."

Ellis laughed, and of course even his laugh was perfect. "Nice to finally meet you all. Jett's told me so much."

Introductions went around, warm and polite, but Sierra caught the silent reactions: Calliope's eyes bugging out,

Raven freezing mid-eyeliner stroke, Thalia leaning close to whisper, "Holy crap! He's like a Greek statue come to life."

When Ellis stepped away to grab a drink, Calliope cornered Jett. "Okay, first... wow. Second, if he doesn't treat you the way you deserve, we're going to have issues."

Raven chimed in, deadpan but deadly serious. "He's gorgeous. Fine. But does he make you laugh? Because if he breaks your heart, we're ending him."

Jett grinned so wide it looked painful. "He's perfect. And yes, he thinks I'm hilarious."

"Good." Sierra hugged him tight. "You deserve someone who gets how amazing you are."

Jett grabbed her hands and spun her in the middle of the room until they collapsed on the couch, wheezing with laughter, faces dusted in glitter Raven had dumped everywhere.

By the time they left for the venue, they were glowing — literally and emotionally — every cheekbone catching the light, the air buzzing with anticipation.

Lauren was already waiting near the front of the line when they arrived. Sierra's heart skipped at the sight of them: black hair falling across their forehead, her old Razor Braids shirt loose on their frame, faded and soft from too many washes. In their hands was a neatly folded, brand-new band tee, held like an offering.

Sierra stepped forward, eyes catching on the shirt. "Want to trade?" she teased, nodding at the new one.

Lauren pressed a hand against the old shirt at their chest. "If you don't mind, I'd like to keep this one."

Something tender spread through Sierra's chest. "Of course. Keep it."

The doors opened, and the crowd surged forward. Their group spilled into the pit, weaving toward the center. The buzz in the air was electric; the kind of energy that meant the night was about to burn itself into memory.

When Razor Braids finally hit the stage, the place detonated. Lights flared like fireworks, the bass line thundered through Sierra's ribs, and the crowd moved as one living thing.

Sierra gave herself over to it completely. She danced with Raven, shouted lyrics with Thalia, and did ridiculous synchronized moves with Calliope that left them doubled over laughing. With Jett, she attempted an elaborate spin that almost dumped them both on the floor.

And then she reached Lauren.

For half a beat, she hesitated. Then she threw her hair and dropped into her infamous twerk, the same one that had cracked them all up that very first night at Neon Pulse.

Lauren's laugh burst out, unguarded, eyes crinkling with delight. Sierra caught the blush climbing their neck, the same blush she remembered from that night months ago, and her heart twisted.

The band shifted into one of their slower, rawer songs, lyrics about being truly seen. Lauren's smile faded into something more intent. Their gaze locked on Sierra, unflinching, as though the words pouring from the speakers belonged to them alone.

Sierra couldn't breathe. Every lyric felt like it had been pulled from their story — the fear of being misunderstood, the relief of finally being seen.

Another song began; this one was of transformation, about becoming yourself when the right person is beside you. Lauren reached for her hand, fingers warm and sure, and never looked away.

Sierra felt tears sting as she tightened her grip. The music swelled, voices all around chanting the chorus, lights flashing red and gold.

Every rational thought screamed this was too fast, too risky. But when Lauren looked at her like that, all her carefully constructed walls felt paper-thin. There was no dramatic pause, no grand buildup. Sierra leaned forward and kissed them.

It wasn't reckless like their first kisses had been, frantic with newness. It was steadier, deeper, filled with the weight of everything they'd been through. A beginning, yes, but also a promise. We can start again. We can do this right this time.

Chapter 48

Lauren stood in Sierra's kitchen, staring at Salem like they were in some kind of standoff. With obvious disdain, he sat on the counter, tail flicking, green eyes narrowed in judgment.

"Come on, buddy." Lauren pulled out a bag of his favorite salmon treats from behind their back. "I know I messed up before, but I'm here to stay this time. I promise."

Salem's ears twitched, but he didn't move.

Lauren shook the bag, and Salem's resolve cracked. His head tilted toward the sound, and Lauren couldn't help but grin.

"Oh, so now I have your attention?" They opened the bag and held out a treat. "These are the good ones. The expensive stuff Sierra pretends she doesn't spoil you with."

Salem stretched forward, snatched the treat, and retreated to consider his options.

"And." Lauren pulled out a small container from their other pocket. "I may have brought a tiny bit of catnip. Just a pinch."

The moment the lid popped, Salem's entire demeanor shifted. He began purring so loudly it sounded like a small motor, then flopped dramatically onto his side and rolled around the counter like he was having the best day of his entire life.

"Oh my God!" Sierra laughed from the doorway. "You furry little traitor. All this time giving Lauren the cold shoulder, and all it took was bribery?"

Lauren cracked up as Salem rubbed his face against everything within reach—the coffee maker, a stack of mail, Lauren's outstretched hand. "I think we're officially friends again."

"He's going to be high for hours." Sierra scooped up the now-blissful cat. "Look at him. He's gone."

Salem purred and head-butted Sierra's chin, then reached out a paw toward Lauren like he was trying to include them in the love fest.

"I missed this." Lauren scratched behind Salem's ears. "All of it. This mess, this joy, this ridiculous cat."

"We missed you, too." The weight of those words settled warm and perfect between them.

·♥·♥·♥·♥·♥·

Later that afternoon, Lauren practically vibrated with nervous energy as they created a temporary group chat, carefully excluding Sierra from the members list.

Anniversary Planning Committee Members: Lauren, Thalia, Tobias, Calliope, Raven, Jett, Ellis

> **Lauren:** Okay everyone, I need your help with something important, and Sierra absolutely cannot see these messages.

> **Calliope:** Ooh, secret mission vibes. I'm already in. What's up?

> **Lauren:** It's almost exactly two years since Sierra and I first met and we're approaching a year since we got back together. I want to do something special to celebrate, but I need it to be perfect.

> **Raven:** Aww that's so sweet! What are you thinking?

Lauren: That's the problem. I don't know. Last time we tried to surprise each other simultaneously, and it was beautiful chaos. This time I want to plan something meaningful.

Jett: Okay, we're definitely helping. Ellis, you're about to get a crash course in Sierra appreciation.

Ellis: I'm honored to be inducted into anniversary planning. What does she love most?

Thalia: Photography, obviously. Art. Her students at the community center. Us. Good coffee. Salem being dramatic.

Calliope: Don't forget she's been talking about wanting to have another gallery showing of her work.

Lauren: Wait, she did? She hasn't mentioned that to me.

Raven: She's been working on this series of portraits from the healing art classes. They're incredible, but she's too modest to do anything with them.

Tobias: What if we organized a surprise showing? Like a real one with an actual venue?

Jett: I know a guy who runs that gallery downtown. He owes me a favor.

Lauren: You guys are amazing, but how do we pull this off without her knowing?

Calliope: Leave that to us. We're professionals in Sierra management.

The surprise came together like magic over the next two weeks. Jett's gallery contact agreed to host a small evening showing. Thalia secretly photographed Sierra's artwork while she was at work and had it blown up. Raven designed elegant invitations. Calliope handled the catering, and Ellis, despite being the newest member of their group, threw himself into setup with the enthusiasm of someone eager to belong.

On the night of the anniversary, Lauren lured Sierra to the gallery under the pretense of checking out a new artist's work.

"I thought it might be nice to get some inspiration." Lauren held Sierra's hand as they walked toward the building. "Plus, you've been working so hard lately. You deserve a night out."

When Sierra walked through the gallery doors and saw her own photographs blown up, mounted, and beautifully lit, her hands flew to her mouth.

"What is this?"

"This is your work getting the recognition it deserves. And also, our two-year anniversary of that day in the park that started it all. Plus, we're almost at our one-year anniversary of being back together." Lauren wrapped their arms around Sierra from behind.

Sierra turned in Lauren's arms, eyes bright with tears. "You did this? All of this? For me?" Her voice cracked, caught between disbelief and a joy so fierce it hurt.

"We did this," Lauren corrected, gesturing to their friends, who were grinning from various corners of the gallery. "The Inner Circle is back in business."

The evening was perfect, intimate but celebratory, with Sierra's healing art series displayed alongside some of her other favorite pieces. Her community center students showed up, beaming with pride at seeing their teacher honored. Even Jonas appeared with a bottle of champagne and several potential clients who were interested in commissioning work.

"I can't believe you pulled this off," Sierra said later, as they stood in front of the centerpiece, a photograph of Lauren from their art class, captured in a moment of vulnerable creation.

"You've always shown me how you see me, and that opened my eyes. I wanted to show you how I see you. How I see your work. You create these spaces where people can heal, where they can be seen and accepted. That's not something you hang in a coffee shop. That's something the world needs to witness."

A week later, Sierra was pacing her living room in a way that made Lauren slightly concerned.

"Babe, you're going to wear a hole in the floor." Lauren sat on the couch, organizing their makeup kit for the next day's clients.

"My parents want to have dinner. Like, a proper dinner. With you. At their house."

Lauren set down the brushes they'd been cleaning. "And that's bad?"

"No! It's good. I think. It's just..." Sierra flopped down beside Lauren. "The last time they met you was for like five minutes at that art thing. This feels official."

"It is official. We're official. One year of being back together officially."

"I know. I just want them to see what I see. How amazing you are, how happy you make me, how much you've grown and healed." Sierra took Lauren's hands. "I want them to love you the way I do."

"And if they don't?"

Sierra's expression grew fierce. "Then that's their loss. But I think they will. Thalia and Tobias have been working on them."

Lauren raised an eyebrow. "Working on them how?"

"Dropping casual comments about how good you are for me. Showing them your social media posts about your therapy progress and art. Thalia may have 'accidentally' left some of your makeup work photos on Mom's kitchen table."

"Your family is terrifying and wonderful."

"They're your family, too. Whether my parents figure that out immediately or not."

The dinner was exactly as awkward as Sierra had predicted, but also warmer than Lauren had dared to hope.

Sierra's mom was making a visible effort, asking careful questions about Lauren's work, which was a far cry from her initial worry about what the neighbors would think. Her father was more reserved but making an effort, occasionally stumbling over Lauren's pronouns but catching himself each time—such a change from the man who'd thrown his napkin down months ago.

"So you do a lot of makeup for photography?" Sierra's mom asked, passing the potatoes.

"Photography, events, some theatrical work. I love the artistic side of it. Making people feel confident and beautiful."

"Lauren did my makeup for my gallery opening," Sierra added. "They're incredibly talented."

"The gallery showing was lovely," her mother said warmly. "We were so proud to see your work displayed like that."

Tobias, bless him, kept the conversation flowing with stories about his latest projects and questions that made everyone laugh. Thalia chimed in with gentle comments which highlighted Lauren's positive influence on Sierra's life.

When Lauren excused themselves to use the bathroom, Thalia followed.

"They're working on it. Dad especially. He asked me last week what pronouns meant and how to use them correctly."

"Really?"

"Really. Mom's been Googling stuff about transgender people and being a good ally. She left a bunch of PFLAG tabs open on her computer last time I was over."

Lauren felt their throat tighten. "They're doing research?"

"They love Sierra, and they can see how happy you make her. They want to understand." Thalia squeezed Lauren's arm. "Just be patient with them. They'll get there."

When they returned to the table, Sierra's dad was showing Sierra photos on his phone.

"Your mother and I have been talking... we'd like to redo the guest room. Make it more welcoming for both of you when you visit. It took us some time to get here, but we want you to feel at home."

Sierra's eyes went wide. "Both of us?"

"Well, of course, both of you," her mother said, as if it was obvious. "You're together, and we can see how happy they make you. It took us a while to understand, but Lauren is part of your life, which makes them part of ours, too."

Lauren felt something tight in their chest finally loosen. Not perfect acceptance, maybe, but genuine effort—and sometimes, effort was the most precious gift of all.

Sierra felt tears prick at her eyes. Months ago, her parents had struggled to even say Lauren's name. Now they were talking about redecorating guest rooms and including them in family plans.

As they drove back to Sierra's apartment later that night, Lauren reached over and took Sierra's hand.

"That went better than I expected."

"My mom called you family. She's never done that with anyone I've dated. Dad is talking about redoing the bedroom for when we visit."

"Your mom saved me leftovers, too. Specifically, for me. With a little note about reheating instructions. She drew a heart in the corner."

They sat in comfortable silence for a moment, processing the evening.

"I love you. Not just for who you are, but for how gracefully you handle all of this. My awkward family, Salem's judgment, the Inner Circle's chaos. You just... fit."

"I love you, too, and I love that your family is trying. I love that they see how happy we make each other."

"They do see it. Finally."

·♥·♥·♥·♥·♥·

Back at the apartment, Salem greeted them with his usual dramatic meowing, clearly offended by their absence. Lauren immediately pulled out the treat bag, and Salem's attitude shifted to pure adoration.

"I can't believe you've turned my cat into a bribery victim." Sierra laughed.

"Hey, it's working. Sometimes love requires strategic treats."

Salem rubbed against their legs.

They settled onto the couch together; Salem sprawled across both their laps like a furry bridge connecting them. The gallery photos from the anniversary celebration were spread across the coffee table, and Sierra kept picking them up and looking at them with an expression of amazement.

"I still can't believe you organized all of that."

"I had help. The Inner Circle is a powerful force."

"We are back, aren't we?" Sierra whispered. "All of us. Different than before, but better."

"So much better." Lauren pressed a kiss on Sierra's temple. "We know what we're capable of losing now. And what we're willing to fight for."

Outside, the city hummed with late-night energy, but inside Sierra's apartment, everything was peaceful. Complete. Like all the scattered pieces of their lives had finally found their way back into place, forming something stronger than before.

Chapter 49

The therapist's office smelled faintly of peppermint tea; a quiet little space tucked above a bookstore downtown. Sierra sat on the couch with her hands folded in her lap, knees brushing against Lauren's. It felt strange at first, sitting side by side like teammates instead of across from each other like adversaries.

They'd been coming here for weeks, both together and in their own individual sessions. It wasn't magic, but it was work they'd committed to... steady, necessary, healing.

"I want you both to talk about what you fear most," Dr. Alvarez said gently, glancing between them.

Sierra took a steadying breath. "For me, it's that you'll leave again. That one hard moment will feel too big, and I'll come home to silence instead of you." Her voice cracked a little, but she forced herself to hold eye contact with Lauren. "I need to know you'll stay, even when it gets messy."

Lauren's fingers twisted together, knuckles pale. "My fear is... that loving me will cost you too much. I'll hurt you just by being myself." They swallowed, eyes glassy. "The night I saw you with Josh, I panicked. I didn't ask questions, I didn't trust you. I just ran. It was easier to destroy everything than risk being abandoned."

Sierra reached over and laced their fingers together. "But I wasn't leaving. I never was."

Dr. Alvarez nodded. "That's the work right there. Naming the fear and then learning new ways to sit with it together instead of apart."

When the session ended, Sierra and Lauren stepped out into the late morning light. Neither spoke for a long moment, but their hands stayed linked as they walked down the block. The silence felt different than before, not heavy, but steady.

Lauren finally gave a small, shaky laugh. "So, do you still want to look at that apartment?"

Sierra smiled, squeezing their hand. "Yeah. I think we're ready."

"This place has good light for your makeup work." Sierra walked through the second bedroom of what had to be their fifteenth apartment viewing. "And it's got that big window you always wanted for color matching."

Lauren stood in the doorway, imagining where their vanity station and product storage could go. "It's perfect. But are you sure you're okay with me taking over an entire room?"

"Babe, your work is important." Sierra wrapped her arms around Lauren from behind. "Besides, I love watching you transform people. You deserve a proper studio space."

Their rental agent, Janet, poked her head in. "The kitchen's been updated, and there's a breakfast nook that gets amazing morning light."

Sierra and Lauren exchanged a look. They'd been cautious for months, rebuilding piece by piece. But their leases were both up next month, and the idea of not waking up together every morning felt wrong.

Sierra walked into the kitchen. "What do you think?"

"I think Salem is going to love that big windowsill in the living room."

"Is that a yes?"

"That's definitely a yes."

Moving day was a kind of joyful chaos only The Inner Circle could create, fueled by coffee, donuts, and far too much commentary about box labels.

Ellis groaned, hefting a carton labeled *Sierra's Photography Collection*. "Why do you own so many books?"

"Knowledge is power." Sierra directed Thalia and Raven as they unpacked essentials. "And some of those are first editions."

"Your girlfriend collects vintage photography books like some people collect stamps." Calliope huffed under the weight of another box. "Jett, please tell me your boyfriend's collection is less back-breaking."

"Ellis mostly collects vintage concert tees and an alarming number of houseplants." Jett carried Salem's carrier with the reverence of someone who knew not to underestimate the cat's opinions.

Lauren emerged from what was now officially their bedroom, holding up two sets of sheets. "Blue ones or gray ones?"

"Blue. They're softer, and Salem likes them better."

Ellis raised a brow. "How do you know Salem has sheet preferences?"

"Oh, he has opinions about everything," Lauren said solemnly. "Thread count, fabric softener brands, which side of the bed gets the best sun. He's very particular."

As if summoned, Salem let out an imperious meow from his carrier.

"See?" Lauren exclaimed. "He's demanding to inspect his new kingdom."

Thalia released him, and Salem immediately began a thorough patrol of every corner. When he reached the living room window, he perched with obvious satisfaction and began grooming.

"Approval granted." Sierra laughed. "We can officially call this home."

That night, after the last box was dragged inside and the Inner Circle finally dispersed, Sierra and Lauren stood in their bedroom surrounded by the mingled evidence of their lives. Her tripods leaned against the wall beside Lauren's makeup kit. Their clothes tumbled together across the unmade bed.

"I can't believe we did it." Lauren's voice was hushed, reverent.

"We did." Sierra stepped closer. "Our room. Our bed. Our home."

Something shifted in the air. The exhaustion from moving day melted into a slow burn that felt like belonging.

"Our first night," Lauren whispered.

Sierra cupped their face. "How does it feel?"

"Like everything finally makes sense." Lauren leaned into her touch. "Like we're exactly where we're supposed to be."

When Sierra kissed them, it was sweet at first, but deepened quickly, urgency sparking beneath the tenderness. This wasn't just want. It was proof. Celebration. A vow carried in touch instead of words.

"I love you," Sierra whispered against their lips.

Lauren's hands slid to the hem of her shirt, fingertips brushing skin. "Show me."

They moved slowly, savoring every breath, every laugh that caught between kisses. Clothes scattered, limbs tangled, moonlight turned their skin silver. Sierra traced patterns along Lauren's chest; Lauren's fingers threaded into her hair. Their rhythm was unhurried, reverent, as if both were memorizing what home felt like in human form.

Afterward, Sierra lay with her head on their chest, listening to the steady heartbeat under her ear with Salem's purring a faint backdrop from the other room.

"Welcome home," she whispered into the dark.

"Welcome home," Lauren echoed, and for the first time, the words felt permanent.

Their first movie night in the new apartment was a christening of sorts. The Inner Circle sprawled across the expanded living room. Calliope and Raven claimed the loveseat. Jett and Ellis lounged on cushions. Thalia and Tobias curled into armchairs.

"I can't believe you two have an actual adult apartment now." Calliope stole popcorn from the bowl balanced on Sierra's knees. "With matching furniture and everything."

Sierra frowned. "We don't have matching furniture."

"Your coffee table matches your TV stand," Ellis pointed out.

"And your throw pillows are part of a color scheme," Thalia added.

Lauren grinned. "We went to IKEA together. It was terrifying and domestic, and I loved it."

Sierra pointed at them. "They argued about curtain rods for twenty minutes."

"Curtain rods matter!" Lauren protested. "They have to hold the weight properly and match the hardware—"

"And this," Jett muttered to Ellis, "is why they're perfect together."

"I heard that." Sierra threw a piece of popcorn at him.

Salem, offended, relocated to the windowsill, where he could supervise in peace.

"What are we watching tonight?" Raven asked.

"Lauren's pick," Sierra replied. "And before anyone complains, they promised it's not another serial-killer doc."

"It's about the history of makeup in film," Lauren said defensively. "Totally different."

Thalia perked up. "Actually, that sounds fascinating. I want to know how they made people look dead in old horror movies."

"See?" Lauren said smugly. "Thalia appreciates educational content."

"Thalia also appreciates gore," Calliope pointed out.

As the movie started, Sierra leaned back and let her gaze drift across the room—friends laughing, teasing, sharing space. This was what she'd missed most when she and Lauren were apart. Not just Lauren, but this sense of belonging. Of family.

Lauren must have felt her watching, because they leaned close and whispered, "What are you thinking?"

"Just how lucky we are. To have all this."

Lauren's smile softened. "I think about that every day."

Chapter 50

Six months into living together, Sierra and Lauren had settled into routines that felt both surprising and inevitable. Lauren made coffee every morning because they woke up first, while Sierra, still useless before caffeine, wandered out of bed in a tangle of messy hair and gratitude. Sierra usually handled dinner because she loved experimenting with recipes, and Lauren always washed the dishes because they found the rhythm of soap and water meditative.

They'd learned each other's quirks and made room for them. Lauren organized everything by color and frequency of use, while Sierra had a system that looked like chaos but somehow made perfect sense to her. Sierra liked the apartment warm and cozy; Lauren preferred a cooler breeze, so they invested in a programmable thermostat and an absurd number of throw blankets. Sierra swore by morning showers; Lauren swore by evening ones. The bathroom counter was a delicate ballet of camera batteries, moisturizers, and makeup brushes, yet they somehow never tripped over each other's space.

One morning, Sierra leaned against the kitchen doorway, the coffee scent drifting through the apartment, and watched Lauren measure beans with scientific precision. Salem sat on the windowsill like their judgmental supervisor. Sierra's heart swelled with a quiet kind of wonder.

"I love how we just... fit," Sierra said.

Lauren didn't look up from their careful scooping. "Even when I rearrange your art supplies?"

"Especially then. I never lose anything anymore." Sierra slipped her arms around Lauren's waist, pressing her cheek to their back. "Besides, watching you organize things is weirdly soothing."

Lauren chuckled softly, leaning into her. "Weirdo."

"Your weirdo."

Sierra kissed their shoulder, and in that small, ordinary moment—the coffee brewing, Salem flicking his tail, the sound of Lauren humming under their breath—she realized something with absolute clarity: she wanted forever. Not just the cohabiting, not just the rhythms they'd fallen into. She wanted a vow, a ring, a name for what they'd already built.

The thought made her knees buckle, so she sat down hard at the table.

"Babe? You okay?" Lauren glanced over, concern flashing in their eyes.

"Yeah. Just... thinking about how happy I am." Sierra smiled faintly. "The best thoughts."

But inside, her chest was thrumming with a secret: she was going to propose.

Valentine's Day arrived with fairy lights and nerves. Sierra had been scheming with Thalia for weeks, who whisked Lauren away for a coffee run while Sierra transformed their living room. She strung the lights across the bookshelves, scattered candles across the floor, and filled mason jars with flowers from the farmers' market. Salem prowled the edges like a foreman inspecting the setup, occasionally pawing at a flower as if testing its durability.

When the key turned in the lock, Sierra's stomach did somersaults. She sat cross-legged on the rug, velvet box in hand, heart hammering.

Lauren stepped inside and froze. "Sierra... what is this?"

"This is me," Sierra said, her voice trembling but sure, "asking you to marry me. This is me promising forever—officially, legally, in front of everyone we love."

Lauren set the coffee cups down with shaking hands and dropped to the floor across from her. Sierra opened the box, revealing a simple white-gold ring with a small diamond that caught the glow of the fairy lights.

"I don't want to spend another day not being engaged to you. I love our life—the ridiculous cat, our friends, your color-coded closets, the way you make coffee, the way you see the best in me even when I can't. Lauren Reeves, will you marry me?"

Tears spilled down Lauren's cheeks before she'd finished speaking. "Yes. Yes, of course yes."

"I love you, too, my fiancée." Sierra lingered on the word, savoring it, then hesitated. "Do you actually like that? Or would you rather I say fiancé, or wife when the time comes, or something else? I don't want to assume."

Lauren's eyes softened, emotion flickering across their face. "Thank you for asking. I like fiancée and wife. Those both feel right to me."

Relief and warmth spread through Sierra's chest. She kissed them again, whispering, "Good. Then I'm going to keep saying it until Salem gets jealous."

Salem punctuated the moment with a long, dramatic meow.

"Too late." Lauren laughed.

"He can wait." Sierra pulled them closer. "I'm kissing my fiancée."

Their celebration started with kisses that tasted like salt and joy, but quickly deepened. They stumbled toward the bedroom, hands never parting, fairy lights glowing in the background.

On the bed, Sierra cupped Lauren's face. "My fiancée," she breathed, testing the word again, savoring it.

Lauren shivered at the sound. "Say it again."

"My fiancée," Sierra repeated, punctuating the word with kisses along their jaw. "Mine. Forever."

Lauren's hands slid under Sierra's shirt, reverent in their touch, mapping the curves they already knew but rediscovering as if for the first time. Sierra's body arched into every caress, her lips finding the hollow of Lauren's throat, the place that always made them gasp.

The intimacy wasn't rushed, wasn't frantic. It was layered with wonder, with awe, with the knowledge that they had built something worth keeping. Every kiss was a promise, every sigh a vow.

"My fiancée," Sierra whispered again, this time into the curve of Lauren's ear.

Lauren's laugh was shaky and wet with tears. "I'll never get tired of hearing that."

"You won't have to. You'll hear it every day."

They moved together like music, like poetry, with the rhythm of people who had memorized each other's bodies but still found new ways to be undone. Sierra gasped Lauren's name; Lauren murmured hers like a prayer.

Later, wrapped in the blue sheets Salem preferred, they lay tangled in the afterglow, the city humming faintly beyond their windows. Sierra's head rested on Lauren's chest, listening to the steady beat of a heart she now felt tethered to in every way that mattered.

"I can't wait to marry you," she whispered, drawing circles on their skin.

"I can't wait to be your wife," Lauren replied, the word tasting sweet and new.

From the windowsill, Salem meowed again, indignant but patient.

"Our cat is jealous," Lauren said with a sleepy laugh.

"Our cat can wait." Sierra pulled her fiancée closer. "I'm not done celebrating yet."

Salem, ever dramatic, flopped onto his side with a thump as if to signal his displeasure. But Sierra barely noticed. The fairy lights still glowed faintly, their joined hands still bore the shimmer of a promise, and her heart still raced with the giddy truth of it all: She had a fiancée.

Forever.

Chapter 51

Their mornings had settled into something beautifully ordinary. Something real. No more waking up in separate beds or wondering what came next. Just two toothbrushes in one ceramic cup, matching mugs with ridiculous puns that made them both laugh, and a perpetually judgmental black cat who absolutely refused to let them sleep past seven.

Lauren always looked impossibly good in the morning light, barefoot, swimming in Sierra's old hoodie like it had always belonged to them, dark hair tousled in every direction. Some days, Sierra would pause in the middle of pouring coffee or checking her phone, caught off guard by a wave of gratitude so intense it made her chest tight. This was her life now. This person, this home, this quiet domestic happiness she'd never dared to hope for.

They'd fallen into rhythms that felt inevitable. Weekly movie nights, always hosted at their place because they had space for everyone. Quiet dinners where they took turns cooking; Sierra had mastered the art of seasoning, while Lauren could make garlic bread that was basically illegal in its perfection. Evenings spent working side by side at their kitchen table, Sierra editing photos while Lauren sketched new makeup looks, their legs touching underneath like the most natural thing in the world. Sierra found herself loving the way Lauren hummed while they worked, or how they'd get ink smudges on their fingers and never noticed.

These weren't grand gestures. They were the moments that built a life.

"Okay, hear me out on this," Lauren said one evening in late spring, curled up on their couch with a wedding planning binder open in their lap and a glass of red wine balanced carefully in their free hand. "The park where it all began. Fairy lights everywhere. Maybe that good taco truck from downtown."

Sierra grinned, looking up from her own wine. "God, marry me already."

Lauren gave her a look of mock exasperation. "I literally already said yes. We've got the ring and everything."

Sierra leaned over to rest her head on Lauren's shoulder, fingers playing with the soft edge of their shared blanket. "It sounds absolutely perfect. Though maybe we upgrade from the taco truck to something slightly more wedding-appropriate?"

"Fine, but I'm holding firm on the fairy lights," Lauren's voice was warm and steady in a way that still made Sierra's heart skip sometimes. "And we don't have to wait forever to make it happen. I've been saving money, and I think I have enough for a small ceremony."

Sierra sat up to look at them properly. "So do I, actually, but yours is the money you set aside to scale up your business."

Lauren suddenly looked vulnerable. "I've been thinking that I want to use that money to build this with you first. The wedding, the life we're making. I don't want you carrying everything on your own. I want to show up as your partner in every way."

"You could show up in a garbage bag and I'd still cry through the entire ceremony," Sierra teased, making Lauren laugh despite the serious conversation. But Sierra caught the deeper worry flickering behind Lauren's smile, the old fear of not being enough.

"Love," Sierra took Lauren's hands in both of hers, "we're already building a life together, and if we're talking about what comes next... maybe we don't stop at wedding planning."

Lauren tilted their head. "What do you mean?"

Sierra's heart pounded, but she smiled. "I mean, if we wanted to... I could come off birth control. We could think about starting a family."

Lauren went still, eyes wide. "Are you serious?"

"I am. One baby, two babies, whatever feels right for us." Sierra squeezed their hands. "And if we do this, then we save together afterward for whatever else you want to do next.

Wedding, family, your business, a house, our hopes and dreams... all of it. We'll make it work together."

Tears welled in Lauren's eyes, their smile radiant. "Sierra, you make me feel whole. In ways I didn't even know I needed. You see me exactly as I am and love me exactly as I am."

Sierra kissed them before the tears could fall, slow and deep, trying to pour all her gratitude and love and overwhelming joy into the connection between their mouths.

When they finally broke apart, she whispered against their lips, "Well, if we're serious about maybe a baby or two, we should probably start practicing."

Lauren raised an eyebrow, grinning. "Practice, huh?"

Sierra stood up and extended her hand with exaggerated formality. "That's going to require some serious dedication."

Lauren took her hand and let themselves be led toward their bedroom, both of them laughing softly.

Their bedroom was dim and golden, lit only by the small salt lamp on Sierra's dresser and the city lights filtering through their curtains. It smelled faintly of lavender and the fabric softener they both loved, creating the kind of sanctuary that lived in the quiet spaces between heartbeats.

Sierra kissed Lauren again, slower this time, her hands cradling their face like she was holding something infinitely precious. Lauren's breath caught when she whispered, "I love you," over and over like an incantation, the words pressing into their skin like a promise.

They undressed each other with a reverence that felt almost sacred. No rushing, no urgency—just the soft slide of fabric, the brush of fingertips, the kind of quiet that made every small sound feel amplified. Lips brushed freckles, hands traced old scars like they were mapping constellations, and every touch carried the weight of everything they'd rebuilt.

When Lauren lay back against their pillows, eyes bright with love and trust, Sierra traced the line of their jaw with her thumb.

"You are the most beautiful person I've ever seen," she whispered.

Lauren's exhale was shaky and full of wonder. "You always look at me like that. Like I'm something miraculous."

"Because you are." Sierra pressed her mouth to the sensitive hollow of their throat. "Because you're loved, now and forever."

What followed wasn't desperate or frantic. It was slow and full of awe and gratitude, every kiss and breath and whispered endearment another way of saying: we survived everything, and we're here, and we're building something beautiful together.

When they finally curled into each other under their favorite quilt, skin against skin and heartbeat matching heartbeat, Sierra ran her fingers through Lauren's hair and smiled into the peaceful quiet.

"One day soon, this might make a baby."

Lauren's hand came to rest over Sierra's heart, fingers spreading wide. "It already made a whole life. This life. Us."

And in the stillness that followed, Sierra closed her eyes and held them close, knowing that whatever the future brought—wedding rings, baby clothes, new dreams—they would face it together. Side by side. Completely whole.

Chapter 52

Six months after they started planning, the same park where Sierra had first spotted Lauren through her camera lens now shimmered with hundreds of fairy lights and the thick, sweet air of a perfect summer evening. Wildflowers bloomed along the pathways, and the scent of champagne and Sierra's mom's homemade macaroons drifted through the warm breeze.

This felt like the true beginning—a start and a full-circle return all at once.

White chairs lined the grass beneath a canopy of twilight and carefully woven lights. Paper lanterns swayed gently from the oak tree branches. Friends and family filled every seat, faces glowing with emotion, tissues already clutched in hands and tucked into pockets.

Sierra's dad stood between them at the head of the aisle, looking distinguished in his navy suit, one arm linked through Sierra's and the other through Lauren's. The altar was an archway of flowers that Raven had insisted on designing, a wild tangle of color that still managed to look elegant. Thalia stood radiant in a flowing lavender dress, while Tobias looked handsome but slightly nervous in his role as Lauren's person.

As they began their walk forward, Sierra's dad leaned close to Lauren and whispered, "Thank you for making my daughter so incredibly happy."

Lauren's eyes immediately went glassy. "She makes me just as happy, Mr. Turner. More than I ever thought was possible."

Then he turned to Sierra, his voice thick with emotion. "I'm sorry it took me so long to understand. But I see how they make you light up, how much stronger you are together. Lauren isn't just marrying into this family. They already are family."

Sierra's throat went tight, and all she could manage was a nod and a squeeze of his hand before the emotion overwhelmed her.

Thalia held Sierra's bouquet like it contained the secrets of the universe, beaming with pride. Tobias stood beside Lauren, practically vibrating with joy despite his earlier nerves. Their mother sat in the front row, somehow holding a very disgruntled Salem in her lap—the cat magnificent in his tiny bow tie but clearly offended by the entire proceeding. His low growls rumbled every time someone dared to clap too loudly.

When the officiant asked if they were ready to exchange vows, Sierra didn't hesitate. She turned toward Lauren, her whole heart visible in her expression.

"Lauren," she began, her voice carrying clearly through the hushed crowd, "from the moment I saw you in this very park, I felt something I didn't have words for yet. When I got to know you, it wasn't just attraction or fascination, it was gravity. You pulled me into a world I didn't know I'd been missing. A world of tenderness and strength, courage, and quiet wisdom. You taught me that love doesn't have to be loud to be real. It just has to be true.

"So I vow to choose you every single day. To stand beside you when life is easy, and especially when it's not. To build our home, one shared morning, one terrible joke, one strategic cat bribery at a time. You are my safe harbor and my greatest adventure. Whatever comes next, we'll figure it out together."

Lauren's hands shook as they pulled out a folded piece of paper, already softened at the edges from being read and reread. They looked up at Sierra and smiled like nothing else in the world existed.

"Sierra," they said, voice thick with emotion, "you saw me. Really, truly saw me, even before I was ready to be seen. You never asked me to be smaller or different or faster in my healing. You just created space, and in that space, I found the courage to become myself. You made being loved feel safe.

"I used to think healing was something that happened in isolation, but you showed me it could happen hand in hand with someone who believes in you. I vow to keep showing up, to meet you exactly where you are, to laugh and cry and fight fairly and love fiercely. I vow to remind you how extraordinary you are when you forget. You are the home I didn't know I was searching for."

The officiant paused, wiping away tears that definitely weren't supposed to be part of the ceremony.

"By the power vested in me, and by the love that brought you both here today, I now pronounce you married. You may kiss!"

The crowd erupted as Sierra and Lauren kissed, slow and anchored in everything they'd survived and everything they still hoped for. There were cheers, applause, and definitely more crying than anyone had planned.

Later, as the reception was in full swing and champagne bottles popped open with fizzy celebration, someone pressed a glass into Sierra's hand. She shook her head gently, setting it aside untouched.

Lauren caught the motion immediately, tilting their head with a curious smile. "Not feeling like celebrating with champagne, wifey?"

Sierra's heart fluttered. "Oh, I'm definitely celebrating. Just... maybe not with alcohol."

Lauren blinked once, then their eyes went wide. "Wait. Are you saying what I think you're saying?"

Sierra nodded, heart hammering with excitement and nerves. "I took a test this morning. I was going to tell you tonight when we got home, but this feels like the most perfect moment possible."

Lauren froze for half a heartbeat. Then their hands flew to Sierra's waist, eyes filling with stunned, reverent joy. "You're pregnant? We're having a baby?"

"Yes, we are," Sierra whispered, placing her hand over Lauren's. "We're doing this."

Lauren let out a sound that was half-laugh, half-sob. "I can't believe it happened so quickly. I hoped, but I didn't dare expect—"

"It happened," Sierra interrupted softly. "We happened."

Sierra's mother, who had been eavesdropping shamelessly from a few feet away, gasped loud enough for half the reception to hear. "Oh my God, I'm going to be a grandmother! I get to spoil a grandbaby!"

Salem, still trapped in her arms, let out an indignant yowl and slapped her cheek with his paw.

Sierra grinned down at him. "Don't worry, Your Royal Majesty. You'll still be the most spoiled creature in our house."

"Well, mostly," Lauren said with a laugh.

They turned back to each other, pressing their foreheads together, Lauren's hands still curved protectively over Sierra's stomach where their child was growing. The fairy lights overhead swayed in the breeze like stars dipping low just to watch.

"I love you so much," Sierra whispered.

Lauren kissed her again, soft and reverent. "I love both of you. All of us."

And there, under the fairy lights with their chosen family cheering around them, surrounded by every person who mattered, including one very judgmental cat, the next chapter of their story began—with overwhelming joy, boundless hope, and hearts so full they could barely contain it all.

Epilogue

Sierra stood at the front of the conference room at the LGBTQIA+ Youth Alliance, watching familiar faces from her community center classes mix with new ones—social workers, counselors, parents clutching informational pamphlets with uncertain but hopeful expressions. Her healing through art program had grown beyond anything she'd imagined, expanding to three other community centers, two domestic violence shelters, and now this.

She adjusted the mic, tucking a strand of hair behind her ear. "When I first started teaching these classes, I thought it was just about putting charcoal on paper, splattering paint, trying to process the noise inside." She smiled at the rows of faces. "But what I've seen is that it isn't really about the art at all. It's about how people look at themselves while they're creating. It's about seeing yourself with even a little compassion when that feels impossible everywhere else."

On the screen behind her, she clicked through slides showing student work, anonymous pieces she'd been given permission to share. A jagged landscape with colors clashing, a face half in shadow, a heart stitched back together with messy red thread.

"These aren't polished." She gestured toward the images. "But that's the point. None of us come into this whole. Art doesn't erase what happened to you, but it gives you somewhere to set it down for a while. A place to pick it up, turn it around, and decide what pieces you want to carry forward... and what you're ready to leave behind."

Her throat tightened, but she pressed on. "When I first picked up a camera again after everything, I thought I had nothing left. But then I realized even the pictures I thought were mistakes told the truth. A blurry edge, a crooked smile, a scar showing. Those were the moments that mattered. Because healing isn't about hiding the cracks. It's about letting them be part of the frame."

The audience was quiet, leaning in. Sierra felt her shoulders ease. For once, speaking didn't feel like standing under a spotlight—it felt like standing shoulder to shoulder with everyone else in the room.

When she wrapped up, a woman in the front row lifted her hand. "Do you ever have other speakers share their personal stories? Sometimes hearing from someone who's walked a similar path can be more powerful than any technique."

Sierra hesitated, then nodded. "We do when someone feels ready. Actually, my partner Lauren has been talking about sharing more of their story." Her gaze softened. "I think their perspective could mean a lot here."

As if on cue, Lauren appeared in the doorway, arriving just as they'd planned after finishing their afternoon client. They'd dressed carefully for this, professional but approachable, in the soft lavender sweater that brought out their eyes.

The director, Nathan, immediately stood. "Lauren, perfect timing. I was hoping to ask you something. Could we step into my office for a minute?"

Lauren and Sierra followed him into his office where he continued. "We're launching a new initiative specifically for LGBTQIA+ youth who are experiencing family rejection or homelessness. Would you consider sharing your story at our first event? We think it could really impact young people who feel like they have no future."

Lauren went still for a moment, and Sierra could see them processing the request. They'd talked about this possibility, but now that it was real, the weight of it showed on their face.

"When?" Lauren asked quietly.

"Next month. It would be about a twenty-minute talk, followed by Q&A if you're comfortable. We'd have counselors available, and it would be a safe, supportive environment. If you're not ready, then whenever you are, we'd love to have you."

Lauren looked at Sierra, who gave them an encouraging nod.

"Yes." Lauren's voice grew stronger. "Yes, I think I need to do this."

·♥·♥·♥·♥·♥·

Three months later, Lauren and Sierra arrived at an auditorium fuller than expected. There were teenagers, young adults, some parents, counselors, and advocates. Sierra sat in the front row, heart pounding with proud nervousness as Lauren adjusted the microphone.

"My name is Lauren." They paused just long enough to make eye contact with a row of nervous-looking kids near the front. "When I was sixteen, my parents kicked me out of our house because I told them I couldn't be the son they wanted me to be."

Their voice was steady, but Sierra caught the slight tremor in their hands as they gripped the podium.

"I used to believe that meant I was broken. That if the people who raised me couldn't love me, no one ever would." They exhaled, voice dipping softer. "I know some of you might feel that way, too. Like you're too much, or not enough, or just... wrong."

A murmur rippled through the audience, a few kids nodding almost without realizing it.

Lauren let the silence stretch before continuing. "I want you to hear me clearly. You are *not* broken. You are *not* wrong. You are *exactly* who you're supposed to be."

They shared their story with raw honesty. The confusion of early childhood, the years of trying to be what others expected, the devastating loss of family, the dark period of believing they had no future. At one point, their voice caught.

"There were nights I didn't think I'd make it to morning," they admitted, eyes flicking to the floor before lifting again. "I thought maybe it would be easier for everyone if I just... wasn't here anymore."

The room went utterly still.

"But I'm standing here because I found people who really saw me. I found a chosen family. I found love that didn't ask me to shrink or change, and eventually, I found the courage to build a life instead of just surviving one."

Their eyes found Sierra in the audience then, and the soft, grateful smile that crossed their face seemed to steady them.

"If you're here tonight and you're scared, if your family doesn't understand, if you feel alone... please know your story isn't finished. There are people who will love you exactly as you are. There are places where you belong, even if you haven't found them yet. Hold on long enough to get there."

When Lauren opened it up for questions, hands shot up immediately. A teenage boy in the third row went first.

"How did you find the courage to keep going when everything felt hopeless?"

Lauren considered the question, then leaned against the podium, softening their posture. "I started small. One day at a time, sometimes one hour at a time. I found one person who accepted me, then another. I created tiny pockets of safety and slowly expanded them. There were setbacks, bad days, but over time the balance shifted toward hope."

A young woman near the back asked, "Did you ever reconcile with your family?"

"No," Lauren replied gently. "And that's okay. Sometimes family is the people who raised you. Sometimes it's the people who choose you. I found family in my friends, in my partner, in communities like this one. Love comes in many forms."

After the event, young people crowded around, some wanting to share their own stories, some just wanting to be near someone who understood. Sierra watched as Lauren hugged a crying teenager, exchanged numbers with a young trans man, and posed for selfies with kids who looked like they'd just met a superhero.

Later, in the car, Lauren leaned their head back against the seat and let out a long breath.

"How do you feel?" Sierra reached over to take their hand.

"Exhausted, but good. Really good." Lauren squeezed her fingers. "Like maybe all the pain actually meant something, you know? Like it wasn't just something that happened to me. It prepared me to help others."

Sierra lifted their joined hands and kissed Lauren's knuckles. "I'm so proud of you. You may have saved lives tonight."

"We saved lives. You showed me that healing could be shared, that our stories could be medicine. I couldn't have done this without what you taught me about creating safe spaces."

As they drove home through the city lights, both of them were quiet, processing the weight and beauty of what had just happened. Their healing had become something larger, a gift they could offer to others still finding their way home to themselves.

Lauren placed their hand on Sierra's belly, where they felt the smallest flutter. "You know what gets me the most?"

"What?" Sierra whispered.

"I spent so many years believing I was fundamentally unlovable. That the parts of me I couldn't change were the parts that would drive everyone away." Their voice was soft, wondering. "And here you are, loving all of me so completely that we created this." They pressed gently against Sierra's stomach. "This little person is going to grow up knowing they're wanted, safe, and loved without conditions."

Sierra felt tears slip down her cheeks as Lauren continued.

"Sometimes I think about that sixteen-year-old kid, sitting on those steps with nowhere to go, convinced their story was over before it started." Lauren looked out at the city lights blurring past. "I wish I could go back and tell them: you're going to find home. Not just a place to live, but people who will choose you every single day. You're going to build something so beautiful from all these broken pieces that you won't even recognize who you used to be."

They turned back to Sierra, eyes bright with unshed tears. "And you're going to help other kids find their way home, too."

Sierra brought Lauren's hand to her lips, kissing their knuckles softly. In the quiet of the car, with the city moving around them and their future growing beneath Sierra's heart, they both understood that some stories don't end. They just keep unfolding, like photographs that reveal new details the longer you look—imperfect and beautiful in every frame.

Bonus Chapter

Salem is based on an actual cat who was part of my life for nearly twenty years. I loved him so much that I write him into my novels whenever I can. After I finished writing this book, I knew Salem needed his own chapter. If you'd like to read what happens from Salem's point of view in a bonus chapter, sign up for my newsletter, and it's yours. You'll also learn the baby's name.

https://link.carlybwrites.com/salem

If you feel moved to leave an honest review on Goodreads, Amazon, social media, or wherever you typically share your book thoughts, I'd be so grateful. It genuinely helps other readers find stories they might love.

Goodreads: https://link.carlybwrites.com/LLGR
Retailers: https://books2read.com/lovinglauren

Acknowledgements

Who knew this would be the hardest part to write? I want to include everyone, but it's so many. Writing a book takes a village. Writing your first one when you're self-published and have no clue what you're doing takes a small country.

First thank you is to you. You took a chance with a brand new author. I'm eternally grateful.

Thank you to my husband. If it weren't for him, I'd have finished this book six months earlier. I'm joking. Mostly. But really, he's been ridiculously supportive through all of this, and I love him more than I know how to say.

To my family (adoptive, biological, and in-laws) and friends, thank you for keeping me upright on the days I was sure I couldn't do it. Krystina, you beta-read this thing and somehow convinced me it didn't suck. Ivy, my sister/bestie/sounding board, you're always the first to read and my biggest cheerleader. Thank you for everything. Sorry, my story made you and Krystina cry. Well... sorry, not sorry. Kris, my bestie, you kept me sane when I was spiraling. Momma Sue, that birthday gift you gave me? It bought my first ISBN. The one for this book. I'm not even kidding. Everyone in my family has been so encouraging, and I'm lucky beyond words.

I've met so many authors along the way who've helped me, but none more than Mick Williams. We bonded over books and proximity, and became fast friends. I mean it when I say I wouldn't be here without him. He helped me so much and introduced me to an entire village of people who've supported me at every turn. To Elisa D. Daniels for being such an incredible friend, author, and inspiration.

Christine from Toxic Love Publishing and author Arsyn Quinn, we stumbled into each other by accident, but now you feel like family. You inspire me constantly. Thank you for reading this and giving me your thoughts.

To the indie author community, thank you for answering every single one of my questions, even the really dumb ones, and for showing me how the pros actually do this.

To my blogging community, who shine a light on indie authors like me. Vanessa Harrelson Keck, you squeezed my story into an impossibly busy schedule, and I'm so grateful. Everyone should check out her blog at https://vanessakeck.wordpress.com/

To the surgeons who literally saved my life twice while I was writing this book, thank you doesn't feel like enough, but thank you.

To all my beta and ARC readers: thank you for taking a chance on me and this story. It means everything.

To Leah, when my editor disappeared right at the due date, you jumped in and knocked it out at lightning speed. You're an absolute rockstar, and I owe you big time.

About the Author

Carly Bryant writes contemporary romance filled with heart-felt emotions, awkward charm, and the kind of love stories that linger long after the last page. Her characters stumble, grow, and learn to love themselves as deeply as they love each other, creating narratives that feel both tender and true.

When she isn't writing, Carly is usually spending time with her husband, three dogs, and countless koi. She's an avid reader with a special love for indie authors.

Follow her at https://link.carlybwrites.com/bryant
https://carlybwrites.com
Or scan the QR code

www.ingramcontent.com/pod-product-compliance
Lightning Source LLC
Chambersburg PA
CBHW030345120726
47901CB00007B/1915